A WHITE MAN'S CHANCE

A WHITE MAN'S CHANCE

BY
JOHNSTON McCULLEY

WILDSIDE PRESS

www.wildsidepress.com

TO
LOURIS

CONTENTS

A WHITE MAN'S CHANCE

A WHITE MAN'S CHANCE

CHAPTER I

A STRANGER OF SPIRIT

AGAIN the whistle of the locomotive shrieked, and the train crept around a short curve and through a narrow cut, rattling its way to the little station of Quebrada.

As a usual thing, it did not stop there. It stopped this day, however, though there was no freight to be thrown out on the little platform. A trunk was tumbled down from the ramshackle baggage-car ahead, and from the single ancient coach at the rear there descended a man.

He was young, of ordinary size. His sombrero was wide-rimmed and gorgeous with decorations. His trousers, his jacket, his stock were of a richness. A diamond flashed at his throat, rings sparkled on his fingers. He held a silk handkerchief in one hand.

He darted forward along the platform and came to the door of the baggage-car. The man inside the car handed out a saddle. It was enormous, and chased with silver. So was the bridle that was fastened to it. And the man wore long silver rowels at his heels.

The train struggled on again and presently disappeared around another curve. The newcomer turned, fists upon his hips, and glanced at Quebrada.

"What a hole!" he gasped.

He saw no human being except an Indian boy sleeping against the side of the depot, with a swarm of flies playing over his face and hands. The breeze from the west churned up the dust now and then, and caused little whirlwinds that died down as if they had not enough energy to combine and cause a storm. Sun-baked, dead Quebrada was before him in all its ugliness!

He threw up his head as if in danger, glanced around again, and then walked briskly to the door of the depot. The door stood open, and he strode inside. No agent was to be seen, but from the opposite side of the partition came the sounds of snores.

The stranger walked directly to the communicating door and kicked it open. The agent was before him, and the brutal assault on the door had not even awakened him. His head hung back, his mouth was open, and from his throat came a volume of sound resembling that of a sawmill.

The latest arrival in Quebrada curled his lips in disgust, and then glanced quickly around the room. Beside the telegraph sounder was a bottle of ink, with the cork out. Beside the ink was a packet of telegraph blanks.

A smile crossed the lips of the stranger as he glanced at these things and then back at the slumbering agent. He stepped swiftly to the table and picked up one of the telegraph blanks. He twisted it around his hand,

and so formed a funnel. With the funnel in one hand and the bottle of ink in the other, he stepped to the side of the agent again.

It was the work of an instant to poise the funnel over the sleeping agent's mouth, and an instant later the bottle of ink had been up-ended, and the black fluid was pouring through the funnel and into the throat of the sleeper.

The agent came to life violently. His head snapped forward, he spat ink, he choked, he clawed at his throat with both hands, he sprang to his feet finally and staggered toward the table. And then he caught sight of the stranger, who had stepped back against the wall and now was standing with his feet far apart and his fists upon his hips again, and laughing raucously.

"You, *señor!*" the agent gasped. "You did that?"

"Who else?" the stranger asked.

"Ha! You shall pay for the insult!"

There was a heavy piece of rock on the table, which had been in use as a paperweight. The agent grasped it, and hurled it with all his strength. He hurled himself immediately after it, having noted the size of the stranger and having decided that it was no greater than his own.

The man against the wall ducked his head, and the rock chipped a piece of adobe out. As the agent rushed, he stepped swiftly to one side, still laughing, caught the agent's right arm, bent it quickly behind his back, and so held him helpless, impotent with rage, gasping, red with anger.

"You had to be awakened, *señor!*" the stranger said.

"A railroad agent is supposed to be awake when a train arrives, is he not? Is it not the usual thing?"

"Nothing was to come on that train," the agent said.

"I came on it, *señor!* Is not that enough? Let us have a certain amount of activity now. My trunk is on the platform, also my saddle and bridle. Out with you!"

He sent the agent spinning toward the door, and followed him out. Then, for the first time, the agent got the sleep fully out of his eyes and saw the gorgeous clothing of the other man, and observed the saddle heavily chased with silver, and a change came into his manner.

"What does the *señor* wish?" he asked.

"There is an inn here?"

"A sort of an inn. Pedro Jorge runs it."

"Then I suppose that I must patronize this Pedro Jorge. You shall carry the trunk."

The agent glanced at the trunk; it was small, and yet had the appearance of being heavy.

"It is against the rules," he announced.

"How is this?"

"I am the agent, and cannot leave the station until closing time, *señor.*"

"There is but one train a day each way, and both of them have passed," the stranger said. "Moreover, there is nothing at all to hold you at the station—and there is a peso to make you carry the trunk."

"A peso, *señor?*"

"I have said it! Pick up the trunk!"

The agent struggled with it, and finally got it upon his back. And then he was horrified to see that the newcomer meant he should carry the saddle, too, which in itself was a good load for an ordinary man.

He started to protest, but the newcomer to Quebrada cut the protest short with a single glance. The saddle was piled on top of the trunk, and one of the reins of the bridle was looped beneath the agent's chin, threatening to cut his throat if the saddle slipped.

"Forward!" the stranger cried.

He urged the agent along the platform and to the edge of the plaza. The Indian boy awoke, took one glance at the scene, and fled screamingly toward a certain hut. A sight of the railroad agent at work was enough to frighten a youth.

"On, brave one!" the stranger was crying. "Straight to this inn of which you spoke. A little more of the speed, *señor!* On!"

The newcomer had touched match to cigarette, and he followed the agent grandly, his head held high in the air, not glancing either to the right or the left. Now and then he flicked the dust from the sleeves of his jacket with the silk handkerchief, and once he tilted his sombrero a trifle to keep the sun from his eyes.

Low and squat, the corners filled with the dust of the mesa, the adobe patched in many places—old, ramshackle, dilapidated—such was the inn at Quebrada.

Across the entire front stretched one great room that served as office, dining-room, and bar. Running back on either side of the patio were wings which contained the kitchen, the servants' quarters, and rooms for rent to wayfarers who might wish a lodging for a night.

Old Valentino was the only servant now, and he was more of a fixture than anything else; and it was only at rare intervals that Valentino was called upon by Pedro Jorge, the proprietor, to sweep the dust and cobwebs from one of the guest-rooms.

For Quebrada had failed to become a metropolis, and wise men always managed to reach the town in the morning, do what trading they wished in the shortest possible time, and quit the place before night fell, that they might sleep in more comfortable quarters.

In addition to the inn, there were a few huts clustered at one side of what was intended to be a plaza, and in these huts there lived certain lazy peons and a few Indians, and a few white men who had descended the social scale as far as the bottom, and descended no further only because it was impossible.

There was a general store, too, that did considerable business with the *haciendas* in the neighborhood at certain times of the year, and the old bachelor proprietor had a respectable adobe house on one side of the village.

The railroad that twisted across Sonora like a steel snake—and a rusty one at that—had the little station-house at Quebrada from necessity, and had established an agent there. For some of the *haciendas* had their freight shipped to this point, and men came for it with great wagons to which half a dozen or so mules were hitched.

But, for the most, Quebrada enjoyed a leisurely existence during the late nineties, and there was not ambition enough in the village to sweep the dust from a walk—had there been a walk. A place to sleep, a few rags to cover the body, peppery food now and then, an occasional drink of cheap wine at Pedro Jorge's place—those things were all that any man desired.

And now it was the siesta hour, and the place looked more dead than usual.

In the big room at the inn, fat Pedro Jorge, who had run the place since the day it was constructed, slept peacefully in a broken chair in a corner. Now and then he snored with considerable energy, so that he rattled the bottles on the bar. His great paunch rose and fell, and the hands that he had clasped over it. His face was purple because of the heat and the continual drinking he did in an effort to stimulate trade.

In another corner of the room there was a table, and here slept two men of the village, one on either side of it, their arms upon the table's surface and their heads upon their arms.

At the end of the bar was old Valentino. He, too, had been at the inn since the day of its construction, and though his hair was scant and white, yet he retained a great deal of the strength of his youth, which had been enormous.

Valentino snored at certain intervals, like an engine expelling steam. His head had dropped forward on his chest, and now and then he raised a hand languidly to brush away a fly that insisted on his nose as a land-ing place. And after a time the fly stung him, and the eyes of old Valentino opened wide, and he heaved a sigh and straightened in his chair and glanced around the room.

He could tell by the sun-line on the wall that the siesta hour was at an end, and yet the others dozed on—for why not, with nothing else to do? Valentino urged himself out of the chair with great difficulty, for the chair was a tight fit, waddled around the end of the bar, gave Pedro Jorge a glance, and then poured himself a drink and quaffed it.

"Swine!" He spoke to himself in a low tone that could not be heard above the sound of the snoring. "And I, Valentino, once servant to a *hidalgo,* have come to this!"

Valentino made a similar remark at least thrice daily, and everybody had grown so accustomed to it that it called forth no comment whatever from the men of Quebrada.

"Swine!" he repeated. "Ah, for the old days of my youth, when I was a man of some consequence in sunny Spain! There were live men then—men who fought and made love and danced and played the guitar. And a curse on the blackest of black days when I was coaxed to come to this Heaven-forsaken Mexico with the promise of great wealth within a year! Here I have remained, and here I shall remain until I expire. It is a punishment!"

Being certain that Pedro Jorge still slept, Valentino poured himself another drink, quaffed it, and wiped the glass and put it away on the shelf.

"Could I but glimpse a *hidalgo* again!" he mourned.

"Could I but let my old eyes rest for a single instant on a *caballero,* a real man of dash and spirit! Ha! I could tell one a mile away, by his walk, the swing of his hips, his manner of dealing with men—and women! Could the impossible but come to pass!"

He sat down in the chair again, determined that he might as well sleep some more.

"Even here, in the old days, it was not so bad," he went on. "Dignified dons had these *haciendas,* then, and there was a touch of old Spain hereabouts. But they could not play politics, and so they are gone. And now the *haciendas* are owned by Americaños, who know not the meaning of leisure, else by half-breed bandits who could not be gentlemen if their lives depended upon it. I say it again—it must be a punishment upon me for something my father did!"

He slumped down in the chair and folded his hands across his breast. His eyes blinked rapidly, and then closed.

At that moment the stranger and the agent reached the door of the inn, and the stranger entered first, the agent following at his heels and depositing the trunk and saddle against the wall.

"The peso, *señor,*" the agent begged.

The stranger tossed him the coin.

"Here we have more sleepy ones," he said. "I shall have to attend to them. You may go."

It was a command, and the agent went, but when he was once outside he ran along the wall of the inn to the nearest open window, through which he could watch.

The newcomer stood before the door for a moment, his hands upon his hips as before and a smile upon his lips. Then he walked to the middle of the room, and turned all the way around, regarding the sleepers one at a time. He listened to the snores of Pedro Jorge and of old Valentino, and viewed a fly that appeared to be considering whether to venture inside the latter's mouth.

Then he stepped swiftly across the earth floor to the end of the bar. He seized a bottle from a shelf, and emptied a part of its contents on Valentino's head. Valentino slept on.

The stranger darted behind the bar again. Beneath it he found a revolver, a formidable-looking weapon of great size and bore. He lifted it, whirled the cylinder, chuckled to himself again, and pointed the muzzle of the weapon toward the ceiling.

As fast as he could work his finger, he pulled the trigger. The long, low-ceilinged room was filled with explosions and smoke. Bullets crashed into the beams above his head.

Pedro Jorge left his chair and came to his feet in a single movement, his lower jaw dropped, his eyes bulging, his hands trembling. Valentino fell from his chair and made a brave attempt to get beneath it. The two men at the table dashed for the door, saw the stranger standing in it with the smoking weapon in his hand, and turned and dashed to a window, scrambling through it in record time.

The smoke cleared away; the stranger laughed.

"Awake!" he cried. "Is this the sort of reception you give a *hidalgo?* Must I use violence to receive

service in this hole of an inn?   Who is the proprietor
here?"

Pedro Jorge waddled forward, still trembling, blinking his eyes, rubbing his hands together and pretending to smile.

"Ah, *señor*, it is the *siesta* hour—" he began.

"The hour is at an end!   You are supposed to be
running an inn, are you not?   Prepare me a room!
Carry my trunk and saddle to it!   Where may I wash
the dust from my hands and face?   Pour me a drink!
Get me more cigarettes!   Service!"

He crashed the butt of the heavy revolver against
the door, and Pedro Jorge and Valentino flinched.

"Pronto!" the stranger cried, flourishing the weapon.

Valentino and Pedro Jorge both ran for the trunk,
and met with a crash before it.   Cursing in undertones,
they picked it up and ran with it from the room.   They
were back almost instantly, and Pedro Jorge took the
saddle, while Valentino rushed behind the bar, picked
up a glass, polished it with his dirty apron, and placed
it upon the bar with a bottle beside it.

The stranger had stepped to the bar and had watched
the polishing process.   Now he reached across, grasped
Valentino's apron, and tore it from his body.   He
ripped it in two and threw it on the floor.   He picked
up the glass and hurled it against the wall, where it
crashed into a hundred fragments.   Then he lifted
the bottle and drank from it, and put it down on the
bar again.

"Let there be no filthiness about me!" he commanded.   "Get you a clean apron!   And get a clean

towel with which to polish your glasses!   And get me
those cigarettes I mentioned, before I lose my temper
entirely!   Service!"

"*Sí, señor!*"   Valentino ejaculated.

"Call me Don José!" the stranger commanded.

CHAPTER II

A LADY OF BEAUTY

Don José strode across the long room to the open door and shaded his eyes with his hand against the glare of the sun while he looked across the plaza. Then he whirled upon old Valentino again, pointed a finger at him, and spoke with authority.

"I shall be abroad on business for about half an hour. At the end of that time, I shall return, and I expect you to have water ready so I may wash, and a meal on the table. And I shall require decent food. If it is not forthcoming, I may lose my temper!"

"*Sí*, Don José!" Valentino cried.

Don José swung through the door and disappeared, and old Valentino stood at the end of the bar, rubbing his fat hands together, smiling, bending forward slightly as if standing on tiptoes to do a man's bidding. Pedro Jorge came back into the room from the patio.

"Ah! At last—at last!" Valentino sighed happily.

"What now, lazy one?" Pedro Jorge demanded.

"He is a real *hidalgo!* It does my old eyes good to observe him! He has the air, the manner—*aire, cortesia! Eleganté!* What spirit, what superb energy! What fine manners! Did you notice the way in which he twirled his silken handkerchief, Pedro Jorge? Did

23

you notice the manner in which his eye flashed? Ha!
There is a man for you—not a cold Americaño, not a
lazy peon, but the finest of men in all the world—a
hidalgo!"

"He has the manner," Pedro Jorge admitted. "But
what does such a man here?"

"Ha! You would ask a *hidalgo* his business, ask
him concerning his comings and his goings? Where
were you reared? Merciful saints! 'Tis cause enough
for him to tear your head from your shoulders!"

"At least, let us give thanks that he is here!" Pedro
Jorge said. "Perhaps we can take from him a *peso* or
two. The saints know that we have need of *pesos!*"

"He will return within half an hour, and wishes
water, that he may wash, and also an excellent meal,"
Valentino said. "I shall prepare the water immediately."

"Prepare it?" asked Pedro Jorge.

"Heat it," said Valentino.

"A man wash in heated water in this weather? Have
you taken leave of your senses!" Pedro Jorge cried.
"He will merely wish to rinse the dust from his hands,
dolt!"

"Ha! Is he not a *hidalgo?* Did I not serve such an
one in my young days in glorious Spain, before I came
to this benighted Mexico to make a fortune that I
never have seen? He will require a tub filled with hot
water, and he will wish the water perfumed. Also, he
will want soap."

"Merciful saints!" Pedro Jorge groaned. "I shall
have to send the boy to the store for some soap. It
has been a long time since we have had any."

"A *hidalgo* always cleanses himself with soap," Valentino explained. "He works it into a stiff lather, and applies it to the skin, and then washes it off with the warm, perfumed water. Perhaps he will wish one of us to fan him as he cools."

"To fa—what nonsense is this?" Pedro Jorge cried. "Is he more than a man?"

"Ha! He is a superman—a *hidalgo!*" Valentino cried. "Blood flows in his veins!"

"And what flows through ours, dolt?"

"Swill! Mere watery fluid! A *hidalgo* has his veins filled with genuine blood, *señor!* And always it is on fire! Always is he ready for a fight, a frolic, to answer the flash of pretty feminine eyes, to play a measure of music—ha! A *hidalgo!* I live to see one again! The moment I opened my eyes and saw him standing before me, I knew it! One cannot mistake a true *caballero, señor,* any more than one can mistake the odor of a skunk!"

"Soap!" mourned Pedro Jorge. "He shall pay!"

"Pay? What is money to a *hidalgo?* Mere coins, mere bits of metal! Pay? But certainly he shall pay, *señor,* and pay exceedingly well. It would be beneath a man of his rank not to overpay. You were wise and you crawled in the dust before him! From this man you can collect money to pay your back taxes and prepare for the future!"

"May the saints be blessed, then, for sending this stranger to my poor house," Pedro Jorge said. "Do you prepare the heated and perfumed water, Valentino, and I shall cook this fine *hidalgo* a meal. Where has he gone?"

"About his business!" Valentino replied gruffly. "Never question the comings and goings of such a man, if you value your hide and peace of mind. He may twist your nose!"

Don José had left the inn with a swinging stride and had walked briskly across the plaza toward the general store. Several natives who witnessed the act marveled at the man's energy at this time of the day, and wondered whether there had been trouble at the inn. Others, who had been spoken to by the railroad agent understood in part, and only marveled the more.

Don José reached the general store and hurried through the doorway. The proprietor was lounging against a counter, and he held conversation with three men of the village regarding nothing much at all. The four of them appeared to be indolent and averse to being disturbed for any reason.

Don José blinked his eyes to get the sunlight out of them, and swaggered toward the four, his eyes meeting and holding those of the man behind the counter.

"Who is proprietor here?" he demanded in a loud voice that caused the three ne'er-do-wells to flinch and retire several paces from the counter.

"I am, *señor*," said the man behind the counter.

"I require a horse. You have horses?"

"I have one noble beast—" the proprietor began.

"A horse, imbecile!" Don José cried.

The proprietor straightened himself and the ends of his mustache bristled suddenly.

"You address me so?" he asked.

Don José reached one hand over the counter and grasped the collar of the proprietor's shirt.

"I am Don José!" he said. "I expect action when I speak, especially when I request information. Have you a horse?"

"You—er—wish to purchase?" the proprietor asked, with a certain degree of courtesy.

"Hire or purchase, whatever you like," Don José said. "Let me have an answer immediately."

"I have a no—er—a horse," the proprietor said.

"Where is the beast?"

"In the corral at the rear of the store, *señor*."

"Lead the way. I shall look at the animal," Don José said.

The proprietor hurried toward the rear behind the counter. Don José hastened after him, but on the outside of the counter, thrusting out his elbows and scattering the three men who stood watching and listening to him. He gave their black scowls scant attention.

The corral was but a step from the back door. The proprietor threw open the gate, and Don José stood beside him and looked in. On the opposite side there was a horse—flea-bitten and lean, his ribs showing, flies buzzing around a sore on one of his legs. He raised his head dispassionately and gently waved one ear.

"There is a horse—" the proprietor began.

"Is this a jest?" cried Don José in his ear.

The proprietor sprang back a couple of paces from the gate and regarded Don José with sudden fear.

"Do you try to make a joke with me?" Don José cried. "That thing a horse? Did I ask for a flea-bitten relic, *señor?* I wish an animal across whose back I can throw a saddle, an animal that can travel over the ground. By the saints, this thing that you have in the corral would not bear the weight of a little child for a distance of a mile!"

"It—it is the only horse I have at present, *señor*," the proprietor wailed.

"Then get me a horse—a real horse! Hire it or buy it—I care not. You shall have your price—but get me a horse! And make the price as it should be, unless you would have me twist one of your long ears. Ass!"

"I—I can send a boy to the nearest *hacienda*—"

"Do not talk about it—do it!" Don José thundered. "I expect service, *señor!*"

"And how much would you be willing—"

"Get me the horse! I'll pay the price! And I shall want him to be kept in the corral and fed and watered well while I am in the vicinity. But get that other beast out of the corral first. He would contaminate a wilderness of horses!"

Don José led the way back into the store.

"One side!" he cried, and thrust the three peons from him again, not gently.

"A saddle? A bridle?" the proprietor was urging.

"I have them. And you have nothing in your stock fit for a gentleman to handle!" Don José replied. "Dust—dust! Never before have I seen so much dust! Why don't you clean up, proprietor? Is this any fit place for a man of rank to enter? I expect to see things cleaner when next I come into your place of business! Ha—what's this?"

Don José had reached the doorway, and now he stood there, almost filling it, shading his eyes with a

hand again and gazing into the plaza. The proprietor
crowded forward and took up a position behind him,
looking over one of his shoulders, and the three *peons*
went forward also, and stooped to peer beneath Don
José's arms.

Before the store a big wagon had been stopped—a
wagon to which four mules were hitched. A *peon* drove
it, and another man had been riding beside it on a
horse. It was a magnificent horse, a black, of strength
and appearance.

But now the rider had dismounted, and he was holding the reins close to the bit, and was attempting
vigorously to administer kicks against the animal's
ribs. Meanwhile, he cursed fluently, and also loudly.

" 'Tis Juan Lopez!" the proprietor told Don José.
"He is the new *superintendente* of the *hacienda* of
Señor William Roberts, an Americaño. It appears that
his mount has displeased him."

"Son of a jackal and coyote!" the angered Juan
Lopez was shrieking. "You would go past the store
and toward the inn, would you, foul offspring of buz-
zard and vulture?"

"That is a jest," the proprietor explained to Don
José. "Juan Lopez drinks so much that his horse
drives straight for the inn of Pedro Jorge as soon as
it reaches the plaza."

"Unmentionable cross between a horned toad and
a rattlesnake!" cried Juan Lopez. "Foul son of a
prairie dog with a ground owl for a mother! De-
formed youngest-born of a sow!"

"The man is fluent," the proprietor suggested. "He
also can swear in English."

"Milch cow! Sheep!" Juan Lopez exclaimed. "Take that!"

His kick landed. The horse squealed suddenly with pain, and tried to rear back and break away. Don José left the shadows of the doorway and sprang into the dazzling sunshine. It appeared that he took but four springs before he was standing beside Juan Lopez.

"Don't dare mistreat that horse again!" Don José said in a stern voice.

Juan Lopez whirled and faced him. Anger was consuming the man, and this was no time for him to take all things into consideration. He noticed the size of Don José, which was not so great as his own, and that was all his enraged senses would allow him to see.

"And what have we here?" Lopez cried. "Do you attend to your own business, *señor!*"

"Treat that horse gently!" Don José commanded. "He is a better horse than you are a man!"

Juan Lopez dropped the reins and cared not that the horse wheeled and ran toward the tavern. He sprang forward, his fists uplifted. He struck wildly.

Don José was not there when the blow landed. He had stepped swiftly aside, and had not even raised his hands.

"Cool your anger, *señor,*" he advised. "If you do not, I shall have to handle you."

Juan Lopez gave expression to another oath. It had to do with Don José, and the newcomer to the village of Quebrada was quick to resent it. He sprang forward and gripped Juan Lopez by the shoulder, twisted his hand, and Lopez found himself upon his knees.

But the *superintendente* was not that easily conquered. He called forth his strength, whirled, was on his feet again, and had whipped a long, keen knife. from his belt. The proprietor of the general store began shouting that such a thing would bring a visit from the *rurales* and would mean a term in *carcel*.

Don José waited for the man's rush. He gripped the wrist of the hand that held the knife, wrenched it, and forced Juan Lopez to drop the knife to the ground. And then he grappled the man about the middle, and raised him above his head, and flung him headlong in the dust and sand.

"Up, cur!" Don José cried. "Catch your horse, and see that you treat the beast well!"

"I shall have revenge for this, *señor!*" Juan Lopez sneered. "You—with your fine clothes!"

" 'Twas not the clothes that conquered you, *peon!*"

"*Peon!* I, a *peon?*" Juan Lopez cried. It was the insult supreme to the man. He was a *peon*, of course, but he had elevated in rank because of good work he had done. Elevate a common fellow, and none will be so quick to declare himself of supreme blood.

Juan Lopez rushed again. Now the man who had been driving the mules appeared to consider this a thing that called for his assistance. Did he aid the *superintendente*, that worthy might give him certain privileges now denied him, might perhaps give him in addition a *peso* to be spent with Pedro Jorge. He sprang from the seat of the wagon.

Don José, it appeared, caught sight of the man in

the air. He had grasped Juan Lopez again, and now he jerked him forward, and so the driver of mules crashed full tilt into the *superintendente*, and they clawed each other's faces vigorously before they realized their mistake, while Don José stood aside and grinned.

The air was filled with curses. They rushed together, their heads bent low. Don José sprang lightly into the air, clutched them by their shirt collars, and neatly cracked their heads together. They sat down, dazed, on the hard ground.

"Go your ways, *peons!*" Don José commanded. "And never attempt again to attack your betters!"

He flicked the dust from his clothes. He heard a woman's silvery laughter.

Don José whirled in his tracks, a smile flashing across his lips, for the laughter found an echo in his heart. Before him was a girl on a horse. She had ridden up during the combat, and he had not noticed her approach.

"By the saints!   A lady of marvelous beauty!" he breathed.

CHAPTER III

SERVANT TO AN ANGEL

THE picture she presented was one to attract instant attention from any man. She wore a riding habit that would have been proper in a city park; her tiny boots were fitted with silver spurs; but on her head was a wide-rimmed *sombrero,* and on her hands were fringed gloves.

She had ceased her laughter when Don José whirled around, but her eyes were still twinkling, and dimples showed in her cheeks, and she was biting at the corner of one pretty lip to keep from letting out more peals of laughter.

Instantly, Don José had forgotten Juan Lopez and the stupid driver of mules. His face was alight, his eyes glistened, his breath came quickly—and for another reason than his recent exertion. His fists were braced against his hips again. He smiled.

When Don José smiled it was as if the sun suddenly had come from behind a cloud. Even white teeth glistened, and delightful ripples seemed to run across his cheeks like ripples on the surface of a pool disturbed by a stone. Yet the smile that answered his seemed to blot out radiance with yet more radiance.

"There is one angel less in heaven," Don José said, half to himself, yet in such a tone that the girl could

33

hear. He glanced above at the sky, as if he half expected to see the hole through which she had fallen.

"Angels do not wear riding habits, *señor*," she replied, smiling at him again.

"I'll take my oath there is one who does."

"It were better, *señor*, if you put your *sombrero* back on your head," she said. "You may be struck by the sun."

"The sun is but a poor thing," Don José returned. "What is being struck by the sun now? Poof! A single glance from your eyes, *señorita*, and the poor sun retires behind a cloud for shame. What man of science was it told us all light comes from that same sun? No matter—he said a falsehood."

"I shall take it unkindly if you do not return your *sombrero* to your head, *señor*."

"A command from the queen is a command!" observed Don José, and he put on his *sombrero*. "If there are further orders—"

"Why were you fighting with those men?" she asked.

Don José turned and regarded them for an instant. They had got to their feet, and were standing side by side, their caps in their hands, looking like schoolboys caught in a prank.

"It is a matter easy of explanation, *señorita*," he replied. "You observe the evil-looking one who is the taller, the one with the squint in his left eye? He was cursing a horse, and kicking at the noble animal's ribs. When I remonstrated with him for it, he saw fit to make an attack upon me. The one standing beside him is a humble driver of mules who rushed to the other's aid. I but cracked their heads together— 'twas nothing!"

The girl urged her horse forward and looked down at the two culprits.

"Juan Lopez, you have been warned about beating horses," she said. "Let this warning be the last. I regret that this gentleman did not give you the beating you deserve. And you, Augustin Gonzales, termed a driver of mules, are as bad as Juan Lopez when you side with him in such a combat. Never seek to defend again a man who mistreats a horse. Go!"

The two men bobbed their heads and went.

"You appear to have a way with these fellows, *señorita*," Don José observed. "May I be of assistance to you? Do you wish to dismount?"

"Have you a desire to act as my servant?" she asked, dimpling once more.

"Your slave, *señorita*, if you wish it!"

"You are rather precipitate, I fear, *señor*."

"Life is short, *señorita*. I have lived for more than twenty-seven years before seeing you—which proves it. The man who wastes time is a fool."

"I was going into the store," she said.

Don José bowed before her, then took the horse by the bridle and led the animal to the store door. He aided her to dismount, and led the way inside.

" 'Tis a foul place, *señorita!*" he said. "Less than an hour ago I ordered this proprietor to clear out the dust and make this establishment a fit place for ladies and gentlemen to visit. And let it be done at once, proprietor! You three men—lazy loiterers! Get to work! Get brooms, rags, soap, and water! Wash those windows! Brush the dust out of the corners. If the proprietor does not pay you, I shall do it myself!"

The laughter of the *señorita* stopped him.

"You expect to get work out of those three men?" she asked. "Do it, and I'll know that you are a leader of men!"

"It is a command!" Don José said. "Continue with your trading, *señorita*. I shall attend to this other matter."

He walked briskly to where the three men were leaning against the counter.

"Did you not hear me instruct you to get water and soap, rags and brooms?" he asked. "Shall I be forced to resort to violence to get work out of you?"

The three men had seen him handle Juan Lopez, and they had no love for such violence. Later, did the opportunity present itself, they might thrust a knife into his back, but they would not stand up before him now. They got brooms, new ones, that made the proprietor wince, and they started to work. One got water and rags, and began washing the windows.

"More speed!" Don José commanded. "The work must be done within a short time. And don't sweep the dirt beneath the counter—take it outdoors! Pronto!"

He drove them to it, and then turned, grinning, to find the eyes of the *señorita* upon him. The eyes of the proprietor were upon him, too, flashing deadly hatred, but Don José did not notice that.

He noticed only that the *señorita* had purchased a basket of goods, and he hurried toward her.

"Since you wish to be my servant, *señor,* you may carry the basket," she said.

"Gladly!"

"And walk two paces behind me, please, as is right and proper in a servant."

She chuckled as she turned her back upon him, and for an instant the smile left Don José's face. The proprietor laughed, and Don José whirled toward him, and he almost choked. Then the newcomer to Quebrada followed the *señorita* from the store.

They walked along the edge of the plaza, Don José two paces in the rear, and presently came to a poor hut set beneath a scraggy palm. Two children slept before the door, a lean dog between them. Just inside a *peon's* wife crooned to an infant. She was fat, greasy, unkempt.

"I have brought you food," the *señorita* said.

"May the saints bless you, *señorita!*"

"And tell your husband that there is work for him if he will come to the *hacienda* to-morrow. But he must work willingly, and not drink as he did before, and gamble away the money he earns. My—servant —will give you a part of what is in my basket."

The *señorita* laughed lightly again, and stepped to one side. Don José bowed and went forward, glancing at the children on the ground and at the woman inside the doorway.

"Let us see," he said. "A cake of soap would be the most appropriate article to leave here, I take it."

"Food!" the *señorita* commanded. "Give her about a third of what is in the basket. We have two more huts to visit."

Don José put out the food, and the *peon's* wife grasped it and muttered her thanks. And then the *señorita* led the way to another foul hut, where more food was distributed, and where a group of dirty children jumped around her and clapped their hands.

And then to the third.

"I'll take the basket now," she said. "There is a sick woman here, and I am going to remain quite some time. And so you may go."

"You would send me away now?" he asked. "An angel should be kind, *señorita*."

"Is this mutiny, *señor?* You refuse to obey orders?"

"But I shall see you again?"

"Quebrada is a small place," she said.

"We do not even know each other's names."

"What is yours?"

"Don José. And yours?"

"If you are interested—find out," she said.

Then she laughed again, and flashed a smile at him, and turned her back and hurried into the hut. Don José remained standing before it for a moment, while two children, forefingers in their mouths, regarded him soberly from a respectful distance.

"*Dios!*" Don José muttered. "Never before have I seen such a lovely *señorita!* Her name? It matters not! I swear by the saints that some day she shall bear mine!"

He started walking briskly away, went a distance

of half a hundred feet, stopped and turned to see whether she was out in the open again and looking after him.

"I knew at the first glance that she was the woman!" he told himself. "Quebrada is a wonderful place!"

CHAPTER IV

A MAKER OF ENEMIES

DON JOSÉ'S trunk, it appeared, was filled with rich apparel. When he came from his room he had donned fresh garments, and if the ones in which he had arrived in the village of Quebrada had been gorgeous, there appeared to be no adequate adjective for the description of the ones he wore now.

He seated himself at a table on which was spread Pedro Jorge's one linen cloth. A *candelero* was in the middle of it, and though the sun was shining brightly outside, yet two tiny candles were burning on the table. Valentino even had carried from his own room a scrawny geranium with a single, faded bloom, and had put that near the *candelero*. And he had unearthed Pedro Jorge's silver, long unused, and had made a brave attempt at polishing it.

Now he hovered near one end of the table, rubbing his hands together, eager to serve Don José and anxious that the *hidalgo* should appreciate the fact that he had on a clean apron. He opened a bottle of wine and put it at Don José's elbow, and a tumbler by its side. And then he disappeared, but returned almost instantly with a plate of thin soup.

Pedro Jorge worked like a maniac in the kitchen over the stove, swearing at times that it was not human

to labor in such heat at that time of the day, and that
this fine Don José should pay amply for it with good
coin.

"He likes the soup," Valentino whispered, his face
beaming, as he came back into the kitchen. "The
roast is done? It is brown?"

"Are you the cook?" demanded Pedro Jorge in a
terrible voice, so that Valentino retired a pace. "Never
before have I cooked for a *hidalgo,* but that is not
saying that I cannot. The food shall melt in his
mouth!"

"Should the vegetables be burned—" Valentino suggested.

"They shall not burn to-day!"

"And the dessert? A pudding? A genuine Spanish
pudding, as I suggested?"

"I shall provide it to the best of my ability," said
Pedro Jorge, with dignity. "One cannot concoct a
masterpiece of dessert within a half-hour, even when a
hidalgo orders it. How did the gentleman like his
bath?"

"It appeared to please him," Valentino replied. "I
did peek in at a crack in the door. He splashed with a
right good will. I shall have to mop up the water
after he has eaten. But he did not use much of the
soap."

"Ha! That is like a fine gentleman!" Pedro Jorge
complained. "And it is excellent soap. I had the boy
get it from the store. I know it is good soap and will
remove the dirt. They use the brand at the Roberts
hacienda for scouring pots."

"By the saints—" Valentino swore. "Small wonder

that he used little of it. It was enough to ruin his
delicate skin!"

"Soap," said Pedro Jorge, "is for the purpose of
removing dirt. That is all I know about it!"

"Service! Service!" roared a voice from the other
room.

Valentino grasped the platter that bore the roast
and hurried from the kitchen. He placed it before
Don José, put a dish of potatoes and beans beside it,
bowed, and bustled out of the room again. Don José
was eating like a man with a hunger.

There entered from the plaza, then, a tall Americaño who went at once to the bar. Don José did not
favor him with a glance. The newcomer to the inn was
slender and broad-shouldered, about thirty years of
age, his face bronzed by sun and wind, and he looked
very much the man.

He pulled off his riding-gloves and slapped the dust
from his breeches, put his hat on the back of his head,
cleared his throat, and looked around.

"Valentino!" he called.

Valentino hurried from the kitchen and went immediately behind the bar.

"*Buenas dias*, Señor Hankins!" he cried. "You
will have a little of the same?"

"Yes. It is a long and dusty ride." Hankins said.
"And the sun appears to be as hot as ever."

"Valentino!" called the man at the table.

"Coming, Don José!" Valentino cried.

He forgot Señor Hankins instantly, and waddled
to the end of the bar and across to the table. He

bowed before the man sitting there, and rubbed his hands.

"More wine!" Don José said.

Valentino hurried back to the bar and took a bottle down from a shelf.

"My drink, Valentino!" Hankins reminded him.

"In a moment, *señor*."

"Why not now? I believe I had my order in first."

"Valentino!" cried Don José.

"I am coming, *caballero!*"

"Hand me my bottle first," Hankins said.

Valentino reached for it.

"Valentino!" Don José insisted.

"Instantly, *cabellero!*" Valentino cried.

He had decided. He ran across the room with the bottle of wine, extracted the cork, filled the tumbler, dusted the bottle and stood it in its proper place at Don José's elbow, and took away the empty one. Back behind the bar again, he reached for Señor Hankins's usual bottle.

"The dessert, Valentino!" Don José ordered.

Hankins did not get his bottle. Without as much as answering, Valentino darted through the kitchen door. Señor Hankins looked across the room at the man sitting at table, and a frown appeared on his forehead. It appeared that he who dined did not appreciate the fact that Señor Hankins was in the place.

Valentino appeared with the dessert and served it. And then he hurried to the bar again. The perspiration was standing out on his forehead in great globules. It was a weary afternoon for old Valentino. Before the coming of the *hidalgo*, Señor Hankins had been the most important of customers, but things were changed now.

"I am glad that at last you can serve me," Hankins said. "What is the meaning of all this? Who is that fellow?"

"*Señor!*" Valentino cried, horrified. "The saints be praised that he did not hear you! That is a *hidalgo* who arrived on to-day's train. That is Don José!"

"Done José what?"

"Just Don José," he said, "and a man dare not ask a *hidalgo* more. Ah, but the sight of him does my old eyes good! I had given up hope of ever seeing a genuine *caballero* again—I had thought such things were but memories!"

"Where did he come from? What is his business?"

"Business!" whispered Valentino. "A *hidalgo* have a business? May the saints have mercy upon us! He is of a blood, that man, of a noble family!"

"But you do not even know his family name."

"It is not necessary, *señor*. Ah, if you could but see his manner, the *aire* he has! The way he walks, the way he commands service! Ha! You can tell a genuine *hidalgo*, *señor*, as easily as one can tell a horse from a coyote!"

"He looks to me," said Hankins, "like an ordinary Mex having his little fling!"

"Pray the saints that he has not heard you!" Valentino gasped.

"Suppose he had?"

"Why, *señor*, he would be sure to resent such a

statement. Have I not said that he is a *hidalgo?* Did he not make the lazy station agent carry his trunk? Did he not order the storekeeper to clean up his place of business? And did he not thrash two men at once because one of them was mistreating a horse? Ha!"

"He appears to be eager to run this part of the country," Hankins said. "So that is the fellow who assaulted Señor Roberts's *superintendente?"*

"Assaulted him, *señor?* Say corrected him, punished him, taught him to obey when a gentleman speaks! Ha! You should have seen it! How he cracked their heads together!"

"More liquor!" Hankins ordered.

Valentino reached for the bottle.

"Valentino!" Don José cried.

"Coming, Don José!"

Hankins was left waiting for his bottle, waiting with a scowl on his handsome face and black rage in his heart. He could have sworn that the man at the table had called Valentino at that instant purposely, and yet he had not even glanced toward the bar.

"You may remove the dishes, Valentino," Don José said. "I dislike to have them before me after I have eaten. And then return here, please."

"*Sí*, Don José!"

Valentino gathered up the dishes and retired to the kitchen with them. He reported to Pedro Jorge that *Señor* Hankins was at the bar, and that he was unable to serve both *Señor* Hankins and Don José at the same time with any degree of success. Pedro Jorge prepared to go to the bar himself.

Valentino returned to Don José's table.

"I thank you for your poor blossom," Don José said, pointing to the faded geranium. "It demonstrates to me that you are a man of good points."

"Oh! Thank you, Don José!"

"A man, I should say, who has seen better days, who has been quite a man in his time."

"That is true, Don José."

"I have taken quite a fancy to you, Valentino. See that you serve me well."

He handed Valentino a *peso*. For once Valentino forbore to bite a coin tendered him as a tip. This made the fourth time that he had received a tip since coming to work for Pedro Jorge twenty-one years before. It was not so bad at Pedro Jorge's at that!

"Valentino!" Hankins called; for Pedro Jorge had not come from the kitchen yet.

"A moment, *señor!*"

"Now!" Hankins cried.

Old Valentino did not know exactly what to do. He certainly did not intend to hurry away from Don José, who gave *pesos*, to attend the Americaño, who was a good man and all that, but who had tipped but once in a year.

Don José now turned slowly in his chair and regarded the man by the bar.

"Valentino," he said, "who is that noisy individual?"

"He is Señor Hankins, Don José, an engineer of mining."

"Allow me to introduce myself," said Hankins, hurrying across the room. "I am Hugh Hankins, interested somewhat in mines and metals. Would it be asking far too much, *señor*, for you to allow this waiter to serve me?"

"Valentino, serve the gentleman," Don José said.

He had overlooked the sneer in the other's tone. Also, by thus graciously granting permission, he scored to a certain extent.

But Hugh Hankins did not appear to be eager to return to the bar now, though Pedro Jorge had come from the kitchen and stood ready to serve him.

"You are a stranger in Quebrada, *señor?*" he asked.

"I never set eyes upon the town until this afternoon, *señor*," Don José replied.

"Ah! You intend to remain with us long?"

"Does one remain long in Quebrada?" Don José asked.

"You are on business, I suppose."

"Who can tell, *señor?*"

"Few strangers come to Quebrada," said Hankins.

"I doubt not that your statement is a true one. I do not wonder at it."

Valentino had returned to the bar, and now he whispered to his employer.

"Observe, Pedro Jorge! Now you will see the difference between a gentleman of Spain, a man of blood, and an ordinary well-bred man. Observe closely!"

Hankins was watching the man at the table put match to the tip of a cigarette. It was to be seen that Hankins felt ill at ease.

"I believe that you are the man," he said after a time, "who assaulted the *superintendente* of the Roberts *hacienda*."

"I rebuked a fellow who was mistreating a horse," said Don José. "You refer to that?"

"I do. Señor Roberts may object."

"You are not Señor Roberts?"

"I am not. But he is my friend, *señor*. And it is an unusual thing for a stranger to interfere in something that does not concern him."

"It concerns me whenever I see a noble animal mistreated," Don José replied.

"You are not interested in mines?" Hankins asked, trying to remain calm.

"Only their output, *señor*, when it is made into rings and such baubles."

"There is a sudden interest in cattle-raising in the vicinity at the present time."

"Indeed? You surprise me. I love a prime steer—"

"Ah!"

"When it is properly roasted and served with an excellent sauce," added Don José.

"I do not believe that I caught your last name," Hankins said, asking himself again to remain calm.

"That is not surprising, since I have not spoken it within your hearing, *señor*."

"Since you are a stranger among us, and evidently a man of means, I am interested, naturally, in your visit, your name, the nature of your business."

"Are you the *magistrado* that you ask such questions?" Don José asked.

Valentino almost choked, and got down behind the bar to hide his laughter. Pedro Jorge turned his face away. Hugh Hankins colored deeply, and his fingers began to twitch.

"I do not like the tone of your voice, *señor!*" he said.

"Then why listen to it?" Don José asked.

Hankins's hands clenched at his sides, and his eyes blazed suddenly.

"*Señor!*" he cried angrily.

"*Señor!*" said Don José, getting out of his chair.

"*Señores!*" said a voice in the door behind them.

They turned. She was framed in the doorway, the *señorita* for whom Don José had played servant.

"Dorothy!" Hugh Hankins cried.

The girl's silvery laughter seemed to fill the room. Don José stepped before her and bowed almost to the floor.

"Ha! You told me to find out your name, *señorita*, if I was interested, and I have," he said. "It is Dorothy!"

"What does this mean?" Hankins asked, looking from one to the other, watching Dorothy's dimples and Don José's smiles.

"The *señorita* and I have met before," said Don José.

"Yes, indeed," she agreed. "He told me that his name was Don José, and he carried my basket when I visited the *peons*. And I saw him punish Juan Lopez and Agustin Gonzales."

"I am afraid that your father will disapprove of you going around with strangers," Hankins said.

The girl's smile was gone in an instant, and her eyes met those of Hankins squarely. Even an angry man should have been able to tell that he had gone too far and that punishment was imminent.

"If my father disapproves, Mr. Hankins, please allow him to tell me so."

"Dorothy!"

"I intended allowing you to ride home with me, but now I am displeased and shall not do so."

"Dorothy, you seem to forget—"

"I forget nothing—not even that I am an American girl old enough to take care of myself. You may follow your own pleasure for the remainder of the afternoon, Hugh. I am going to have cakes and wine with Don José."

She deliberately turned her back upon him and walked to the little table in the corner of the room. Don José, ignoring Hankins, darted before her and pulled out a chair. The smiling Valentino hurried for little cakes and wine.

Hankins walked to the far end of the bar, and sat down there with a bottle before him, rage in his face. But well he knew the young lady who lunched with Don José! He would gain nothing by trying to assert his rights. Already he had transgressed to such an extent that he would have to sue for pardon. But—as for this Don José who had come from nowhere and refused to tell his business—

"I suppose I am doing a very naughty thing," Dorothy was saying to that Don José, "but I cannot help it. Since we are lunching together, we should know each other better. We know only half of each other's names."

Don José raised a hand in protest.

"I pray you not to tell me your family name," he said. "If you did that I could not call you Dorothy.

Let it remain a mystery with me at present. And, to make it equal, I shall withhold the remainder of my name, also."

She laughed and agreed. Nor did she stop to think that Don José cleverly had avoided revealing his identity.

"I shall ask no questions," he went on. "It is enough for me that I have found an angel here in Quebrada. Ah, *señorita,* but the sight of you warms the heart of a man!"

"Be careful, Don José. I am betrothed."

"I feel sorry for the man."

"Indeed?"

"Because he is to lose you," said Don José.

She could not meet his eyes now, and her face flushed suddenly.

"I am betrothed to Señor Hankins," she said. "And I am just punishing him because he was rude to me."

"Until you are actually his wife, I may hope," Don José told her.

"I find I was right when I said you are precipitate."

"What man would not be in your presence, *señorita?* Is it not the privilege of man to attempt to win the woman he loves?"

"How you speak! You never saw me until a short time ago."

"That was my misfortune, *señorita.*"

"And already you are speaking of love," she said, trying to laugh lightly.

"Why not—if I love, *señorita?* What silly things we see in some corners of the world—a man and woman loving each other, yet pretending that they do not, unspoken words trembling on their lips, a wait for a certain moment to arrive. Ha! Either a man loves or he does not! And, if he does, why delay speaking about it?"

"Please," she begged.

"Now that you understand, I am willing to change the subject."

"I almost feel like laughing at you—and I do not want to do that," she said.

Hankins left the end of the bar.

"Dorothy, are you ready to start?" he asked. "If you have finished your interesting conversation with the unknown stranger whose business is a mystery—"

"Hugh Hankins!" she cried, springing to her feet. "Don José is my friend, and I would have you know it!"

"But—"

"And I intend to ride home alone!"

She turned to Don José and granted him a smile, and then hurried from the inn. Hankins followed her as far as the door, and there he whirled around to give Don José one look that spoke volumes. Then he went out.

And Don José laughed and ran quickly to a window, and watched the *señorita* crossing the plaza with her head held high in the air, and Señor Hankins at her side, attempting to explain and ask pardon, gesturing wildly with both hands like a Frenchman in a moment of excitement.

"Valentino," Pedro Jorge whispered to his aged

servitor, "did you notice the look on Señor Hankins's face as he glanced at this Don José?   It was pure enmity, and nothing less.   Valentino, this high-born *hidalgo*, makes as many enemies as you do mistakes, which is quite a few.   May the saints protect him!"

CHAPTER V

VALENTINO GOSSIPS

AN instant the sun burned the country, then a scarlet haze was spread over it, and then came the dusk, for the sun had dropped behind the western hills.

In the inn at Quebrada old Valentino lighted the candles; for Pedro Jorge refused to spend money for kerosene when candles were cheaper. For the most part, the candles were set in the tops of empty bottles, but Valentino had unearthed two *candeleros,* one for Don José's room and the other for the table in the corner by the window, which was to be regarded hereafter as sacred to Don José.

Now the children were playing around the plaza, and the men and women of the village sat before their adobe huts and talked in shrill voices, discussing the events of the day. Don José was the general subject.

Some had it that he was a high official of the Mexican government, and that as a result of his visit there would be more taxes and men impressed for the army. Others declared he was a wealthy owner of land come from the south to purchase broad acres and institute an era of prosperity for Quebrada, at which statement the men scowled, for they had learned that prosperity came only through work, a thing they abhorred and at thought of which they flinched.

54

Others declared that he was the scion of a noble house, come here to visit the lands of his ancestors. That was the more romantic belief, and so it prevailed.

There had been a time when *hidalgos* from Spain had owned the broad acres, and upon their *haciendas* had been villages, and great herds, and large storehouses for goods; and some of them had possessed such great estates that it took a good horseman a day to ride from the door to the front gate, as the saying was.

Then evil times had come, and the old régime had melted away, and some of the great *haciendas* had been cut up into smaller ones. Men found metal and worked the ground. Railroads came and horseflesh deteriorated. Romance, as it had been known, died, and business took its place, and there was hustle and bustle, and the fine old days of the *hidalgos* were at an end.

From the States to the north had come shrewd men who made several dollars grow where but one had grown before. They erected fences and built their buildings, and insisted that things should be clean and sanitary, but they did not demolish the fine old houses of the *hidalgos*.

Some they repaired, and they still served as living quarters. Some still retained on their walls old paintings of the men of blood who once had lived there. And was it anything unusual that the scion of a noble family should visit the home of his ancestors?

It was well understood among the people who knew of such things that the nobleman who had erected the house always had it called for him. Others might purchase it, but to those who knew it always was the Gonzales *hacienda* or the Vega *casa*, or whatever it happened to be.

And that house always stood open to the sons of its builder. He was free to enter it and look at the portraits of his ancestors, and dream of the days when his fathers strode across the great rooms and cried their commands to native servants.

That was it, the people of Quebrada decided. This Don José was the son of some noble house, and he had returned to look upon the place of his ancestors; and because of his high-born pride he forbore to state his family name. The people of Quebrada would respect that feeling as they respected the man.

Valentino was responsible for the starting of that tale, for he could not help boasting of the fact that the inn was entertaining a *hidalgo*. He spoke with enthusiasm of Don José's manner of conduct, and lied somewhat.

And the story went out to the *haciendas* of the vicinity through servants who had been in the village, and some of the Americans said that such a thing was foolishness and rot, but each hoped that his *hacienda* was the one the *cabellero* had come to visit, since such a thing would give them added prestige in the eyes of the people of the land.

Sitting below the window, Don José overheard men on the outside speaking of these things, and he smiled warmly and chuckled, and called for Valentino to fetch more wine, declaring that the best in the house was weak enough.

When candles were burning in all the houses, and in

the store across the plaza, Valentino slipped into his own room and took from beneath his bunk an aged guitar. It was black with age, and there were nicks in the casing, but the strings were good and the instrument had an excellent tone.

Valentino said nothing when he went back into the big room, but he put the guitar against the wall a few feet from Don José, and then he retreated to the bar again and began polishing glasses—with a clean towel.

Half an hour passed, during which Don José sipped his wine and puffed at his cigarette and looked out over the plaza at the moon. And then he turned his head and saw the guitar, and gave a little exclamation of pleasure and picked the instrument up. Valentino's face was wreathed with smiles.

Don José plucked gently at a string. He settled the instrument in his lap, and he plucked at the remaining strings. And then he began to play softly, so that Valentino and Pedro Jorge scarcely could hear. Gradually the playing became louder, and presently Don José burst into song. He sang in a low, sweet voice at first, and then the music seemed to get into his soul, and his voice filled the big room and rolled through the windows and across the plaza.

It was a dainty love-song of ancient Spain that he sang, and there were tears in the eyes of old Valentino when he had finished; and from the plaza came a burst of applause.

"It appears that I have an audience," Don José said; and then he sang again.

It was a song of the Spanish cafés this time, a bit of a naughty song that had been written cleverly, and when he had finished there was more applause and a great deal of laughter, and shouts from the plaza asking that he sing more.

And so Don José complied, and for an hour played the guitar and sang, and then some men of the village grew bold and entered the inn, and Don José played a dance, and they kicked up the dirt of the floor happily.

Then Don José asked that they be served with wine at his expense, and then told them to begone.

Valentino plucked at Pedro Jorge's sleeve.

"Did I not say that he is a *hidalgo?*" he asked. "Not only is he one, but he is a great one! He has been here less than half a day and has done everything, even to making love to a *señorita.*"

"The *señorita?* Ha! She is to wed the Señor Hankins."

"So it has been whispered. But the priest has not mumbled the words yet, and until he has this Señor Hankins runs the risk of losing his bride. If this Don José wishes her, he will have her. I knew *cabelleros* in my youth."

"Valentino!" Don José called.

Valentino hurried across the room and stood before him.

"Sit down. I wish to talk with you," Don José said.

"I can stand, Don José. It would scarcely be proper for me to sit in your presence."

"Very well. If you grow tired, lean against the wall."

"I could not grow tired talking with you, Don José."

"Um! Tell me of this Señor Hankins and the lovely *señorita* who were at the inn this afternoon."

"Señor Hankins is an Americaño, an engineer of mining, and handles a certain hole in the ground near here which is said to give forth gold in large quantities."

"He has wealth, then?"

"It is understood that he has a little, but is rapidly earning more. He may have great wealth soon."

"How is that, Valentino?"

"He is to wed the *señorita*, they say. She is the Señorita Dorothy Charlton. Her father owns a large *hacienda* near here, Don José, about ten miles to the north."

"Ah! And her father is wealthy?"

"Not as a man of your station would count wealth, Don José, yet he has ample, it is true."

"Explain about the girl."

"Gladly, Don José. It is common knowledge, since servants of the *hacienda* have overheard their people talking and have passed the intelligence along. The Señorita Charlton is a foster-daughter of Señor Roberts, who owns the *hacienda*. It is said that Señor Roberts was a friend of the *señorita's* father. When he died, Señor Roberts adopted the girl. Her father died a very wealthy man, away up in the States, in some village they call Boston."

"I have heard of the village," said Don José dryly.

"I never did before, but I am not a traveled man. However, this Señor Charlton had other friends, and they were to be the trustees of his fortunes. The wealth was to go to the *señorita* entirely when she became a bride, and in the meantime she was to have what you call the interest."

"I understand. Continue, Valentino."

"But there is a condition."

"Ah! Generally there is a condition!"

"These trustees, it appears, are to decide whether the man she marries is a worthy man. When the *señorita* announced that she was betrothed they were to make an investigation of the man. You understand, Don José? Her foster-father alone was not to decide. It appears that the *señorita's* father loved her foster-father, but did not think he was a man to judge other men."

"Get to the point of the tale!"

"This Señor Hankins meets the *señorita* here and impresses her, and it is said that he impressed her foster-father also. However, they became betrothed. And so those men in the village of Boston, up in the States, are to investigate, and the marriage cannot take place until that is done. And should they decide that the man is not worthy, then the *señorita* gets the interest only, as long as she lives, and not the principal."

"And if she marries despite an adverse report, her husband will not get to handle the fortune," said Don José.

"Precisely, *señor.*"

"And so this Señor Hankins, I take it, is eager to make a good impression on the trustees."

"It is said the trustees are sending a Yankee to do the investigating," Valentino went on. "Those at the *hacienda* are awaiting him. Señor Roberts is feverish about it. No doubt, he said not long ago—and one of his house servants repeated it—there will come some dignified, gray-whiskered gentleman from this village

of Boston, a man who does not know this country, and
who wears a stiff shirt and a small hat; and he will
not be comfortable, and because of his discomfort will
say that Señor Hankins is not worthy.   Those at the
hacienda are eager to please this man when he comes."

"I do not wonder at it," Don José said.   "There are
many peculiar things in this world of ours.   And the
señorita—in reality what manner of girl is she?"

"Ah, *señor!*"

Old Valentino stood on the tips of his toes and
kissed his fingers at the ceiling.   He threw wide his
arms in a gesture meant to represent an utter inability
to find words to express his thoughts.   He rolled his
eyes.

"As good as that?" asked Don José.

"You have seen her, *señor!* The light of the southern
stars is in her eyes.   The deep scarlet of the poinsettia
is in her lips.   The golden sunshine is in her flowing
hair.   Her long lashes curl like the tendrils of a vine.
The blush of the rose is in her cheek.   Her throat is
as white as the driven snow on the mountain peaks.
Her feet and hands are as dainty as delicate flowers.
Her voice is sweet music, *señor*.   And she is as graceful
as a gazelle!"

"That is the way she appeared to me," Don José
admitted.   "I but wished to know whether other men
saw the same."

"And the kind heart of her!   She cannot bear it to
see a thieving native whipped.   She cannot endure it
to hear a dog whimper.   She pets the little children;
she exchanges whispers with the birds!"

"And is this Señor Hankins worthy?" Don José

asked. "Can he be worthy of such a paragon of a *señorita?*"

"No man could be wholly worthy of her, except possibly yourself, Don José. As to this Señor Hankins, I take it that he is a straightforward man in business. It appears that the Americaños treat him with respect, though with not any great degree of admiration. He is strong and handsome, and no doubt would make a model husband."

"No woman can be happy with a model husband," said Don José. "That is a peculiar philosophy, yet it is true. Life with such would be too well-balanced and would become monotonous. Besides, there is no such thing in all the world."

"You have wisdom, Don José."

"So has the donkey that flops his long ears at the flies. I thank you for your gossip, Valentino. You are an excellent man."

"Thank you, Don José."

"You may fetch me a glass of brandy. I shall retire soon, for I am tired because of travel."

Valentino hurried for the brandy. Don José got up and stretched himself and walked to the door.

There were no lights in the adobe huts now, but there were in the store and the merchant's house. The dusty, sandy plaza was a thing of beauty under the moonlight. Here and there across it couples walked. From the distance came the soft strains of a guitar. Somewhere a woman laughed.

"I should prefer to have it night all the time, did I exist in Quebrada," Don José said.

"Here is the brandy, *señor.*"

"I say it again, Valentino—you are an excellent man. I shall rise early, and will want an excellent breakfast."

"You shall have it, *caballero*. Is there anything special you would like?"

"There is," Don José replied, "but you could not get it for me!"

CHAPTER VI

AT THE HACIENDA

Don José vouchsafed no important information the following morning, to the consternation of old Valentino, who was up before break of day and with his own hands prepared the most gorgeous breakfast that ever had been prepared at the inn of Pedro Jorge.

The guest ate the meal with evident relish, told the beaming Valentino that it was an excellent one, and then went out before the inn to look at the horse the merchant had obtained for him.

It was, in truth, a noble animal, and Don José took currency from his money-belt and paid the price without haggling, to Valentino's entire satisfaction. Then he had Valentino carry the heavy saddle and bridle from his room, and these he put on the horse, after which he tethered the animal to one corner of the inn and went inside for his riding gauntlets.

When he emerged Valentino noticed that Don José also had a belt around his waist, a very superior belt, and that a holster hung from one side of it, and from the holster was sticking the butt of a revolver.

"What does this road that runs toward the north pass?" Don José asked.

"Several *haciendas* within the twenty miles," Valentino replied. "All are owned now by Americaños.

64

The Señor Roberts of whom I spoke last evening has the second on the right-hand side of the road. There is a driveway sheltered by giant trees that were planted no man knows how many years ago."

"I shall ride toward the north," Don José said. "I shall return in time for the evening meal, which I trust will be up to the standard set by that of last evening."

"I shall attend to it personally, Don José."

"I say it yet again—you are an excellent man," Don José replied.

And then he mounted the horse, picked up the reins, touched his spurs to the animal's flanks, and rode swiftly toward the north.

"Ha! He rides like a true *caballero*, too!" Valentino exclaimed to Pedro Jorge, who had come sleepily into the room. "Notice how he sits back in his saddle? Did you ever see anything more graceful than that?"

"Valentino," said Pedro Jorge, "it has come to my mind that we know little concerning this pretty gentleman, and that he is a sort of a man of mystery. We do not know his family name, and we do not know his business in this locality. It is highly unusual for such a gentleman to visit Quebrada. And he is running up an enormous bill. He drinks nothing but the best wine; he eats like a king; and we were forced to purchase soap for him."

"*Señor!*" Valentino gasped, horrified. "You doubt the *hidalgo's* honor? He has a belt stuffed with good money—I saw him pay the merchant for the horse."

"What the merchant gets does not come into

my purse," said Pedro Jorge. "We must endeavor
to ascertain something more regarding this gentleman."

Then Pedro Jorge went about his business, and
Valentino, still horrified, helped himself to a drink
when Pedro Jorge was not looking. That a *hidalgo*
should be doubted on the question of funds was
something worse than cold-blooded murder and almost high treason in the mind and estimation of old
Valentino.

Don José urged his mount at a fair rate of speed and
soon was out of sight of the village. He topped a
small hill and brought the horse to a walk. Now he
rode leisurely and looked about him.

Everywhere was dust and sand and rocks broiling
in the sun. Here and there in the distance could be
seen patches of green, where some *hacienda* owner had
obtained water and raised grain. There were herds
grazing to right and left—cattle, horses, sheep. Far
away on the horizon was a film of smoke that came
from a mine.

He seemed to be the only person on the highway
this morning, save a few *peons* going from one place
to another, and to these he gave not the slightest attention. He urged his horse into a gallop again and
began to cover ground.

In time he reached the driveway old Valentino had
described, and without hesitation turned his horse into
it. He rode slowly beneath the overhanging branches
of the huge eucalyptus trees, looking at the orchard
on either side, where nuts and olives grew.

Two men glanced at him and observed his magnificent apparel, and spoke to each other concerning his probable identity, and then went on with their work of digging irrigation trenches. Don José apparently had not seen them.

He reached the house finally, and saw no living being before it. Don José tethered his horse, flicked the dust from his clothes, wiped the perspiration from his face with his silk handkerchief, and stepped across the veranda and opened the front door. He found himself in a large living-room; and there was nobody else there.

The room was well furnished, he saw. It was more than comfortable. There was a huge fireplace at one end of the room that suggested coziness for chilly evenings. There were ample rugs on the floor and pictures on the walls, some of them old oil portraits.

Don José walked slowly around the big room, looking at these articles, and then he sat down in an easy chair before the fireplace, put his *sombrero* on the table before him, and made himself comfortable generally.

He heard voices in an adjoining room, but saw no one, and as the minutes passed Don José regarded the old portraits, a smile of satisfaction on his lips and an eager light in his eyes.

A door opened on one side of the room, and Miss Dorothy Charlton started to enter. But she backed out hastily, making not the slightest noise, and faced her father and mother.

"He—he is here!" she whispered mysteriously.

"Whom do you mean?" her mother asked.

"The man I met in Quebrada—the man the *peons* are talking about. He came to the village yesterday— a *hidalgo* of noble blood, the men say. It is being whispered that he is come to pay a visit of respect to the home of his ancestors. And to think that it should be our house! To think that persons of noble blood once lived and ruled here!"

"Dorothy, you are silly and romantic," her mother retorted.

"Is that surprising in a girl who is about to become a bride?" her father asked, smiling at her. "I shall go in and interview this gentleman."

Roberts was a big man, with gray hair, and health glowed in his face. He swept into the living-room, closing the door behind him, and stamped across to the fireplace.

Don José was upon his feet in an instant, bowing and smiling, his eyes twinkling.

"You are Señor Roberts?" he asked.

"I have that honor, *señor.*"

"You may call me Don José, *señor.* I have done myself the honor of calling upon you this morning."

"Be seated, *señor,*" Roberts said. "Did not somebody hear your knock?"

"My knock?" Don José asked.

"At the door, *señor.*"

"Oh! I did not knock at the door, Señor Roberts. I should have done that?"

"It is customary, I believe, when entering the residence of a stranger."

Don José looked a trifle pained, as if he did not

really understand, and then a flash of comprehension appeared to illuminate his features.

"Ah, yes!" he said. "I must plead ignorance, *señor*. Perhaps I was too enthusiastic."

"Enthusiastic?" Roberts questioned, sitting down in a chair on the other side of the table.

"Once these broad acres were owned by noble families who came out of Spain," Don José said. "You know that, *señor*. But evil days came, and the families moved away, and others purchased the *haciendas*. But the spirit of such places never changes, *señor*. It seems to me that I can close my eyes and see dignified *dons* and lovely *donas* walking around this room. I can hear the twinkling of guitars, the soft songs of sunny Spain. I can see the lazy natives sleeping in the corners. It is as if those portraits on the walls were live men and women, *señor*. You comprehend?"

"This was once the estate of your family?" Roberts asked.

"A man dislikes to speak of lost fortunes and former grandeur," Don José said. "To descendants of those old families these places are as shrines. Is it not so, *señor?* Sitting before the portraits of his ancestors, a man may meditate on the times and the manners. May he not, *señor?* As to knocking at your door— perhaps you do not understand the custom, *señor*. A man may enter the home of his ancestors as if he still belonged there, so long as he conducts himself in a proper fashion. It is his right to look at the old scenes and dream of the days of his youth."

"It seems to me that I have heard something to that effect," said Roberts.

"If I intrude, of course, *señor,* I shall take my leave at once," Don José went on to say. "I would not have you think that I am not a proper man."

Roberts was beginning to pride himself that he knew and understood those of the Latin race. He got up from his chair and bowed and addressed Don José quite courteously.

"I appreciate the delicacy of your feelings in this matter, *señor,*" he said. "It is no more than just that you should pay this visit of respect. Go about the place as it pleases you, I beg of you, with the exception of the ladies' rooms, of course."

"Of course," echoed Don José.

"And if you wish to remain until the evening, and partake of a meal or so with us—"

"You are kindness itself, *señor!*"

"It is a great old place. I fell in love with it myself the first time I saw it, and could not rest until its purchase had been completed. You will notice that I have changed very little in the house. I put in certain plumbing, of course—baths. And there is a new fountain in the *patio.*"

"Needed improvements, no doubt," Don José said.

"So make yourself completely at home, *señor,* and pardon my absence for a short time. I have some orders to give my superintendent," Roberts told him.

Then the owner of the *hacienda* stalked across the room to the doorway, bowed to Don José, and passed out, of a mind that he had conducted himself with fine Old World courtesy in the presence of this scion of a noble house.

Left alone, Don José walked around the room again, and then picked up his *sombrero,* and wandered out to the veranda.

As he reached it, he stopped. On one corner of the veranda was a cozy nook, shaded with curtains, dressed with flowers and foliage. There was a comfortable bench there, and sitting on the bench was Miss Dorothy Charlton.

"*Señorita!*" Don José gasped, as if the mere sight of her was enough to take his breath away.

Dorothy whirled at the sound of his voice and flushed prettily.

"Good day, Don José," she said. "Are you still eager to be my servant?"

"Always, *señorita!*"

"Sometimes I grow angry at servants and box their ears."

"Ah, *señorita!* I have been told in the village that your heart is so tender you cannot bear to hear a dog whimper. You are an Americaño, are you not?"

"Yes; I came from Massachusetts."

"And you like this land?"

"I adore it!" she said. "It must have been wonderful here in the old days."

"Ah, *señorita!*" he said, and rolled his eyes. "Picture the old *dons* in their gorgeous costumes, the lovely *donas* with their fans and mantillas! Picture the little native children rolling in the dust! The tinkling of a guitar comes from the distance, the breath of a languid song of love and romance! Down the winding trail lumbering *carretas* make their way, carrying grain, and olives, jars of honey, possibly the members of some family, with a *caballero* riding alongside, his gallant steed plunging, the sun glistening from the silver on his bridle and saddle!   A breath of perfume is in the air, an atmosphere of peace and contentment and love—"

"It must have been wonderful," she breathed.

"It was wonderful, *señorita!*   It was as wonderful as you are yourself!"

"But that was so many years ago.   You must have been—quite small," she said.

"Indeed, I was quite small, *señorita*.   But even a small boy may notice things.   And I have heard tell—I have read.   Were we but back in the old days—"

"And if we were—"

"Then I should be making furious love to you, *señorita!*   And there would be an old *dueña* sitting not far away, regarding us out of the corners of her eyes, pretending that she was ready to eat me if a thought, a word, a gesture was not exactly to her liking."

Dorothy Charlton laughed happily.

"At night, when the moon was full and bright, I should stand beneath your window and play the guitar and sing," Don José went on.   "And perhaps some other *caballero* would wish to do the same, and we would have high words and our hot blood would boil. And then there would be knives drawn, and perhaps a little blood spilled."

"*Señor!*   I should not have liked that!"

"Ha!   What is a little blood?" Don José cried. "Shed in the name of love, it is shed for a noble purpose! In those old days I should have gone to your father and asked permission to seek your hand, and there would have been a great feast, with you at one end of the long table and me at the other, and all the guests between us to keep us apart, while we should have been eager to rush to each other's arms. That is what would happen, *señorita,* were we back in the old days. If it could happen now—"

"I am betrothed," she said simply.

"Ah! I had forgotten it for the moment, *señorita.* Your pardon. I was carried away with my own eloquence. And I should not speak so to you, of course. I suppose you Americaños think I am a greaser. That is the term, I believe. It is a delicate thing. I have to deal with the times and the manners. What does it profit a man in this country, *señorita,* that he is of Castilian blood and of a proud family that has done much to enrich history? This Sonora, this northern Mexico, almost the entire country, is in the hands of Americaños now. And these men from the north cannot, it appears, differentiate. Either a man is a white man or a greaser, to them."

"I understand, *señor.*"

"And the white man is to have every courtesy, every chance to win what he desires. And a greaser is a thing to sneer at, a thing to ridicule. All who are not white men are greasers; they cannot see the difference."

Don José appeared to speak with some bitterness, and then stepped away to lean against the railing and look down the driveway. Dorothy left the bench and stepped up beside him, and put her hand upon his arm.

"I understand fully, Don José," she said in a low voice. "Rest assured that I differentiate."

"I thank you, *señorita*," he cried. "You are graciousness itself."

"And if you wait until I get a hat, I shall be proud to show you around the place," she added.

CHAPTER VII

"SOME DAY HE'LL BUST!"

JUAN LOPEZ, the *superintendente*, his face aflame with hatred, dodged between two of the adobe huts, went inside the orchard fence, and approached one of the men working at the irrigation ditches. He pointed to the ground as if giving orders, but he spoke in a tense whisper:

"He is here!"

The other man did not raise his head. He continued to heap the earth to one side, and he spoke from the corner of his mouth so that others working near could not overhear him.

"Who?" he asked.

"The man who handled us in the plaza at Quebrada, dolt! The fine gentleman who cracked our heads together. He rode up some time since on a fine horse, with his bridle and saddle heavy with silver. He was dressed in gorgeous apparel, and he entered at the front door as if he owned the place. Now the *señorita* is talking to him on the veranda. And I heard Señor Roberts himself request him to remain for the evening meal."

"That means," said the other, "that it will be night when he returns to the village."

"Exactly, dolt. At times you demonstrate your possession of common sense," Juan Lopez told him. "There will be a moon, of course, but there are many places of shadows between here and the town."

"What would you suggest?"

"That you do not eat too heavily this evening, but get away from the table as soon as it is possible, and meet me where the driveway runs into the highroad. I shall make it my business to see to it that there are two horses ready."

"It is understood," the man replied.

"And pile the dirt higher, dolt!" Juan Lopez cried in a stronger voice. "The water will seep through as you have it now, and flood the orchard where we do not wish it flooded."

And then he went on to the next man and rebuked him for his small show of energy.

As he left the orchard Juan Lopez beheld a horseman riding up the driveway, and recognized him for Señor Hugh Hankins. This Señor Hankins made a point of getting at the *hacienda* each day, if only for an hour or so with the *señorita*, and Juan Lopez, knowing that the *señorita* was talking to Don José on the veranda, and knowing that she was betrothed to Señor Hankins, was of a mind that the latter might call Don José to task because of his jealousy.

Even a cold Americaño, Juan Lopez supposed, gave way to jealousy on occasion.

The eyes of Señor Hankins narrowed a trifle as he got down from his horse and walked up the veranda steps, but he did not betray the annoyance he felt because of Don José's presence. Señor Hankins was a gentleman, and not a rogue. There were certain qualities in his character open to criticism, of course, but most men are found with those.

Dorothy Charlton greeted him warmly, but denied him the usual kiss because of the stranger's presence.

"Ah! You are paying the *hacienda* a visit, *señor?*" Hugh Hankins asked.

"As you see, *señor*. Señor Roberts has been gracious enough to ask me to make myself at home for a short time, and the *señorita* has been kindness itself."

Hankins knitted his brows and sat down beside the girl, noticing the manner in which she looked at Don José. He had not heard the gossip, and so knew of no reason why Don José should be there. Such gentlemen running around the country should state their business openly, he thought.

Dorothy smiled upon them impartially, and then excused herself for a time, saying that she wished to consult her mother on a matter, and the men were left alone.

Don José took cigarettes from his pocket, and Hugh Hankins accepted one, and they smoked.

"It is a great country," said Hankins, by way of opening a conversation.

"Marvelous in some ways," Don José assented. "By the way, *señor*, I have understood that you are betrothed to the *señorita*. You are to be congratulated."

"Thank you, *señor*," Hankins returned.

Don José had very cleverly and delicately intimated that he realized the other's claims on the girl. That wasn't so bad, Hankins thought.

"Are you interested in cattle, *señor?*" Hankins asked. "I have understood that some *hacienda* owner from the south was coming to inspect the herds hereabouts."

"As I remarked last night, *señor,* I love a prime steer when it is properly roasted."

"Ah—I had forgotten," Hankins said. "And you are not interested in mining, either, I believe you said. Just riding through the country for your health?"

"My health is excellent, *señor.*"

"I am rejoiced to hear it," Hankins returned. "We have so few strangers visiting in this locality that we are interested when one arrives."

"That is polite of you," said Don José.

"I trust that your visit will arouse no suspicion among the men of the countryside, *señor.* It has been whispered around that there is to be a draft for the Federal army, and the men love their homes too much to fight. They would have small politeness for a recruiting officer."

"No doubt," said Don José.

"They really hate one almost as much as they hate a gatherer of taxes."

"I never have gathered taxes, and never expect to gather them," said Don José. "By the way, that is an excellent horse you have, Señor Hankins."

Hankins bit his lip, but kept his temper.

"Yes; it is a good beast."

"I purchased one from the merchant in Quebrada. It appears to be an excellent animal, and I paid an excellent price for him. But when a man purchases horse-flesh he wishes the best."

"Precisely," Hankins replied, looking across at the orchard. "Will you pardon me, *señor,* if I leave you alone for a time? I have some business to transact with Mr. Roberts."

Instantly Don José was upon his feet and bowing.

"Pray do not let me detain you, *señor,*" he said. "Business is something that calls for instant attention, I have heard."

"Ah! You have never been in business?"

"Do I resemble a business man?" asked Don José, twirling his silk handkerchief.

Hankins hurried inside the house and found Roberts going over his books.

"Who is the mysterious stranger?" he asked.

"The man on the veranda? He calls himself Don José."

"And that is all that anybody has been able to get out of him," Hankins said. "He fences skilfully with words when a man attempts to learn his business. I always suspect a man who fails to tell his full name."

"Oh, he appears to be harmless enough!" Roberts said. "And there is a romantic reason for him being here, I believe. It has been whispered that this house was once the property of his ancestors, that these old portraits are of some of his family. You know the custom, Hankins—these fellows are entitled to return to the ancestral home and meditate on the past."

"So that is the story, eh?"

"He intimated as much. He is of noble blood, a *hidalgo,* a *caballero,* as they call it."

Hankins laughed. "Be careful, Roberts!" he warned. "Be careful for your own sake—and Dorothy's."

"What do you mean?"

"I distrust this mysterious, fashionably dressed gentleman, that is what I mean. Be on guard, Roberts, and do not give him too much liberty. He may be nothing more than a smooth scoundrel. *Hidalgo,* eh? Roberts, I have studied the breed throughout Mexico and Central and South America, as you know. He is a greaser—a greaser pure and simple!"

"He is courteous to an extreme," Roberts said.

"He is now. But it is assumed, if I can read a man. He is only playing a part, playing at being a man of noble blood. I have regarded his features carefully. Courteous, eh? For a time, perhaps. But he is a greaser, Roberts, and don't you forget it! He's a greaser—and sooner or later it will come to the surface—he'll blow up, he'll bust!"

"He appears to have plenty of money."

"That is nothing. He would have to have some money to play the part, naturally. And we do not know how he got it. I'd be on guard, Roberts."

"Of course, I'll not let him pull the wool over my eyes," Roberts said.

"Have you heard from Boston, by the way?"

"Only a letter saying that they will send down a certain Mr. Blenhorn. It is merely a matter of form, of course, keeping within the letter of Mr. Charlton's will. I have no doubt that the report will be favorable to you."

"I wish it was over with!" Hankins said. "It is a sort of nonsensical thing, isn't it?"

"But the fortune would be lost if the terms of the will were not complied with," Roberts said. "I'd not worry about it, Hankins."

Hänkins gave a start of surprise.

"What's the trouble?" Roberts asked.

"That Don José! As I looked up I was sure that I saw him at the window."

"Nonsense!"

"I tell you that I did, Roberts. I'd be careful about that fellow. He may be a common thief."

"He probably is lonesome and glanced in to see whether we were through with our conference," Roberts said. "You're nervous—you've been working too hard. When you are married, you should take a long honeymoon, and forget about mines and metals for a couple of months or so."

"Two weeks will be all I can spare, Roberts. We are just getting things running nicely. All we fear now is more graft by these confounded officials. I had a suspicion, at first, that this Don José was nosing around in their behalf."

"You are entirely too suspicious."

"I wish it was over. I wish that chap would come from Boston and give his approval. I'll not feel exactly safe until Dorothy and I are husband and wife."

"Worrying about Dorothy now?"

"Why shouldn't I? She is young and romantic. I was about the only decent marriageable white man around here, and how can I feel certain that I'd have won her if there had been a lot of competition? And this Don José—"

"What about him now, in Heaven's name?"

"Dorothy is seeing entirely too much of him, Roberts. I noticed the way she looked at the fellow. He's a handsome brute; he wears those confounded gorgeous Spanish clothes. What chance has a common white man against a romantic setting like that?"

"Why, Hugh—"

"I'm a bit afraid, I tell you. She's romantic, and she may fancy herself falling in love with him. What chance has a white man against a combination of good, swarthy looks, gorgeous apparel, poetry, music, and romance? I want a chance, Roberts—a white man's chance!"

"Rot! Dorothy isn't as changeable as that. Let's go out on the veranda and have a glass of wine with this *hidalgo*."

They had the wine, Don José being courtesy itself.

Then came the evening meal beneath soft lights, during which Don José's wit seemed to sparkle. And then they sat out on the veranda again for a time, and Don José played the guitar and sang.

Finally, Don José took his departure. He kissed Mrs. Roberts's hand, bowed over that of the *señorita,* thanked Roberts for his hospitality, expressed the hope that he would meet Mr. Hankins at some future time, and went toward his horse.

"Never shall I forget this visit!" he cried, having mounted his beast. "It shall live long in my memory. *Buenas días!*"

"*Señor, á Dios!*" Roberts cried.

He turned and faced the others.

"A gentleman out of the past," he said. "Courteous —and harmless. It was refreshing to have him here for a few hours."

"Do not forget what I told you," Hankins said. "I know the tribe! He is an impostor. His fine courtesy

is all put on. And when the proper moment arrives
the greaser streak will show itself—he'll bust!"

Don José, humming a bit of song, rode happily down
the driveway and turned into the highroad, urging his
horse at a gentle lope toward the village of Quebrada.
He came to the top of a small hill, and rode down into
a tiny ravine where the crags cast dark shadows despite the bright light of the moon.

In the shadows, Juan, Lopez and Agustin Gonzales
were waiting!

CHAPTER VIII

A BATTLE IN THE DARK

DON JOSÉ allowed the horse to pick his own way through the loose gravel at the bottom of the ravine, scarcely touching the reins; and he still hummed the song. He rode slowly through a streak of moonlight and went into the deeper shadows again. Flame split the darkness—a bullet shrilled by his head.

Don José made two moves as one. He hurled himself from the saddle, and he whipped his revolver from the holster and fired. And at the same instant he darted to one side and crouched behind a bowlder at the side of the road.

The horse gave a snort of fear, reared, plunged forward, and ran along the road toward the distant town. For a moment then there was not the slightest sound. Somewhere in that darkness, Don José knew, was a man who had attempted to murder him. He was waiting now to ascertain the effect of his shot.

Don José reached out and picked up a stone. He held it poised in his hand for an instant, then hurled it far to the right. It struck the gravel and made a noise.

Instantly the darkness was split by another flame, and Don José, smiling that his simple stratagem had resulted so successfully, shot twice at the spot where he had seen the flash. And then he darted silently to the left again, for a distance of half a dozen paces, and found another bowlder and crouched behind it.

His shot had drawn fire from two directions, and he realized now that he contended against a brace of foes. This was a business more serious than he had thought at first. Here were desperate robbers, no doubt, who had noticed him riding to the *hacienda*— thieves who had noted his fine apparel and diamond rings.

He regretted now that he had sprung from his horse's back—it would have been better to have ridden past the thugs. But he had acted on impulse, and it was too late now for regrets.

His horse was running like a wild animal toward Quebrada, he supposed. Perhaps, when it arrived there, the men would think there was something wrong and send out a party to investigate. But the party would arrive too late to be of service.

"This is a business that I must settle for myself," Don José mused.

He scarcely breathed; he made not the slightest sound. And he strained his ears to catch some noise that would betray the whereabouts of his foes—but he heard nothing.

Several minutes passed without event, and then he sensed that a man was crawling over the gravel toward him. Don José did not fire in that direction— he listened.

"I am sure that we got him that time," a voice whispered.

"There is no noise," another whispered in reply. "Let us ride on!"

"We must make it appear proper, dolt. We must take his money and his diamonds and disarrange his attire. Then those who find him will think that bandits have done this thing. The *rurales* will search the hills instead of the *haciendas*."

Don José almost whistled. So robbery was not the compelling motive for this attempt at assassination. Why then should he be waylaid and fired upon? Why should these men seek to take his life?

Those questions were important, but they could be answered at a later time, he told himself. At this moment the thing to do was to ascertain the identities of his assailants and to conquer them.

"I cannot find the body," one of them was whispering now. "This is about where he was when I fired."

"Careful! He may be only wounded. Or possibly he was not struck at all."

Don José heard them crawling nearer. He gripped his revolver by the barrel and waited.

He heard a man breathing almost at his side; he knew that a foe was crawling over the bowlder behind which he was hidden. Suddenly he put up a hand, grasped the man by his throat, and struck with the butt of the heavy revolver.

But in the darkness he could only guess at distances, and the blow fell upon the man's shoulder. He gave a shriek of fright and pain and began to fight.

Don José was upon his feet now, attempting to conquer the man quickly, for he heard the other give an exclamation and stumble toward the scene of the fray.

He felt the wind of a knife that missed his cheek by a scant inch; he heard his antagonist hissing in his ear.

Don José jerked backward, and his assailant came with him. But the thug had good fortune with him this night, for he managed to remain upon his feet. Again the knife flashed, and Don José felt a sting in his left arm above the elbow, and knew that blood had spurted from the wound.

Hot anger surged into his heart then and he began fighting like a maniac.

"Ha, scoundrel!" he cried. "Attack your betters; eh? By the saints, it were well to send your foul soul hence!"

The second man had closed in now, and it appeared that both of them were afraid to use a knife for fear they might strike each other instead of Don José. Whereas they could not tell at times whether they fought friend or foe, Don José had the advantage of knowing that any man he attacked was an enemy.

He spoke no more, but he fought like a wild man. He tripped them, he hurled them aside, he picked them up and threw them down, using his revolver as a bludgeon, but making no attempt to shoot.

It appeared that his two foes were enraged and determined, too, for they did not run at this show of resistance. Once more they closed in, and Don José felt a knife flash past his cheek again, and heard one of the men give a shriek of pain, and knew that the knife had missed him and found lodgment in the wrong body. He felt blood spurting over his face and hands and breast.

"I shall be a mess!" he thought.

Now the three of them were upon the ground again, battling like crazed men. Don José crashed the butt of his revolver against a head and heard a groan of pain. Once more a knife scratched at his arm.

"Volar!" one of the men shrieked.

So they had enough and were going to flee, eh? Don José did not wish that until he had ascertained their identities. He would know the names and faces of these enemies who sought to slay and then rob to mislead others as to the motive for it. He wanted to know the men who sought his life.

He fired the revolver again, so that by its flash he could locate them well. But it happened that both their faces were turned away at the instant, and so his trick availed him naught. Both men were upon their feet again and dashed away. Don José hurried after them, firing once more and calling upon them to halt.

But fear gave wings to their feet. They hurried to the highroad and along it. Don José heard them cursing and shrieking to each other to hurry. And then he heard the thudding of galloping hoofs. They were gone.

He stood beside the bowlder for a time, breathing heavily. Finally he went out to the road and stumbled along it toward the distant village.

He made as little noise as he could, for he feared more foes might be waiting in ambush, else his assailants would waylay him again farther along the highway.

Gradually he made his way out of the little ravine of the shadows and came into the bright moonlight at the top of the hill. He continued down the road for a short distance, and then, blessing the bright moon, he took stock of the damages.

His sleeve had been slashed with a knife, but the arm had not been cut deeply. Blood drenched his breast, however, and was on his face and hands. He wiped it off as well as he could with his silk handkerchief, brushed the dust from his clothes, and glanced around.

"A mess!" he told himself. "My clothes are ruined and drenched with a man's blood, my horse is gone, and there are several miles of dusty road between me and that hole of a Quebrada. A mess!"

He started walking briskly along the road.

The moon was high in the heavens now, and the highway was like a silver ribbon winding across the mesa. It was deserted, too, with not even a *peon* trudging along it.

Don José whistled an air beneath his breath and made what speed he could, stopping now and then to rest and contemplate the dust that was mingling with blood on his clothes and causing more of a mess. He reached the top of a hill and looked ahead, but could see no lights.

Old Valentino would be worrying, he doubted not; for he had said that he would return in time for the evening meal, and now it was some three hours past that time and he was not near the village yet. He wished for the hundredth time that the horse had not become frightened and run away.

On he trudged, carrying his heavy *sombrero* in his hand a part of the time, wiping the perspiration from his face with his sleeve, thankful, at least, that this was not midday with a hot sun pouring down from the heavens.

And so he came to the crest of another hill, and in the distance he could see the few twinkling lights of the village, for which he gave thanks. He quickened his pace a bit and hurried down the long slope. After all this he would need another meal and a bottle of wine and more heated water that he might take another bath.

He was not far from the village now. He hurried around a curve in the highway—and came upon his horse. The animal was standing beside the road cropping at a small bunch of grass.

Don José exulted and threw himself into the saddle. He put spurs to the beast's flanks and dashed along the highroad toward the town. He came to the end of the plaza and galloped across it and stopped before the door of the inn.

"Take my horse," he directed a *peon* standing near. "Remove saddle and bridle and carry them inside and put the animal to the merchant's corral. Here is a *peso*."

The man grasped the bridle. Don José sprang from the saddle and strode into the inn.

Valentino had been true to his instructions. The table was ready in the corner, and candles were burning upon it, and the faded geranium was in place.

And old Valentino himself, with a cry of pleasure, stumbled from behind the bar when Don José entered and hurried forward. And then Don José stepped nearer the bar, where the light was stronger, and Valentino caught sight of his appearance.

"*Caballero!* You have been slain!" he cried.

"Not quite."

"You are wounded! You bleed! Pedro Jorge, come quickly and fetch water and towels!"

"Nonsense!" Don José cried. "It is nothing."

He was standing beside the bar now, and the half-dozen men who had been there retreated to the end of it. They had seen his blood-drenched clothes and wondered at his plight.

Valentino stood before him, trembling, concern in his face, trying to speak, wishing that he could do something and not knowing exactly what to do.

"What—has happened, Don José?" he gasped. "You have been badly wounded!"

"A small scratch on the arm," Don José replied. "Prepare some water so I may wash."

Valentino groaned and hurried into the kitchen. Don José turned toward Pedro Jorge, who was behind the bar, and who, guessing his need, had set out the brandy bottle and a glass. Don José gulped down the fiery liquor.

"I shall require a meal after I have bathed," he said.

"It shall be ready, Don José. You do not need medical assistance?"

"Nothing of that sort. You appear to believe that I am gasping my last breath!"

"If the *hidalgo* will pardon—the sight of him—"

"I do appear to be somewhat bloody, eh? Well, it cannot be helped. Perhaps I shall have a tale to tell when I have bathed."

Valentino announced that the water was ready, and

Don José retired to his own room. Then the *peons* crowded forward to the bar, asking a multitude of questions.

"You heard as much as I did, dolts!" Pedro Jorge exclaimed. "Do I know how the man came to be all bloody? Think you that I assaulted him myself?"

"I felt some fear for him at the first glance," Valentino said. "But he does not appear to be weak from loss of blood. Here is some mystery!"

"He rode north early in the morning," Pedro Jorge offered. "You remember, Valentino?"

"And said that he would return in time for the evening meal, and he is almost four hours late for it. There is certainly some mystery about it."

"I wish we knew more concerning him."

"Is it for men like us to question?" Valentino demanded. "Cannot a *hidalgo* have his little battles without common folk interfering in them?"

"Had he been slain his bill would have remained unpaid, and it is an enormous one!" Pedro Jorge said. "Allow your mind to dwell upon that fact!"

"Be quiet, for the love of the saints!" Valentino gasped. "Suppose he had heard you?"

It became evident then that Don José had been rapid with his bath, for he came into the room again and hurried to the table as if nothing had happened. Pedro Jorge hastened into the kitchen, and Valentino followed him to get the soup.

Don José ate with evident relish and appetite, Valentino bending over him and anticipating his wishes; and finally he ordered the dishes removed, touched a match to the tip of a cigarette, and leaned back in his chair.

"A scratch on the arm—it was nothing," he declared. "Merely the prick of a knife."

"You fought?" Valentino questioned boldly.

Pedro Jorge was listening from the bar. The *peons* who had been in the room crouched in a corner, their ears open. They would not have missed this for a great deal; on the morrow they could tell the rest of Quebrada how they had heard Don José relate with his own voice the story of his experiences.

"*Sí*, I fought!" Don José replied to Valentino's question. "I rode north to make a certain visit, and spent the day in that manner. And after night had fallen I started to return to the village. At a certain place in the road men set upon me."

"Ha! The scoundrels!" Valentino cried.

"Several of them fired at me from the darkness," Don José continued, with a twinkle in his eye that none perceived. "I dismounted immediately and urged my horse to gallop on ahead. And then I made my way carefully through the darkness, eager to locate my foes."

"You fired at them?" Valentino asked.

"I could not see them," Don José said. "I listened for their steps. One approached me and I grappled with him. I struck him behind the ear with the butt of my revolver.

"And then another came upon me out of the dark and struck at me with a knife. It ripped my sleeve and sliced my left arm."

"Ha! The dog!" Valentino cried.

"Then a third rushed upon me, and I grasped two of them and hurled them together, cracking their heads. At this juncture several more came running to the scene."

"A mob of scoundrels!" Valentino cried.

"They sought my blood, my life, it appeared. They slashed at me with their keen knives, and I was compelled to keep dodging their blows."

"In the darkness?" Pedro Jorge asked.

"By this time we were out of the shadows and in the bright moonlight, where I could see what I was doing," Don José explained. "One of them I tripped, and then I picked him up and hurled him at the others. They rushed upon me again, and striking at me one of them struck a friend with the knife, and his blood gushed upon me and ruined my clothing. Then I drew my revolver and fired one shot over their heads. They ran to their horses and dashed away."

"Ha! They had horses?" Valentino cried.

"Excellent horses, judging from the speed with which they left the scene. And so I caught my own horse then and rode back to the inn."

"The *rurales* should know of this at once!" Valentino exclaimed. "These bandits should be pursued and placed under arrest. They should be thrown into the *carcel* to rot! To attack a *hidalgo* on the public highway—"

"The *rurales* would have to ride swiftly to catch them," Don José observed. "Serve all here with wine and place it to my account. I am fatigued and will retire."

Pedro Jorge and Valentino filled the glasses, and the

men drank to the health and future prosperity of Don
José, after which Don José drank to Quebrada and its
citizens, and then started for his room, old Valentino
leading the way with a candle in his hand.

"Don José," he said at the door, "if there is any
danger let it be known, and I shall watch outside your
window throughout the night. It will be a pleasure."

"There is not the slightest danger," Don José said.
"But allow me to say again that you are an excellent
man."

He took the candle and entered the room and closed
the door behind him. He put the candle on the little
table, and then placed his fists on his hips and bent
backward and laughed so that tears streamed down
his cheeks.

"That was a beautiful mess of lies!" he told himself.
"But they were necessary. They expected some wild
tale and would not have been satisfied with the truth!"

CHAPTER IX

ACCUSED OF CRIME

Don José did not tumble into his bed immediately; he stood with fists upon his hips and contemplated the room.

There was a single door that opened into the hallway, and which had a serviceable lock. There was a single window that overlooked a pile of emptied tin cans and bottles, and the window always was open. The bed was a narrow one and was directly beneath this window, so that a guest could get all the fresh air he liked, though it carried on it odors of a garbage heap.

The moonlight came through the window a bit, but not with much strength, and when the candle was out it caused elusive shadows to play across the bed.

Don José grunted to himself and removed one of the blankets. He rolled it so that it resembled a human body in form, and put it beneath the sheets. Then he took the other blanket and spread it in a corner of the room, investigating first with the candle to be sure it was not spread over some scorpion's family.

He blew out the candle, rolled up loosely in his blanket, and prepared for slumber. From an adjoin-

ing room came the snores of Pedro Jorge, who had lost
no time in retiring after his guest had gone to bed.

The moon shifted so that only the faintest trace of
its light showed across the window. Don José stirred
in his sleep and instantly was wide-awake. He heard
not a sound save the snores from the next room and
the soft rustling of palm fronds in the breeze, but he
sensed the near presence of a human being.

He slipped from his blanket quietly and crouched
in the darkness near the wall, his eyes upon the window. Presently he saw a faint shadow there, and he
crept along the wall step by step, cautiously, every
sense alert.

He knew now that there was a man outside his
window. And he was waiting for the next move. He
could see the man's head outlined against the moonlight, saw a hand raised, and realized that the hand
contained a knife. The nocturnal visitor was looking
down at the bed beneath the window.

As Don José watched the hand holding the knife
was raised higher and then drove downward. At the
same instant Don José sprang. He gripped the wrist
of the hand that held the knife and jerked forward
with all his strength.

But the man, it was evident, had braced his feet
against something outside, and Don José failed in his
attempt to pull him into the room. He jerked back
snarling and tried to strike with the other arm. He
dropped the knife, wrenched backward, drew Don José
halfway on the bed, and jerked free.

Don José went through the window after him, determined to discover the identity of this persistent man

with murderous intent. At the same instant the moon drifted behind a cloud. And at exactly the same instant there came a thunderous report and shriek of alarm from old Valentino.

The man had escaped—there could be no doubting that fact. Don José could hear the sound of galloping hoofs.

"Ho, there, Valentino! Put up your cannon!" he cried as there came a second explosion and a murderous slug whistled past his head. "Would you slay me?"

"May the saints preserve us! Is that you, Don José?"

"Who else?"

"Ha! I have been on guard, Don José. I feared that your assailants might annoy you during the night. And it is a nice night for remaining out of doors. It appears that I dozed a trifle and awoke to see somebody at your window, so I fired."

"And almost tore my body in two with one of the slugs," Don José said.

"May the saints be thanked that I did not!" Valentino cried, approaching. "What is this? You are dressed? I—I beg your pardon, Don José."

Old Valentino was almost overcome with his embarrassment. Here he was investigating some business in which he had not the slightest concern, he told himself. Who was he to question if a *hidalgo* left his room by means of the window and returned in the small hours of the morning?

It was an excellent time then for Don José to explain that he had seen the man at his window, and had sprung out after him, but for some reason he did not; and within a few hours he wished devoutly that he had.

Pedro Jorge came charging around the corner of the building now, clad in a red nightshirt that reached scarcely to his knees and was half patches.

"What is it?" he cried. "Has there been murder done? Somebody is slain?"

"Thank the saints that there is not!" Valentino groaned. "I was guarding Don José's window and awoke to find a man climbing through it and so fired the revolver. But the man was Don José himself, and I almost slew him."

"Ass!" Pedro Jorge cried. "That comes from sleeping in the moonilght instead of in a proper bed. Go instantly to your room! You are not hurt, Don José?"

"Not as much as a scratch, thank you!" Don José replied. *"Buenas noches!"* And he sprang through the window and was in his room again.

Pedro Jorge and Valentino walked around the corner of the building and entered the inn, and both took brandy.

"This is a peculiar business!" Pedro Jorge said. "Are you trying to slay our best customer? You would kill him before he as much as pays his bill?"

"I swear that there was somebody at his window. I fired—and then Don José called upon me not to murder him."

"Where do you suppose he could have been at this hour of the night?" Pedro asked.

"Who knows, *señor?* Perhaps there is a love affair—"

"Ha! There is not a woman in the village at which such a man would look a second time!"

"Perhaps it was to take a stroll in the moonlight."

"Then why should he crawl through the window? Is there not a door that is always unlocked? Could he not walk through the hall and make his exit properly? There is some mystery here! What about that fight he had earlier in the night? What about the blood upon his clothing? Ha!"

"I am not eager to question the acts of my betters!" Valentino declared.

He stalked away with considerable dignity and went to bed. Pedro Jorge drank another bit of brandy, shook his head in doubt, and followed, and soon was snoring again.

Morning came, and Don José appeared for his breakfast in fresh clothes and with a smile upon his face, as though the events of the night previous had been nothing. He replied to Valentino's question that never had he felt better in his life, and he began eating breakfast with a display of appetite that gave his words truth.

Came a shriek from the end of the plaza; a chorus of shrieks from feminine throats!

"Some *peon* is beating his wife," said Valentino.

"Or the merchant has refused credit and that is the wail of the one refused," Pedro Jorge added.

The shrieks continued, and Pedro Jorge waddled to the door. Don José continued eating his breakfast as if he had heard nothing. Pedro Jorge beheld men and women running toward the merchant's house, which stood just off the plaza and not far from the store.

Before the door of the house was a feminine servant, and she was doing the screeching. She waved
her hands, beat them together, hammered at her
chest, and howled words that could not be understood
by those about her.

"Perhaps the merchant has a fit," Pedro Jorge said.

Without removing his apron he hurried across the
plaza to ascertain the cause of the commotion.

There was quite a crowd before the door of the
merchant's house now, and the local *magistrado* had
arrived, and two *rurales* who were stationed at Quebrada a part of the time were there.

The *magistrado* was shrieking to the servant to
speak in an intelligent manner, and because of his
threatening attitude the servant was howling the more.
The *magistrado* pushed her to one side and entered
the house.

Almost immediately he was back in the doorway
again, his face white and his hands trembling, and he
called to the *rurales*. They rushed into the dwelling.

The reason for the servant's screeching was before
them. In the front room was the merchant lying in
a pool of blood. A knife had been thrust through
his heart, and his head had been battered, and his
throat was slit almost from ear to ear. It was evident that he had been dead for several hours.

The *magistrado,* ranking those present, took command of the situation and ordered the *rurales* to keep
out the crowd. Word went forth that the merchant
had been foully murdered, and that he had been robbed
also since his desk had been broken open and papers
were scattered about.

Here was excitement for the village of Quebrada!
A shooting affair in the plaza, with death at the end
of it and the victor fleeing toward the north, was not
an unusual occurrence; but here was a cold-blooded
murder and a case of theft, where the perpetrator was
unknown, and the mystery of it added spice.

"Who could have done this hideous thing?" the
magistrado asked. "There is no stranger in the town."

"Except this Don José," said one.

"Ha! What is known concerning him?"

"He has said nothing except that his name is Don
José," a man replied. "He purchased a fine horse
from the merchant, and yesterday he rode toward the
north and did not return until night."

"And he had much blood on his clothes," added a
peon who had been at the inn when Don José arrived.

"What is this?" the *magistrado* asked.   "Pedro
Jorge, what do you know of the man?"

Now the *magistrado* collected the taxes in the vil-
large, and he had been lenient with Pedro Jorge, and
also he spent many a *peso* with the innkeeper for wine.

"I would like to speak to you privately, *señor*," Pedro Jorge said, glancing around at the crowd; and the
magistrado asked him inside the merchant's house.
Pedro Jorge acted like a man who had evidence to im-
part.

"What is it?" the official demanded.

"In the first place, *señor*, this Don José has funds
and whatever happens, I wish you would see to it that
I am paid my bill. It is an enormous bill—I even had
to purchase the man soap."

"You shall be protected, Pedro Jorge."

"This Don José rode away early yesterday morning, it is true, saying that he would return in time for the evening meal and did not come back until four hours after that time, and then with his clothing drenched with blood."

"Ha! What said he?"

"He told a weird tale about having been attacked by almost a score of bandits, who shot at him and assaulted him with their knives. There was a tiny cut on one of his arms, and he made the remark that the blood on his clothes had come from the veins of another man."

"Ha! That is significant. Proceed, *señor.*"

"Old Valentino, who appears to think that this Don José is a noble *hidalgo,* was afraid the man had deadly enemies, and last night watched outside his window. He slumbered, awoke to see a man crawling in, and fired off my big revolver. And, behold, the man was Don José himself!"

"What time was this?"

"About two in the morning, *magistrado.*"

"What was the man doing out at that hour?"

"That is the question," Pedro Jorge said.

"The evidence appears to be sufficient," the *magistrado* remarked. "Is this Don José now at your inn?"

"*Si, señor!*"

"We shall pay him a visit. Do not fear, Pedro Jorge—if the man has funds you shall receive the money due you."

The *magistrado* led the way across the plaza, flanked by the two *rurales*. Pedro Jorge was at his heels, and behind flocked the men and women of the village.

Don José was just finishing his breakfast, was just lighting a cigarette. He looked up with a smile as the throng entered and raised his eyebrows when the official stopped before his table.

"I am the *magistrado*, *señor*. I find it my duty to ask you a few questions."

"But certainly!" said Don José. "Valentino, fetch wine for the *magistrado*."

"No wine, thank you! This is a serious business. There has been murder done!"

"In Quebrada? Is this a jest? I had thought that nothing ever happened here."

"It is no time for levity, *señor*. What is your name?"

"Don José."

"Don José what?" the *magistrado* asked.

"Is not plain Don José enough? What are your questions?"

Valentino hovered near, alarm in his face. How dared the village *magistrado* address a *hidalgo* in such a high-handed manner? It would not have surprised Valentino had Don José twisted the *magistrado's* nose.

"The merchant has been slain!" the official went on. "He was killed with a knife in the living-room of his house and his desk was robbed."

"This is news!" said Don José.

"Is it, *señor?*"

"What do you mean by that tone?" Don José asked. "Surely you are not making an attempt to connect me with the crime?"

"Certainly not, Don José!" Valentino cried.

"Silence!" the *magistrado* exclaimed, and old Valentino winced, though he desired to face the official bravely.

"You are a stranger in our village, Don José," the *magistrado* said. "What is your business?"

"Must a man have a business?"

"It would be better for you to tell the whole truth in reply to my questions."

"Shall we say, then, that I am merely traveling?"

"Tourists do not visit Quebrada, *señor*. There is nothing here to attract them. You called upon the merchant soon after your arrival, did you not?"

"I did."

"And purchased a horse? But first you spoke to him in a harsh manner and ordered him to clean the dust from his wares, did you not, *señor*?"

"The place needed cleaning."

"Where did you go when you rode away from the village yesterday morning?"

"To the *hacienda* of Señor Roberts."

"You had business with this Señor Roberts?"

"Would it not be more to the point to ask Señor Roberts that?" asked Don José.

"And when you returned to this inn your clothes were covered with blood!" the *magistrado* charged, shaking his finger at Don José. "Do not deny it!"

"I have no intention of attempting to deny it, *señor*, since it is the truth. My clothes were absolutely ruined, to tell it all."

"Ha! And when alarm was raised concerning your

adventure you said that the blood came from the veins of another man, did you not, *señor?*"

"I did," replied Don José, "and it did."

"From whose veins, *señor?*"

"I have not the slightest idea."

"You have not the slightest idea? You fight with a man and spill his blood and have it drench your clothes, and yet you have not the slightest idea regarding his identity?"

"You have guessed it!"

"You still refuse to give your entire name and state what brought you to Quebrada?"

"My name is Don José and I was brought on a train."

The *magistrado* turned to the *rurales*.

"Search his room!" he commanded.

Don José grinned and puffed at his cigarette and blew a cloud of smoke toward the ceiling.

Presently the *rurales* returned, and one of them handed a bloody knife to the *magistrado*.

"It was found in his room, behind the bed and next to the wall," the man reported.

"Ha!" the *magistrado* cried. "Do you still deny your guilt in the face of this, *señor?* Can you smile when you look upon this bloody weapon?"

"I know nothing of the knife," said Don José.

He thought that it must be the one dropped by the fellow who had tried to crawl through the window the night before, but he was not sure.

"Another thing! You slipped from your room during the night, and did not return until early in the morning," the *magistrado* charged.

"A fellow tried to get at me through my window and I sprang out after him," Don José explained.

"You were fully dressed?"

"I had not removed my clothes because I expected some such visitor."

"Why?"

"I was attacked on the highway, and did not know who attacked me, or their reason for it, and I thought that perhaps they might try it again at the inn."

"The story is very thin!" the *magistrado* announced. "Your answers have not satisfied me, *señor*. I shall have to hold you for further investigation, and I do not doubt you are guilty!"

"Hold me?" asked Don José.

"In the *carcel, señor!*"

Old Valentino gave an exclamation of horror.

"Why, you would not dare do such a thing!" he told the official. "You would treat a high-born *hidalgo* in such a brutal fashion? You would treat him like a thieving *peon?* Put such a man in the foul *carcel?* Ha!"

"Silence from you!" the official cried. "How do you know that he is a *hidalgo?*"

"Ha! He has the air—the manner! And I have eyes! I have observed him! By the saints—"

"Silence! And this man goes to the *carcel,*" the *magistrado* said again.

Now Don José tossed aside the cigarette he had been smoking, put his heel upon it to extinguish the fire, and got slowly to his feet and faced the *magistrado,* the smile having gone from his face. His chin

was thrust forward a little, and his eyes had narrowed
and now glowed.

"All this is nonsense!" he cried. "I go into your
foul jail? You call me a murderer?"

"You are to be held for a rigid investigation, *señor*,"
the official declared.

"One side!" Don José cried.

He struck out quickly and thrust the *magistrado*
from him with sudden violence, and in such manner
that the official struck against the two *rurales* with
full force and caused them to lose balance for an instant.

"One side!" Don José cried again; and now he
charged at the crowd before the door.

There was an immediate uproar. The *magistrado*
called upon those in the doorway to stop the fugitive,
to prevent an escape. The *rurales* struggled to get
upon their feet. Children shrieked and fled to the
four corners of the room. Women screeched and
fought to get away from the open door.

"One side!" Don José cried for a third time.

And now he was at the door—he was through it.
And old Valentino, who had struggled through the
throng at Don José's heels, whirled suddenly in the
doorway and threw up Pedro Jorge's big revolver.

"Back *señores*, or I fire!" he cried.

The *magistrado* and the *rurales* stopped in their
headlong rush—stopped to stare in astonishment at
this unexpected menace that confronted them.

"You put no *hidalgo* in jail while I am alive to prevent the act!" Valentino screeched. "Back, scum!

Go, Don José! Get your horse from the corral and take a saddle and bridle from the merchant's store. I shall hold these villains until you have gone some distance! Ha! By the saints, my blood is young again!"

CHAPTER X

MASTER OF THE TOWN

HUGH HANKINS left the mine that morning at an early hour, for a shipment of machinery that was badly needed was expected at Quebrada, and he was aware from sad experience that the only manner in which to get it promptly was to be on the scene and have it attended to himself.

He rode easily along the highway, glancing back now and then at the smoke of the mill and speculating what it meant to him in dollars. He thought of Dorothy Charlton, too, and wondered what manner of man he was who would come from Boston to investigate him and decide whether he would make a worthy husband. He thought of everything and everybody, including Don José—and he galloped around a bend in the road to behold Don José bearing down upon him, his horse maintaining a good rate of speed.

Hankins pulled his horse to a walk and frowned. He did not like this Don José, though he had no real reason for disliking him. He told himself that it was impossible for him to be jealous of such a man merely because he had paid a visit to the Roberts *hacienda*. He had a premonition, though, that it was not well

110

for him that the life-paths of himself and Don José had crossed at this time.

Don José stopped his horse, swept off his *sombrero,* and bowed. He was smiling as usual.

"A fair morning, Señor Hankins!" he said.

"It is, indeed," Hankins replied with studied courtesy. "You are abroad early."

"It was earlier at rise of the sun," Don José observed. "Why should a man possess a horse if not to ride him?"

"You are going out to take a look at the mine?" Hankins asked.

Hankins still had a little fear that Don José was a man sent by federal officials to nose around and make an investigation in an effort to discover something that would form a basis for a demand for more taxes, more graft. Hankins had been bothered considerably by such things.

"Is your mine in this direction?" Don José asked, innocently. "I had not thought of visiting it, but perhaps I may some time when you are there. I have heard that it is a very valuable mine."

"It will be when a considerable work has been done on it and a great deal more money spent," Hankins replied, on guard. "Do you expect to remain in the vicinity long, *señor?*"

"Who knows?" asked Don José. "A man is not always master of his actions."

"Ah! You speak as a man who is subject to orders."

"Are not all of us, more or less?" asked Don José.

"You will pardon me now, *señor,* I know, if I ride on. I have an excellent reason for haste."

Don José bowed again, touched his horse with the spurs, and galloped away in a cloud of dust. For some time Hugh Hankins remained on his horse in the middle of the highway, gazing after him.

"There is some mystery about that fellow," he told himself. "And he is no *caballero!* He's an ordinary greaser—and some day he'll bust!"

And then he rode on toward the town.

Having galloped around another bend in the road Hankins saw bearing down upon him a small company of horsemen. They rode in a whirlwind of dust and appeared to be getting all the speed possible out of their mounts.

Hankins swung his horse to one side of the highway to allow them to pass, supposing that here were some American cowboys who worked on a *hacienda* of the neighborhood, for there were several who had only Americans to handle their herds.

They dashed up to him, shrieked at their horses and at one another, stopped to surround him, all babbling questions at once. Hankins saw that two of them were *rurales* and the other half-dozen were men of the village, one of them the merchant's assistant.

"What is the trouble?" Hankins asked.

"Has he passed you? Did he go this way?"

"Who?"

"This Don José."

"I passed him but a short time ago and we talked some," Hankins replied. "What is the trouble?"

All rode on except one, who remained to explain.

"The merchant has been foully murdered!" he said. "He was robbed also. This Don José is being pursued for the crime, the *magistrado* having decided that he be held. He made his escape from us at the inn. There is an abundance of evidence against him."

The member of the posse galloped on in an effort to overtake his fellows. Hankins spurred his horse and dashed madly toward the distant town.

So this fine Don José had "busted" already, had he? He was a common murderer and thief!

Suddenly Hankins forgot the machinery he was expecting to find at Quebrada. He had remembered Dorothy Charlton. The fellow had spent the greater part of a day at the Roberts *hacienda*.

Was it possible that he had been looking over the ground there in contemplation of some crime? Was Dorothy in danger? Were her foster parents safe?

Hankins took a cross-trail and made for the Roberts *hacienda*. Those he passed on the road noticed that he was punishing his horse cruelly, and marveled at it, for generally Señor Hankins rode in a leisurely manner. He came to the driveway and galloped up it, and saw Dorothy at the end of the veranda picking flowers.

"Thank Heaven that you are safe!" Hankins cried, running up to her.

"Why, Hugh, what has happened?" she cried.

Roberts and his wife hurried out to the veranda, having heard his furious approach.

"This pretty Don José who was here yesterday—he has murdered the storekeeper at Quebrada and robbed him, and a posse is chasing the fellow now. They have conclusive evidence against him."

"I cannot believe it!" Mrs. Roberts exclaimed. "That man? A man like him a murderer and thief? There must be some grave mistake, I feel sure!"

"No, it cannot be true!" Dorothy declared.

"There it is!" said Hankins, turning to Roberts and throwing out his hands in a gesture of despair. "I told you so! The fellow has the glamour of romance about him, and women are attracted by it. Dorothy, be fair! Discount the man's foreign birth and good looks and romantic ways. Give me a white man's chance!"

"Why, Hugh!"

"I met the fellow, and afterward the posse pursuing him. I rode here the moment I heard of it. I was afraid for you."

"Why be afraid for us?" Roberts asked.

"Why the fellow was here yesterday! He might have been merely looking over the ground, seeing whether there was anything here worth stealing. I told you that he was a common greaser. There was a reason for his fine manners. I'd be careful, Roberts! Have some of your men armed, and let a few of them stay near the house. This fellow may pay you a visit."

Roberts hurried away to find his *superintendente*. The man was in the orchard overseeing trench digging. Roberts told the tale in a few words, and did not notice that the eyes of the *superintendente* flashed peculiarly.

"Have half a dozen men scattered around the house," Roberts instructed. "And be sure that we are well guarded to-night. The *rurales* will catch the fellow, no doubt, but we must be on our guard until

they do.   Where is Agustin Gonzales?   He will be an
excellent man to place in charge."

"Agustin Gonzales is unable to work today, *señor*,"
the *superintendente* explained.

"Is he drunk, Juan Lopez?"

"No, *señor*.   He had a trifle of an argument with
one of the other men, and there is a small knife-
wound in his side.   But in reality it is nothing."

"Confound the fellow—he always is fighting.   Well,
do the best that you can."

Roberts hurried back to the veranda.   And he arrived just in time to hear a spirited defense of Don
José from the lips of Dorothy.

"I will not believe it!" the girl was saying.   "He is
not that sort of man at all.   I can imagine him slaying another for an insult and during a quarrel.   But
he is not a thief.   One look at his face would convince any one of that."

"Let us not bother our heads about the fellow,"
Hankins said finally.   "Yesterday he was here for a
few hours—to-day he is gone—that is all there is
to it!"

Hankins rode on to Quebrada then, for he was
anxious to find out about his machinery. And he found
that resentment against Don José was strong in his
breast.

As for Don José, he did not visit the mine, but he
approached near it.   From the top of the hill he looked
back and saw the pursuit spread along the road. He
guessed that the *magistrado* had offered a reward for
his capture.

He came to where the road forked and stopped his

horse to look around him. Nearby there was a wild jumble of rocks, and Don José rode into the midst of them, so that he was hidden from the road. He lighted a cigarette and waited.

It was but a few minutes before the pursuit reached the spot. Don José concerned himself only with seeing that his horse made no noise and listened to the conversation.

"We must separate here," the leader was saying. "Half of us must take each road. We can come together three miles further on. It is my opinion that the fellow is making for the border and hopes to cross into the States."

They shouted at one another and rode on.

Don José waited until he could hear the beating of their horses' hoofs no longer, and then he made his way back to the road and galloped toward the town.

He laughed to himself as he rode, and urged his horse to make good speed, and presently came within sight of the village. He made no effort to ride around the place, but followed down the highway, only he was alert.

Don José had a mental census of Quebrada. The best men were in the chase. There remained only the station agent, the *magistrado,* who was old and lacking in courage, and Pedro Jorge and Valentino, also old, besides certain *peons* who could be cowed with a look.

He galloped to the rear of the inn, dismounted, tethered his horse, and entered a door from the *patio.* He went at once to his room and got his belt and revolver. And then he walked on to the door of the main room.

"All the time I guessed it," Pedro Jorge was saying. "I did not relish the manner in which he acted. Valentino thought that he was a *hidalgo* and bowed before him, but I was suspicious of the man. Have some more wine, *magistrado*."

"It will bring a certain prestige to our village," the *magistrado* was saying. "It will be the first time I have presided over a trial of a murderer."

"Ha! You are not presiding yet!" Pedro Jorge exclaimed.

"Oh, they will catch the fellow! For how can he escape, with two of our *rurales* pursuing him? But for that fool of an old Valentino we should have him in the *carcel* now.

"He is nothing ferocious to capture—and, besides, he is not armed. I could capture the fellow myself!"

"Have some more wine, *magistrado*," Pedro Jorge urged. "And please do not forget your promise to see that my bill is paid from the money found on the man when he is taken!"

"You shall have the amount of your bill, Pedro Jorge, and I care not if you include a few extras. And I shall request that the man be executed here after he has been convicted and sentenced. It will attract attention to Quebrada—and possibly get the name of the village in the newspapers. And all of us, I feel sure, would love to see an execution! Is it not so, *senores?*"

He glanced at the others in the room.

"*Sí! Sí!*" they shouted. Many of them never had seen anything as lovely as an execution.

Don José threw open the door at that juncture and faced them. The *magistrado* suddenly let his wine glass drop to the floor.

Pedro Jorge gave one glance and then started to get beneath the bar. The others in the room crouched against the nearest wall, fear written in their faces.

"By the saints—" the *magistrado* swore.

"Hands up!" Don José commanded. "Make the slightest move that I do not order and there shall be a funeral service at the little church! So you could capture me yourself, eh, *magistrado?* 'Tis your duty just now to send somebody in chase of your posse. When last I saw them they were riding like the wind into the north. Unless they are fetched back they soon will be across the border and on the way to the frozen north. Where is Valentino?"

No man answered him. Don José glanced rapidly around the room and saw Pedro Jorge's back.

"Come out of that, Pedro Jorge!" he ordered. "Tell me—where is Valentino?"

"In *carcel, señor.*"

"Why is he in jail?"

"The *magistrado* had him sent there, Don José, because he aided you to escape."

"Ah!"

There was a wealth of meaning in Don José's simple exclamation. He glared at the *magistrado,* and that official flinched and prepared to beg for his life.

"He shall be released," Don José went on to say. "But there is something else to be done first. Pedro

Jorge, do not worry about my bill. Here is twice what I owe you. And you will allow my trunk to remain in my room—I am still a guest at this hole of an inn."

"*Sí*, Don José! Whatever you say!" Pedro Jorge cried, pouncing on the piece of currency.

"I need assistance now. I shall require your services, Pedro Jorge, and also those of the *magistrado*. Kindly come with me. You other men are to come along, too. In fact, I insist upon it! Do you understand?"

He waved a hand toward the door—the hand held the revolver. The *magistrado* shuffled forward, his face white, and his hands trembling, and Pedro Jorge followed at his heels, the perspiration standing out on his forehead. The others in the room joined the procession.

Don José stopped them at the door of his room.

"The *magistrado* will get my saddle," he directed. "Pedro Jorge, you get the bridle. Pronto!"

In an instant they were out in the hall again.

"My horse is in the *patio*," Don José said. "He wears saddle and bridle that I borrowed from the store. Put my own saddle and bridle on the beast and then return the others to the store at your leisure. I expect prompt service."

He got it. The *magistrado* staggered beneath the weight of the heavy saddle, but he bore it bravely and swiftly to the *patio*, and began taking the other from the horse's back. Pedro Jorge exchanged the bridles.

"And so old Valentino has been thrown into the *carcel* because he was loyal to me, has he?" Don José said. "We must have him out at once. One moment, *señores!*"

He mounted the horse, gathered up the reins, and then turned to face them.

"We shall do old Valentino all honor," he said. "We shall parade to the *carcel,* and the *magistrado* himself shall open the door and bring Valentino to the freedom of the open air again. And if, after I have ridden away, Valentino is once more incarcerated, I shall punish the *magistrado* severely when I return. You will form in line, *señores*, and the brave *magistrado,* who could capture me himself, shall lead my horse. I may mention that I am fairly accurate with the revolver that swings against my hip."

They formed in line as he had commanded and the parade began. It went around the corner of the inn and straight across the plaza toward the *carcel*. From the *adobe* huts women and children ran to view the spectacle.

They thought at first that Don José had been captured and was being taken to prison, but they thought differently when they observed that he was smoking a cigarette, and that his hands were not bound, and that he now held in one hand a revolver, the muzzle of which menaced the *magistrado's* back.

They reached the *carcel* and Don José dismounted. He bade one of the men hold his horse, and promised dire punishment if the man proved disloyal. And then he bowed to the *magistrado* and motioned toward the door.

"In you go!" he exclaimed. "You will tell the man in charge that Valentino is to be released immediately, but you must unlock the cell door yourself—and ask his pardon for having incarcerated him. I expect obedience!"

He got it. The trembling *magistrado* went to the door and called the jailer, and made his wishes known. With his own hands he unlocked the door of the cell and led old Valentino forth to the freedom of the open air.

"Understand, Valentino, you are free!" Don José said. "And if you are troubled again about this matter, I shall punish certain persons, if it takes me years to do so! Now we will all go back to the inn."

The parade was formed again and went across the plaza. They crowded inside the inn, Don José following them, after he had glanced down the highway and made sure the posse was not returning unexpectedly.

"Wine, Pedro Jorge!" he cried. "Serve every man here with the best wine in the house—and charge it to yourself!"

"*Señor?*"

"Charge it to yourself, I said, as a punishment."

There were tears in Pedro Jorge's eyes as he poured out the wine; there was a light of expectation in Valentino's. Ha! Here was the very pattern of all ideal *hidalgos!*

"You are refreshed, *señores?*" Don José asked presently. "Then I shall take leave of you for a short time. *Magistrado,* when I find the man who slew the merchant I shall bring him to your *carcel* myself, Señores, *á Dios!*"

He hurried from the inn and vaulted into the saddle. He turned to wave his *sombrero* at them; he smiled as he watched them crowding the doorway, the white-faced *magistrado* in the fore. Pedro Jorge's face was purple with wrath because of the wine he had been forced to give away. Valentino beamed.

"It is almost the *siesta* hour—take your rest!" Don José cried to them.

And then he dashed across the plaza and turned into the highway that ran toward the·north. And he saw Señor Hugh Hankins riding toward him through the dust!

CHAPTER XI

DON JOSÉ GETS A ROSE

Now that the menace of Don José's actual presence was removed, it was no more than natural that bravery should return full force to the *magistrado* and those with him.

The official, too, saw Señor Hugh Hankins riding toward the village, and he darted out into the plaza and screeched with the full power of his lungs for Señor Hankins to take prisoner this Don José, who had terrorized the village and now was escaping.

The *magistrado* accompanied his screeches with violent gestures; he waved his arms and beat his breast and shook his fists toward the flying horseman because of his outraged dignity and his wrath.

Señor Hankins perceived Don José bearing down upon him, riding swiftly, his horse with belly close to the ground and head thrust forward. He saw the *magistrado*, also, and the others in the plaza making their wild gestures, and he heard their shrieks.

Señor Hankins guessed at once that Don José had eluded the posse, had committed some fresh atrocity, and now was fleeing the consequences of it. Señor Hankins swung his horse squarely across the road at a

narrow place where there was a stone fence on one
side and a deep gulch on the other.

To tell the truth, Hugh Hankins made the move as
a response to impulse, and had in his mind no definite
plan for stopping Don José or capturing him. It happened, too, that Hankins was not armed. And he
thought he was confronting a man who had blood upon
his hands, and who was desperate because he knew
that capture would mean an ignoble death.

Don José stopped before him in a cloud of dust, pulling his horse back on its haunches.

"*Buenas dias, señor!*" he said. "You will please
me by pulling your beast to one side of the road. I
cannot pass when he stands as he does, and I am
afraid that this mount of mine is not horse enough
to vault over you."

"You are running away!" Hankins charged.

"I am riding away," Don José corrected.

"From the consequences of a murder and robbery,
I suppose," Hankins said.

"Ah! You have heard the tale?"

"And what new crime have you committed now?"

"A most serious one, I am afraid, *señor*. I have
forced Pedro Jorge to give a crowd wine and charge
it to himself. He will wail for a month, I doubt not!"

"Turn back!" Hankins commanded suddenly.

Don José threw back his head and laughed.

"You ask me to turn back?" he cried. "I have no
quarrel with you, Señor Hankins, and you will be a
very wise man to cause none between us. I am in
haste and your horse is blocking the road. And you
are not armed, I perceive, whereas I have an excel-

lent revolver with me, and it is loaded with first-class cartridges. One side!"

Don José whipped out the revolver as he spoke, and the smile left his face and a look of determination came into it. His lower jaw shot forward, his eyes became piercing, he scowled.

Hankins raised his hand as if to protest, but Don José spurred his horse forward and alongside the mount of the other man, and then he bent over until his face was within a foot of Señor Hankins's.

"Dismount!" he commanded. "And do it quickly, *señor!*"

Hankins looked him squarely in the eyes and decided that here was a man who would carry out a threat. He dismounted slowly, for there seemed nothing else to do. It would avail him nothing to refuse and receive a slug of lead through his vitals.

But he took his time about it, and his face was white with anger, and his eyes flamed into those of Don José. In that instant each knew that enmity had formed between them for all time.

"We may meet on more even terms one of these days, *señor!*" Hugh Hankins said.

"It will be a pleasure," Don José replied. "Do not feel badly about this, *señor*. An unarmed man can accomplish nothing in the face of a weapon. I perceive that you have good common sense as well as courage. I am in haste, as I said, and do not care to have you following at my heels, and hence I am forced to take your horse. I shall release him after a time."

He seized the reins, spurred his own mount, and

dashed along the highway toward the north, leading
Hankins's horse beside him. He rode like the wind,
and stirred up as much dust as the wind could have,
and finally disappeared around the nearest curve. And
then he released Hankins's horse and continued along
the highway.

The sun was blazing now, and, after a time, Don
José rode with some leisure, sparing his horse. He
mopped the perspiration from his face with a silk
handkerchief, brushed the dust from his clothes, and
began humming a song.

Mile after mile he rode in this fashion until he
came within sight of the Roberts *hacienda,* and then
he grew suddenly alert and on guard.

Men were working in the fields and orchards, and
they seemed to give him no attention. He galloped
slowly around the bend in the road and came to the
entrance of the driveway. And there, beneath a
spreading tree, he saw Dorothy Charlton feeding pig-
eons.

She glanced up quickly when she heard the beating
of his horse's hoofs, and one hand went to her breast,
and her face turned white for an instant, but she soon
regained her composure. She had been riding, and
her horse was grazing some distance away, too far for
her to reach instantly.

"Buenas dias, señorita!" Don José called.

He stopped his horse, swept off his *sombrero,* and
bowed from the saddle.

"Is it not a beautiful day?" he asked.

Now she confronted him, hands clenched at her
sides, and looked at him bravely.

"You are bold to speak to me, *señor*," she said.

"I beg your pardon!"

"Have you eluded the posse that was pursuing you? Have you washed the blood from your hands? They are saying that you killed an old man and then robbed his desk of all the money it contained!"

Don José threw back his head and laughed.

"And surely you cannot believe such a wild tale, *señorita*," he said.

"I did not think it possible, *señor*. But they are saying that the evidence is strong against you."

"Circumstantial evidence only, *senorita*, which is the most unjust thing in the world."

"You have said little concerning your name and business," she went on. "You have made the countryside suspicious of you. If you are not guilty, why do you not explain things? Why do you run away from those who pursue?"

"Those are fair questions and deserving of fair answers," he said. "The evidence is damning, I must admit! And the silly *magistrado* would have thrown me into the *carcel*. You have lived in this country long enough, *señorita*, to appreciate what that would have meant—no chance for defense, a mockery of a trial, perhaps my execution made the occasion for a day of feasting. And so I naturally refused to be incarcerated. For how can I find the real murderer if I am not at liberty to search for him?"

"You are trying to do that?"

"Certainly, *señorita*. By doing that I can remove the stain from my own name. Do you think a *hidalgo* would allow suspicion to attach itself to his name? Do you think that he would allow men to look at him from the corners of their eyes? Ha!"

"I—I am almost persuaded that you are innocent, *señor*," she said, meeting his eyes again.

"Almost? It shall be my task to convince you," he replied. "I would not have you suspect me for the world, nor your foster parents, nor even Señor Hankins, who, I fear, does suspect me now."

"Why do you not tell your name?" she asked. "Why do you not come out plainly and say in as many words that you have come to Quebrada for the purpose of visiting the home of your ancestors. Would not that force men to believe in you, *señor?*"

"Who knows?" he said.

"And there are all sorts of rumors flying about. Some say that you are an official who will impress men for the army, and others that you have come to oppress the poor by collecting more taxes. Tell the facts, *señor*, and these rumors will cease."

"The dear people must have a topic for gossip," he explained. "Without one, life for them would be unendurable."

"At least, tell the facts to me," she begged, smiling up at him, dimpling.

"Ah, *señorita*, it is difficult to refuse any request you make. But to tell you would be to rob you of woman's birthright—the right to experience curiosity," he said. "And that would be an unkindness, *señorita*. Can you not trust me? Does not your woman's instinct tell you whether I am the proper sort of man?"

"Perhaps it does," she replied. "But the people of

the countryside do not all possess a woman's instinct, *señor*. The posse is still pursuing you?"

"I believe so. I have not seen it since it rode past me and went violently toward the northern border. Undoubtedly somebody will catch it in time and turn it back."

"And you have no fear, *señor?* Would you rather ride with danger than tell the truth and drive all danger away?"

"Ha! Then you do not believe me guilty?" he asked.

"I cannot bring myself to think that you could commit such a foul crime!" she answered.

"I thank you, *señorita!* It is a great deal for a man to have a woman believe in him. And even Señor Hankins thinks that I am guilty, and I have no doubt that he has joined the pursuit by this time."

"If you will explain things to Señor Hankins he might help you. He is not without influence."

Don José remembered the look that had passed between himself and Señor Hankins last and chuckled.

"It is much better for a man to fight such a thing out by himself," he observed.

"You are very peculiar in some ways, *señor*," she said. "Have you stopped to think that you may be seriously injured if the posse comes up with you, or that you may have to wound a man?"

"I have thought considerably about it, *señorita*," he admitted. "But a man must take a chance now and then—it adds spice to his existence."

She had stepped close to his horse's head now, and

was plucking the thorns from a rose, and did not look up at him when she spoke again.

"And so you refuse absolutely to explain the mystery to me?" she asked.

"Think how much better it would be, *señorita*, to speculate as to my identity and reason for being in this neighborhood," he said. "The explanation may be so prosaic that you will feel cheated out of a romance."

"Then I shall not urge you against your will, *señor*. And may I be allowed to express the hope that you will be free of your difficulties soon?"

"You are kindness itself, *señorita*," he assured her.

More difficulties were approaching, but neither of them realized it at the time. From the far distance Juan Lopez had seen Don José—and had recognized him.

He had called half a dozen fellows to him, those Señor Roberts had ordered armed to guard the place, and now they slipped along the deep irrigation ditches and through the trees and high grass, attempting to get near their man.

Juan Lopez had explained plainly that, no doubt, the *magistrado* of Quebrada would give a handsome reward for the *hidalgo*, and the men were eager. As for himself, he was determined to take the *hidalgo's* life, and Agustin Gonzales, his accomplice, had the same notion. They could not forget how Don José had fought them off in the little ravine of the deep shadows.

But Don José, apparently, saw nothing except the sweet face of the *señorita* standing at his horse's head, and she was intent on their conversation, and neither realized the menace.

"I fear that I must ride on," Don José was telling her. "I cannot wait here until the posse is at my heels. It would be ideal to spend the entire afternoon in such pleasant conversation, but it would not be good common sense."

"May good fortune ride with you, *señor*, if you really are innocent," Dorothy said.

"You do not fully believe it yet?"

"Yes, I believe it," she replied, looking up at him.

"And the rose, *señorita*—the one you are holding! Would you give it to me as a token of trust?"

"Why, *señor*—"

"As a token of trust, *señorita*."

"A rose? It is nothing," she said, but flushed as she spoke. "Of course you may have it, *señor*."

She started to hand it up to him, still smiling at his eagerness to receive it. At that instant Juan Lopez sneezed. It was a disastrous sneeze for Juan Lopez. He had crawled within a short distance of Don José, and was about to raise his revolver and fire. A weed tickled his nose and filled it with dust—and he sneezed!

The sneeze put an end to the stealthy approach, of course. Juan Lopez sprang to his feet, shouting his orders to the others. Don José glanced up quickly and instantly realized his danger.

None could see exactly what happened, but suddenly he had jerked out his revolver and had fired, and Juan Lopez was nursing a broken wrist, and his own weapon had fallen to the ground.

There came a fusillade then, and bullets flew about Don José's head. Dorothy Charlton dropped the rose in the dust of the highway, covered her ears with her hands, and darted back half a dozen paces, her eyes wide with terror. Don José fired again, this time over the heads of the men nearest, and galloped away.

They took after him on foot, mindful of the reward, and fired at him wildly. And suddenly he wheeled his horse and was dashing back straight at them.

They scattered to either side of the road. They had fired all their càrtridges, and some were trying frantically to reload. Don José ran his horse straight down the dusty highway, laughing and shouting at his foes. Dorothy Charlton looked at him in wonder.

Then suddenly he swung down from the saddle. His left hand touched the ground and he swung upright again. He waved his hand—and Dorothy saw that the rose was in it.

"I have it!" he cried, waving at her. *"Señorita, á Dios!"*

CHAPTER XII

AN UNAVAILING SIEGE

Now it happened that the posse grew tired of riding into the north, especially since they found no trace of the fugitive and were told by several along the road that no horseman had galloped that way; and so they turned about and made for Quebrada again, realizing that somewhere along the way they had ridden past their quarry.

The men at Señor Hankins's mine had heard of the murder and robbery by that time, and had decided to join in the manhunt, as it would break the monotony of handling hard rock and extracting gold from ore. Some fifteen of them, all mounted, and half of them Americans, galloped out to the main road in time to join forces with the men from the village.

They came in time to where the trail forked, and near where they met Señor Hankins, who had obtained possession of his horse again, and he gave them the latest news regarding Don José. So the entire band rode forward toward the north, following the road that led to the Roberts *hacienda*.

There was some fear in the heart of Hugh Hankins now, for he knew that Don José had ridden in that direction, and he placed little faith in the men Señor

133

Roberts had on guard at his place, knowing considerable about the breed.

So he led the small army himself, and urged the
men who followed to their utmost speed, sweeping
down hill and up hill, galloping through little ravines,
raising a cloud of dust that would have done credit
to a regiment of cavalry.

Don José, riding back down the highroad and searching for a trail that he might follow toward the hills,
came to the top of a small elevation and looked ahead.
Within two hundred yards of him, and bearing down
upon him with the greatest possible speed, he beheld
Hugh Hankins and the men at his back.

At the same instant Hankins caught sight of Don
José. His cry to his followers was heard above the
pounding of their horses' hoofs. They glanced ahead,
too, and observed the man they sought and promptly
gave chase.

Don José found himself in somewhat of a predicament now. Before him rode Hankins and the
crowd; behind him was a furious and wounded Juan
Lopez and the men of the *hacienda*. On either side
of the highway, there was soft plowed ground, through
which no horse would be able to carry a rider with any
great amount of speed.

Neither did Don José have time to hesitate and consider the emergency. He wheeled his horse promptly
and dashed back from whence he had come, bending
low over the beast's neck to escape any chance bullets
that Hankins or the members of the posse might send
in his direction, and watching for the menace of the
hacienda men ahead.

These men were still near the end of the driveway. Dorothy Charlton had mounted her horse and was riding slowly toward the house. All saw Don José returning, and noticed that he was pursued; and the men of the *hacienda* took cover and prepared to give him a warm reception.

He did not dare attempt to ride through them now. They were in such a position that surely one of them could stop him with a bullet, or at least stop his horse, which would be almost as bad with Hankins and the posse following so closely. In such event either capture or death would be certain.

But he was past the acres of plowed ground now. Suddenly he pulled his horse sharply to the left, and the animal cleared the high fence as if it had not been there. Don José galloped through an orchard toward the distant *hacienda* buildings.

The posse swept up the road and started in pursuit, some of them taking the fence in Don José's wake, and others continuing to the driveway, some cutting back to a lane and thus making an attempt to hem the fugitive in and cut off his escape. Juan Lopez and the men of the *hacienda* ran quickly along the driveway, shouting an alarm.

Dorothy Charlton had been quick to understand the situation. She experienced a sharp, quick mental struggle, and decided that this man was innocent and worthy of aid. She urged her horse forward and galloped toward the big barn. Springing from the saddle, she threw open the big door and waved wildly to Don José.

Don José galloped through the orchard, cleared another fence, and sprang from his horse before the door, leaving the animal with trailing reins. He ran inside the barn, where Dorothy was waiting.

"They are surrounding you," she gasped. "You cannot escape to the hills now, for they surely would overtake you since the trails curve so. Hurry through the barn, go to a *peon's* hut, disguise yourself! I'll rush out, and then you bar the door, and they'll think you have barricaded yourself and intend making a defense."

"Quick thought, and an excellent one, *señorita!*" he said.

She did not wait longer. She hurried from the barn again, pretending to be much alarmed, and Don José slammed the big door shut and barred it. Dorothy, her hands held over her ears, ran back to the veranda of the house.

Up swept the posse, and Hankins plunged from his horse's back and hurried up to the girl.

"He—he went into the barn," she gasped.

"He did not harm you?"

"No—he left his horse and went into the barn and fastened the door."

"He's going to make a stand in the barn!" Hankins cried to the others of the posse. "Surround the place —quickly! Do you want him to escape again?"

Don José had wasted no time. Having barred the front door, he ran rapidly through the big structure, glad that there were no workmen in it for him to encounter. He darted through the rear door, which he slammed shut after him, and, keeping the barn between himself and his pursuers, hurried a short distance to the group of *adobe* huts used by men of the *hacienda* as homes, and entered the nearest.

An old man was there, a half-breed who sat in a corner eating a bit of bread. He looked up at Don José in surprise at this unexpected entrance, and then struggled to get up upon his feet since he saw one of his betters before him.

"Not a word!" Don José commanded. "Not as much as a faint whisper or you die!"

He flourished the revolver as he spoke, and the old man cringed against the wall, his face ashen.

"I—I am but an old *peon*—" he began.

"Silence!" commanded Don José. "I can see that much, fool! You live here alone?"

"*Sí señor!*"

"Nobody is liable to come in?"

"No, *señor;* nobody ever comes to my poor hut."

"Remove your clothes!"

"*Señor?*"

"Quickly! Do you wish to die a horrible death before your time? Off with your worn jacket—off with the ragged breeches! Quickly! Off with the old shoes—and get me your torn hat!"

The old *peon* did not pretend to understand what all this meant, but he started to obey, for he did not like Don José's manner, and, also, one of his superiors was commanding. He was deaf to a certain extent, and did not hear the cries of the men outside surrounding the barn. His hands trembled so that he scarcely was able to carry out Don José's orders, but he made shift to do so, and soon crouched in one corner of his hut, almost naked.

"Ugh!" exclaimed Don José as he glanced at the clothes in a pile at his feet. "This is a terrible thing, but it is necessary, I suppose. Confound this business! I am beginning to dislike it. This is worse than facing the posse!"

He watched the old man as he picked up the clothes, but he did not fear that a sudden screech of the *peon* would betray him. It was plainly to be seen that the old man was terrified and had no thought of resistance in his head.

He drew on the ragged breeches over his own gorgeous raiment. He pulled the big, old shoes over his fine boots. He picked up dust from the floor and dashed it over the breeches where his own fine clothing was showing through.

Then he put on the ragged jacket and threw more dust over himself. He wet his hands and smeared damp dust over his throat and face and hands. He ran to the little fireplace in the corner and got ashes and he smeared them on his hair and rumpled it at the temples. He picked up the *peon's* hat—a battered, dirty *sombrero*—and pulled it down well over his head.

And then he gave particular attention to the old man who cringed against the wall. "I cannot have you giving an alarm to my enemies," he said. "I shall have to bind and gag you, I am afraid. You have nothing to fear—I shall not harm you!"

Hanging from a peg in one of the walls were some bits of rope and straps of leather. Don José took them down and lashed the old *peon's* hands behind his back. Then he forced the terrified man to lie down, and lashed his feet and legs together and affixed a gag, then stood back a pace and contemplated him.

"If you attempt to escape as soon as I have gone out I shall return and punish you severely!" Don José said. "That is well understood? Nod your head! And because I dislike to rob an old man of his clothes and bind and gag him, here is some salve for your wounded feelings! You can see it?"

Don José exhibited a bill of generous denomination, and the eyes of the old man glistened. It was a large fortune for a *peon,* especially an old man who had no ambition and very little hope left.

"I place it here beneath this pan," Don José went on. "Then nobody will steal it when they find you here. Enjoy yourself with the money. You understand?"

The old man nodded again, and again his eyes gleamed. He would be willing to lose his clothes and be bound and gagged every day for such payment. Don José smiled down at him, and then turned around, bent his shoulders, and shuffled feebly to the door.

Hankins had assumed command of those who besieged the barn. It was entirely surrounded now, and men were behind what cover they could find; and Hankins was holding a council of war with the two *rurales* and Juan Lopez.

"He has barricaded himself, I suppose," Hankins was saying. "He undoubtedly will put up a fight since he is cornered and knows what capture means. We don't want to lose any men if we can help it. Have all the horses taken around to the other end of the veranda or a stray shot may wound one of them."

Half a dozen men ran to carry out his orders.

"We must rush the building and batter down the doors," Hankins continued. "Once we get inside great care must be taken. Find cover, search for the fellow. Get him alive, if it is possible, but at any rate, get him!"

Juan Lopez and Agustin Gonzales exchanged glances. Don José would not be taken alive if they had the fortune to get a chance shot at him, they decided.

Roberts was standing on the end of the veranda now, and Dorothy was by his side, declaring that she was in no danger there, and that she wanted to watch developments.

"Give the rogue a chance to surrender, Hankins!" Roberts called. "Let us have no killing if it can be prevented!"

Hankins walked a short distance toward the barn and called out:

"Within there, Don José? Come out and give yourself up, and I guarantee you'll be taken safely to the *carcel!* If you do not, we shall come in for you!"

He waited, but there was no answer.

"After him!" Hankins cried. "All rush in at once when I give the signal. Take care of yourselves. Watch out when you batter down the doors!"

He gave the signal. From every side the men rushed in, getting close to the walls of the barn, making their way as quickly as possible toward the doors. Some remained under cover a short distance away, watching the windows and ready to prevent an escape in that direction.

They began battering at the doors. An old man came slowly from the group of huts and made his way

toward the house. He was bent; he walked with a
shuffling gait; he seemed not to appreciate the fact
that there was a man-hunt near him. He glanced
once at the men battering at the doors and shuffled a
little faster toward the house.

Dorothy Charlton stood beside her father on the end
of the veranda, her hands held over her ears as if she
expected to hear the sound of a shot at any instant
and did not wish to hear it. She felt sure that Don
José was innocent. She wondered whether he had gone
on through the barn and to the huts or had remained
to be caught in the big building. She felt that she almost hated Hugh Hankins because he was in command of the men surrounding and attacking the barn.

"Look at that old man!" she heard her father ex-
claim. "The fool will be getting himself shot if he
doesn't go away."

Dorothy looked where her father pointed and saw
an old, dirty *peon* shuffling toward the corner of the
house. She did not recognize him at first—there were
so many and they were coming and going all the time.
Moreover, she imagined that Don José, if he had got
through the barn, had crept along the irrigation ditches
and made his way toward the distant hills.

She looked at the barn again and saw that the front
door was giving way. She glanced again at the old
peon, who was facing the veranda now. She met his
eyes—and he winked!

Dorothy Charlton caught her breath in a little gasp,
and the red flamed into her face. What did the old
rascal mean? she asked herself. She glanced at him
again. His head was turned now so that she could see

his face well, but her father and the others could not. And now his lips curled in a smile that she knew well, and his eyes seemed to take fire and flash, and he winked again.

And then it seemed that her heart almost stood still and her face grew suddenly white—for she recognized him now despite the ashes in his hair and the old clothes and his stooped shoulders and aged manner of walking.

She saw that it was Don José disguised before her, and she feared some of the others would recognize him, too. Why hadn't he made the most of his opportunity and gone toward the hills? But Don José seemed inclined to flirt with danger. Having realized that she recognized him, he deliberately turned away and hobbled back toward the barn.

His horse was still a short distance in front of the door, where he had dismounted. Now Hankins whirled around and caught sight of the animal—and saw the old *peon*, too. It seemed to Dorothy that her heart stood still again.

"Here, you!" Hankins cried. "Lead that horse around the corner of the house! We'll be inside in a minute, and there'll be firing, and we don't want the horse hurt."

"*Sí, señor!*" Don José called in a quavering voice.

Dorothy scarcely could keep back a smile now. It was an excellent joke on Hankins, and he should know of it one day, she promised herself. She slipped away from her father's side and walked the length of the veranda and went down the steps at the other end.

Don José was speaking to the horse, urging the

beast to step with more life. He was past the veranda steps now—and comparatively safe. The men were still battering away at the door of the barn. Once inside they soon would discover that their quarry was not there.

Don José led the horse around the end of the veranda and stopped. He came face to face with Dorothy, and reached up to remove the battered *sombrero*.

"Don't, *señor!*" she whispered. "You are not in safety yet!"

"I shall mount my horse and ride, *señorita*," he said. "I can be half-way to the highroad before they can start after me. I can stampede their mounts—"

"There is danger in that! There is danger as long as they pursue, *señor*. You must go into hiding. Do you wish always to ride about the country and dodge a posse? Walk around to the *patio*."

"What would you do, *señorita?*"

"Do not ask questions. Hurry—and I shall meet you there."

Without waiting for his reply she turned around and hurried to the front door. She went through the house and waited in the *patio*. There was scant danger of Don José being observed since all the servants were out in front watching the battle at the barn.

"Come!" she commanded when he turned the corner.

She opened a door and bade him follow her. She opened another door and thrust him into a room.

"Under the bed and back against the wall!" she commanded.

"But, *señorita*—"

"And hurry! When they find you are missing they'll search. And no man will search in here."

"And why not?"

"It is my own room," she said.

"*Señorita,* I cannot—"

"I am an American girl, *señor*. And you are a gentleman. Let us have no false modesty at such a time. Listen!"

From outside came a chorus of cries and shrieks of baffled rage. The posse had discovered that Don José was not in the barn!

CHAPTER XIII

EVENTS OF THE NIGHT

NIGHT was upon Sonora, a beautiful moonlight night that cast a glamour of beauty and romance over an ugly landscape. The mesa had taken on certain soft tones, and the trees were touched as if with silver, and the dusty highroad looked like a peaceful stream flowing sluggishly around through the hills on its way from the border to the village of Quebrada.

At the *haciendas*, lights were burning in the houses, and here and there the strains of music could be heard, for it was long after the hour of the evening meal, almost the standard bedtime in fact. In the huts some of the *peons* already had gone to their bunks, and others sat before their doors to dream of things that never would come to pass.

At the Roberts *hacienda* Hugh Hankins was taking his leave, for he was forced to return to the mine.

"I cannot explain it, unless the fellow hid in the high grass and afterward made his way to the hills," he was saying. "There is some mystery about his disappearance."

"What matters it, since he is innocent?" Dorothy asked.

"But we do not know that he is."

"I know. I talked to him out at the end of the driveway."

Hankins threw up his hands in despair.

"There it is!" he exclaimed. "She defends the fellow. He has infatuated her with his foreign manner. He is like the breath of romance to her. What chance has a white man?"

And then Hankins rode away, a bit gruff in his manner, and the others went back into the house.

Two hours later a dark form slipped through the window of Dorothy's room and got to the ground. Soon afterward Dorothy herself crept through the house and went to the end of the *patio*, where Don José had gone to wait for her.

"It is as I said, *señorita*—there is only a chance," he explained. "Don't you think I had better do this thing alone?"

"And have me miss the adventure?" she asked. "Was it not agreed between us that I should help?"

"Come, then!" Don José said, chuckling. "Never was there such a *señorita!*"

They crept away from the house, keeping in the shadows as much as possible, followed a deep irrigation ditch, and made their way to the cluster of *adobe* huts in the rear of the big barn. They crawled forward until they were near a certain hut—and on the dark side of it. And there they crouched, breathless, and listened.

Almost all the *peons* had retired now, and there was scarcely a gleam of light to be seen, yet a streak of light came from the hut against the wall of which they crouched.

Lifting himself carefully, Don José peered through a window. Juan Lopez, the *superintendente*, and Agustin Gonzales, his accomplice, were talking, a bottle of wine between them, their heads close together. Don José got down from the window.

"They are inside," he whispered to Dorothy. "Let us listen!"

"The thing must be done!" Juan Lopez was saying. "And the only safe way is to find this man people think is a *caballero* and put a bullet through his heart. Then there will be no questions asked, for word has gone forth from the *magistrado* to get him either dead or alive!

"He is but a common human man and merely has been fortunate so far," Juan Lopez declared. "He cannot escape the neighborhood with the entire countryside searching for him, with Señor Hankins the head of the chase. Sooner or later his good luck will desert him. Is it not always so? Our hope is that he will not be taken alive, for that might mean disaster to us."

"But even if he is captured alive, how can it concern us?" Gonzales asked.

"Dolt! There always is a chance of things going wrong," Juan Lopez said, lifting the wine bottle again and stopping long enough to take a big drink.

"How can things go wrong in this? Does he know we were the men who attacked him in the little ravine the other night?"

"Perhaps not," Juan Lopez replied. "But it is possible that he may have certain suspicions. The man knows that we hate him for the manner in which he

handled us in the plaza at Quebrada. Cannot he put
one and one together and make a pair?"

"As to the other business—" Gonzales hinted.

"If this *hidalgo* is slain everybody will be quick to
declare that he killed the merchant, and that he has
received his just deserts for the crime. If he escapes
there always will remain a doubt. If he is taken and
brought to trial, his good luck may stand by him, and
he may be cleared of the charge, and then people will
begin to look around for the guilty man."

"And then—"

"And then we will be in some danger," Juan Lopez
said. "Anybody but a dolt would perceive that."

"Let us go away at once," Gonzales begged. "We
have the money—and it is enough."

"Some six thousand *pesos* we took from the merchant's desk—*si!*" Juan Lopez replied. "The money
would be enough for our purpose. We could go to the
border and cross into the States and live like kings for
a time. But if we run away now people will suspect.
They will search for a reason for our going, and something may happen to lead them to believe that we killed
the merchant and robbed his desk. We shall not go
away until this *hidaglo* has been slain!"

"If only it had been done that night at the inn—"

"He has the luck of *el diablo!* He must have been
awake and on guard that night. I had thought to
kill and rob the merchant and then slay this Don
José. We failed, but at least the crime has been
fastened on him."

Don José grinned in the darkness behind the hut,
and in some manner his hand encountered that of

Dorothy Charlton, and he felt a slight pressure. Dorothy was rejoicing that she had decided upon a man's innocence and it had been proved afterward.

"Remain here," she said. "I shall get father as a witness."

She slipped away through the shadows and made her way toward the house. She hurried around to the *patio*, entered, and rushed to her father's room. She put out a hand and touched him gently. The owner of the *hacienda* instantly opened his eyes.

"Not a sound! Do not wake mother!" she whispered.

"Dorothy! What is the trouble?"

"Hush! Dress as quickly as you can and meet me in the hall."

"But—"

"Please—and do not wake mother!"

She hurried from the room, and Roberts got out of bed and reached for his clothes. Soon he was outside —beside her.

"You must come with me," she said. "I helped Don José escape this afternoon, and hid him, because I knew that he was innocent. And we have just been listening at one of the huts and have heard things that prove his innocence. He is waiting there now. Come!"

They hurried through the house and to the veranda, and then slipped quietly toward the barn, and went around it to the cluster of huts. They made not the slightest sound as they approached the one where Don José was listening.

"Inside this hut are your *superintendente* and Agustin Gonzales, *señor*," Don José whispered. "You are in ample time to hear an interesting conversation. Listen!"

"No; I'll not do it!" Juan Lopez was saying. "To run away now, as I said before, would be to direct suspicion toward us. And as long as this Don José is alive we are in grave danger. Let us remain here and slay him and then go to the States. Can you not wait a few days to begin spending the merchant's money? What would everybody think if we were to leave now? I have an excellent position here, and they would wonder why I left it. I shall write to a certain cousin of mine in Arizona, and have him write to me saying that there is an opening there, and then I'll have an excuse for going. And I shall take you along to give you a good job."

"Perhaps that will be best," Gonzales said.

"Have another drink of the wine," said Juan Lopez. "The merchant's money paid for it. Did you hide your share, as I told you, that it may not be found on your person?"

"It is beneath the floor of my hut," Gonzales replied. "I wish we had found more in the merchant's desk."

"We are fortunate to have the sum we have now," Lopez told him. "Never before had I seen a man fight as that fat old merchant fought! I thought we never would kill him!"

Don José pressed Roberts' arm, and Roberts sucked in his breath sharply.

"You have heard?" Don José whispered.

"I have heard, *señor*. The scoundrels! And trying to fasten the crime on you!"

"The only thing for me to do," Don José explained, "was to maintain my liberty until I could catch the murderers. Remain here with the *señorita*, Señor Roberts, while I enter the hut and make these men prisoners. Then, when there is no danger, you may come in also."

"They are desperate men!" Roberts said.

"They are, but cowardly murderers, and one of them has a broken wrist, due to my markmanship this afternoon. Wait here, Señor Roberts, with the *señorita*, and I shall not be long. You may enter when I call."

Don José grasped his revolver firmly and slipped around the corner of the hut. He braced himself before the door, and then hurled it open suddenly and confronted the pair before they had time to get upon their feet.

"Hands up!   Pronto!" he cried.

They snarled their hate at him like wolves, but they were prompt to obey.

"Stand back to the wall!" he commanded.   "Put your faces against it and keep your hands elevated else I'll riddle both of you—murderers! Steady there!"

They had flinched at his word; he fired a bullet into the wall beside them, and was delighted to see them cower.

"You may come in now, Señor Roberts!" he called.

Roberts came bustling in, words of condemnation for the pair bubbling from his lips. Dorothy followed and stopped in the open doorway.

"There are some straps in that corner, Señor Roberts," Don José said. "Also, there is a length of rope.

Will it be too much trouble to have you tie the hands
of these men behind their backs?"

"It will be a pleasure, *señor*," Roberts said.

He got the straps and the rope, and Don José made
the two men stand a couple of paces apart. Roberts
did his work well, pulling at the knots with such violence that he made the prisoners cry out. He searched
them for weapons, taking a wicked-looking knife from
each and a revolver from Juan Lopez.

"Turn around!" Don José commanded.

They turned to face him, fear and hatred mingled
in their countenances.

"So you made an attempt to slay me, did you?" Don
José said. "I suppose that I should shoot you down
for that, but we'll allow the law to deal with you for
the merchant's murder."

"We didn't do it!" Juan Lopez shrieked.

"Three of us heard you confess it. And we heard
you say where you had buried a part of the money, and
heard you plan to visit the States after you had slain
me. You shall never see the States—neither of you!
Out the door—march!"

Roberts called, and the *peons* came tumbling from
their huts, astonished to find the *hacienda* owner there
at such an hour, and the *señorita*, too, and frightened
a bit when they beheld Don José.

"One of you fetch my horse and put saddle and
bridle on him," Don José directed. "Señor Roberts,
kindly have a man fetch another horse, a good one,
with bridle only on him."

Roberts gave the order, and they went toward the
veranda, the prisoners closely watched.

"I shall put both of them on the horse and lash them there!" Don José explained. "And then I shall take them to Quebrada and hand them over to the *magistrado*. You will kindly write a note to that official saying that you overheard these men confess their crimes!"

Roberts hastened inside the house to write the note. Don José stepped close to Dorothy.

"I never shall forget that you had faith in me, *señorita*," he said.

"It was my woman's instinct, *señor*."

"Whatever it was, I thank you for it. We have had an adventure—we have captured murderers together. Perhaps the saints will be kind and let us have another!"

"If the chance comes I shall be with you, *señor*," she replied; and then she hurried into the house.

The men came from the stable with the horses, and Don José sent one of the *peons* for more rope. And then he forced his prisoners to mount and lashed their feet together beneath the horse's belly. He fastened the men together, too, and tied the horse to his own saddle. Roberts came out with the note which Don José put inside his blouse. And then Don José mounted his own horse.

"You do not need help?" Roberts asked.

"I fancy not, *señor*," replied Don José. "These men do not appear formidable at the present moment."

"Can you forgive us for doubting you?"

"Things did appear black," Don José answered. "You are forgiven freely, *señor*, and all the others."

"And come out and have a meal or so with us," Roberts begged.

"Gladly," said Don José, his smile flashing.

"This, the home of your ancestors, is open to you, *señor*. Leave that wretched inn at Quebrada, come here and remain with us as long as you desire."

"Perhaps I shall accept that invitation, if you really mean it," said Don José.

"I do mean it, *señor*."

"Then I shall be starting with these criminals. It is a long ten miles to town."

He bowed from the saddle and started his horse. He galloped slowly along the driveway beneath the trees, paying not the slightest attention, it seemed, to the two men on the other mount, who were not riding any too easily.

When he turned into the highway he lighted a cigarette, and between puffs of smoke he sang of love and youth. The prisoners ground their teeth in rage.

At times Don José spurred his horse, and then there were howls and imprecations behind him, to which he paid no attention. He rode slowly through the little ravine of the shadows, where the fruitless assault had taken place, and he called the attention of his prisoners to it.

"Here there was once a battle," he said, "and the lesser force won when the superior force began knifing each other by mistake. The superior force afterward ran away, I have heard it said."

He came finally to the top of the last hill and started down the slope toward Quebrada, and now he was singing at the top of his voice. From the darkness behind a ledge of rock two horsemen darted and bore down upon him.

"By the saints, 'tis he!" one of them exclaimed.

"Halt! Put up your hands!" the voice of Hugh Hankins cried. "We have you now, Don José!"

"As I live, it is my old friend, Señor Hankins!" Don José exclaimed.

"Up with your hands or I fire!"

Don José elevated his hands.

"What violence!" he said. "And what is this nonsense all about, *señor?*"

"Who is that with you?"

"A couple of prisoners, *señor*. One was the *superintendente* of the Roberts *hacienda* until a short time ago. The other is a particular chum of his. They have recently confessed to the murder of the merchant!"

"What's that?" Hankins cried.

"Force him to release us, *señor!*" Juan Lopez began begging. "It is all a lie! He is but contriving at his own escape! Force him to let us go!"

"Señor Hankins, reach inside my blouse and you will find a letter that is there," Don José directed. "Señor Roberts wrote it, and in it he says how he heard these two men confess."

Hankins took out the letter, alert lest Don José seize him as he did so. He read it swiftly by the light of matches while the other men guarded Don José.

"It is true!" he said when he had finished. "Roberts wrote it, all right!"

"But this Don José forced him to write it!" Juan

Lopez cried. "He entered the house and made Señor Roberts write it at the point of a pistol! Then he captured us when we tried to interfere and brought us on the road to town."

Hugh Hankins looked suspicious.

"Let all of us go to the *carcel*," Don José proposed. "And send for Señor Roberts, if you doubt my word."

"Ride on and we'll ride beside you," Hankins directed.

They rode on. Don José continued singing the song of youth and love! They came to the plaza and crossed it and stopped before the inn.

There was a light in the inn, and the man with Hankins dismounted and opened the door—to find the *magistrado* drinking wine with Pedro Jorge and Valentino.

It was an excited trio that charged out and into the plaza at the man's call. Don José was sitting on his horse easily and puffing at a cigarette again.

"Ha, Valentino!" he cried. "It was impossible to-day that I return here for the evening meal. But I shall want for something to eat within a very short time. Can you get it for me? I have been busy capturing murderers!"

"You shall have an elegant meal, Don José!" the delighted Valentino cried.

"Cold meat will do—that and a bottle of wine."

"I shall get it immediately."

"Not so fast!" Hankins exclaimed. "We are not certain about this business yet, Don José. Perhaps this note was written in good faith, and perhaps it was not."

"Well, what do you intend to do about it, *señor?* Going to consider it all night?"

Hankins related the facts to the *magistrado,* and that official scratched his head.

"We shall have to keep this Don José in the *carcel* until we can communicate with Señor Roberts," the *magistrado* said after a time.

"You would dare do such a thing after he has captured these murderers?" Valentino screeched. "You would thus affront a *hidalgo?* By the saints—"

"I have no intention," interrupted Don José, "of spending the remainder of the night in a foul prison room. I am renting a room at the inn, and there I shall sleep after I have eaten something. To this room there is but one door and one window. So you can have men guard it easily, *señores.* And this you must do, or I shall use some small influence that perhaps I possess to the detriment of a certain *magistrado.*"

Now the *magistrado* did not care to lose his position, for there were certain ways of making money in an easy manner as long as he held it; and, also, he was beginning to believe that perhaps this Don José was a government official in disguise who might wish to glance into his books—and he might find there certain things that would cause the *magistrado* to be sent to the *carcel* himself. And so the official scratched his head again and pretended to be deep in thought, though his mind already had been made up.

Finally he spoke:

"That is an agreeable plan," he admitted. "Cer-

tainly I have no wish to incarcerate an innocent man,
especially if it be a man who has been the instrument
to bring criminals to justice. You shall sleep in your
own room at the inn, Don José—but the window and
the door shall be well guarded."

CHAPTER XIV

A TERRIBLE SIESTA HOUR

THE following morning it was ascertained that the note written by Señor Roberts was genuine, and that he had overheard the confessions of the two murderers, and so the *magistrado* apologized humbly to Don José and ordered all the guards removed; and Hugh Hankins, having seen his machinery started toward the mine, galloped in that direction himself to attend to his business.

Having eaten his breakfast and praised the attentions of old Valentino, Don José walked about the village for a time, sweeping off his *sombrero* to *peon* women and making faces at the children and passing the time of day with the men.

This manner of acting caused more suspicion, for, as a general rule, a man who appeared to be anybody at all never approached a *peon* unless it was to administer a kick or cuff, and had a habit of striking at children with stick or riding crop, and spoke of the women as unmentionable wretches who should have known better than to bring ill-looking offspring into the world to clutter it up.

Don José spent the *siesta* hour in the big room at the inn, and a terrible *siesta* hour it was, according to what Pedro Jorge related afterward. It appeared that this *hidalgo* had no sense of the proper fitness of things.

By the saints, the *siesta* hour had been invented as a short period of time during which a hard-working innkeeper could rest from his labors and catch a bit of sleep! It was a sacred hour, no less, during which it was permitted a man to call his soul his own. Was not such the intention, *señor?*

But this nervous, energetic Don José—!

As the *siesta* hour began, Pedro Jorge took his favorite crippled chair to his pet corner, propped it against the wall so that it would not topple over, and lowered his giant self into it slowly and carefully, grunting his keen satisfaction when he discovered that it would bear his weight yet another day.

He settled himself comfortably, folded his hands over his enormous paunch, and closed his eyes. Yesterday, during the *siesta,* he had been contemplating his youth and certain love affairs of his bravado days, and had not finished when he awoke. To-day he hoped to be able to continue the reverie, beginning where he had left off.

Valentino sat in his usual chair at the end of the bar, his head drooping on his breast, his eyes blinking slowly like those of some great owl attempting to see in the glare of the day.

Don José was in the corner by the table beneath the window, and he was smoking a cigarette. He sat low in his chair, his legs were sprawled, and his *sombrero* was on the table before him.

Valentino began to snore gently, starting a crescendo

that was no less than wonderful. The first snore was like the initial breath of an afternoon sea breeze, as gentle as a zephyr and about as irritating. The second was the sound of a little wave on a pebbly beach, enduring for a breath longer and receding with a timid hiss that died away as if in the distance.

Then came one of more power, a forte snore that was noble and somewhat impressing and of longer duration. It was the storm at sea heard from the shore of a cove. And then a distant rumbling was heard. It was not terrifying at first, though there was a quality of mystery in it; it approached gradually, and grew louder until it seemed to beat upon the ear.

The strength of the gale, the terrifying shriek of the hurricane, roar of the typhoon, whirlwind of the tornado, deafening crash of the angry heavens rolled into one! On it came and louder it grew, until it was as if a man's ears could stand no more, and then it broke in a crash that hinted at the final end of everything—oblivion!

An instant of deep silence—and then the initial breath of the afternoon sea breeze again, and the entire program repeated! Valentino's snore was a symphony terrible in theme.

Don José flinched at the crescendo and turned in his chair to look around. Valentino knew it not. Don José glanced at Pedro Jorge, whose mouth was open, and who snored also, but whose snores did not have the poetry those of Valentino contained. A tender smile appeared about the lips of Pedro Jorge—his dream was progressing favorably, as he had hoped it would.

Don José flinched again as old Valentino reached the heights, and then he smiled and sat up in his chair.

"Service! Service!" he cried suddenly and in a voice like thunder.

Pedro Jorge came from his dream with a sudden start. Old Valentino sprang from his chair, rubbing at his eyes and glancing around the room.

"Service!" Don José cried again.

Pedro Jorge and Valentino looked astonished. They glanced at each other and then at Don José.

"Do you not understand, imbeciles?" Don José asked. "Must a man ask half a dozen times to receive attention in this hole of an inn?"

"It is the *siesta* hour, *señor*," said Pedro Jorge, as a man speaks of a sacred thing. He spoke also as if he felt sure that Don José must have lost track of the flight of time.

"What of it? Service!" Don José demanded. He pounded on the table with one of his fists.

"But—" Pedro Jorge began.

Such a thing never had been heard of before, Pedro Jorge felt sure—demand service during the *siesta* hour? Could a black raven be white or the sun a delicate green? Did the men of Mars speak Spanish with an English accent? Ha!

"If I am forced to get up from this chair and resent this impertinence—" Don José began.

Valentino cut him short.

"Coming at once, Don José!" he cried. "What did the *hidalgo* wish? May I get a pillow for his back? Does the *caballero* wish a draft of wine before he slumbers? Would he have old Valentino fan the flies away?"

"It seems to me," said Don José, "that I heard the *magistrado* has placed a man in charge of the store of the dead merchant. That is correct?"

"*Si*, Don José!"

"This is my last cigarette. I wish for some more. Go and get them for me."

"*Si*, Don José! You—that is—you do not wish them for some little time, of course?"

"Immediately!"

Valentino almost grew pale in the face. He waddled to the door and glanced out at the plaza—a sun-baked, burning, dazzling plaza, across which the black heat-wave danced in countless rows. Valentino flinched at the sight, and licked his lips, and glanced back at Don José like some dog who did not wish to do a trick. But he found no mercy in Don José's look.

"I am quite sure, *caballero*, that I have a part of a packet of cigarettes beneath the bar," he said.

"Dolt! I always open a fresh package and smoke all of them myself!"

"Pedro Jorge intends to keep them in stock after to-day."

"Indeed! And what has that to do with the present moment?"

Valentino looked out at the plaza again.

"I wish that it would rain," he observed.

"Do I get my cigarettes?" Don José demanded. "Must I leave this comfortable chair and see about things?"

Valentino shivered. A man who ran wild through

the countryside, who outwitted posses and captured murderers and thieves, and all that—such a man should never be allowed to leave his chair to see about things!

"I—I will get the cigarettes immediately, *caballero*," Valentino whined.

Pedro Jorge gave a sigh of thankfulness and settled down in his chair again. Valentino shuffled to the bar, got his old *sombrero*, put it upon his head slowly, and crossed the room like a man going to his execution.

He stopped in the doorway and glanced at Don José once more, as if to implore him for a show of mercy, but Don José's eyes were hard. Valentino went on out into the burning sun and started toward the store.

Pedro Jorge was in the midst of his dream again already. He was thankful that there had been no task for him to do. This was an awful thing—making a man work in the *siesta* hour! If he had been asked directly to do such a thing he would have rebelled. He would have told this *hidalgo* that the best people observed the *siesta*, and that he refused—absolutely refused—

"Pedro Jorge!"

The innkeeper opened his eyes and regarded Don José with some hostility.

"Get up out of your chair, fat one. You can do your sleeping to-night. Just now I expect service!"

"Now, what?" Pedro Jorge asked bravely. "What now, Don José? You will find matches at your elbow—"

"Get up! I want my trunk carried here to the door!"

"Your— Did you say your trunk, Don José? You wish it carried from your room and placed here by the door?"

"That is my instruction. Do I have to ask twice?"

"The train is not due for two hours, Don José, and always is from two to three hours behind time," said Pedro Jorge. "There will be ample time to carry out your trunk later, if you are going to take the train."

"I wish it carried here now!"

"But think, Don José! Perhaps before the train arrives you will want something out of that trunk. And what then?"

"I am not going away on the train, blockhead! I am going to retain my room here, and pay you for it, but I am going away with my trunk for a few days."

"What madness is this?" Pedro Jorge asked.

"Get the trunk!" Don José commanded.

He sprang to his feet and put his hands on the table. He vaulted over it and confronted Pedro Jorge angrily. Pedro Jorge got out of his chair with considerable speed, considering his size, and retreated a pace. Don José's attitude was menacing, to say the least.

"I—I shall get your trunk," Pedro Jorge said, and he hurried out of the room.

In the hall he stopped and shook his fists toward high heaven, and declared upon his oath that never before in the history of the world had such a thing occurred! He called the saints to witness that this high-

born *hidalgo* had been touched by the sun in his extreme youth, and hence was not right in his head,
wherefore he, Pedro Jorge, keeper of an inn, suffered
agonies to which he was not entitled.

Then he went to Don José's room and got the trunk.

It was not exactly a heavy trunk, but to Pedro
Jorge, who seldom handled baggage of any sort, it appeared to be filled with solid rock. He puffed and
groaned, and finally had it in the hall, and he sent it
end over end along the hall and to the doorway, and
tumbled it into the room.

There he stopped to wipe the perspiration from his
face and throw a glance of reproach at Don José, who
appeared not to appreciate it, or even understand what
it meant. More puffing and groaning and the trunk
was across the big room and where Don José had
commanded that it should be put.

Valentino returned at that moment with the packet
of cigarettes. Don José received them and tendered
a tip, and Valentino called down blessings on his head
and retired to his chair. Pedro Jorge had gone to his
chair also, but he knew that his dream had been ruined
for all time.

Don José opened the package of cigarettes and
touched match to one, and peered through the window
at the sizzling plaza. Valentino's famous crescendo
snore began again—Pedro Jorge's head was nodding
on his breast.

"Service!" Don José screeched.

Pedro Jorge sat upright in his chair; Valentino came
to his feet like a soldier in the presence of an officer.

"Isn't there a fellow across the plaza who owns a cart?" Don José asked.

"*Sí, señor!*" Valentino said.

"I wish this fellow to haul my trunk out to the *hacienda* of Señor Roberts."

"Undoubtedly he will be eager to do it, Don José," said Valentino, and sat down again.

"Go and see about it," Don José directed.

"At this moment?" Valentino asked.

"Certainly! I want him to be ready to start within half an hour. He shall be well paid."

"I am not quite sure that the man can be found at this moment," Valentino said. "Perhaps, after a time—"

"Go and see!" Don José commanded.

Valentino reached for his battered sombrero again, put it on his head, and marched slowly to the door. He gave Don José a look that seemed to say a certain *hidalgo* was falling rapidly in Valentino's estimation, but Don José was looking through the window.

Valentino went out. Pedro Jorge, his eyes closed again, was smiling, chuckling, in fact, at Valentino's errand. It was an excellent joke on old Valentino to have to do such a thing during the *siesta* hour. Twice he had been compelled to cross the sizzling plaza—

"Pedro Jorge!"

"Don José?"

"I have decided to waste no more time here. Go you to the corral of the merchant and get my horse, and when you have him here put saddle and bridle on him."

"Don José! You would not ride abroad at this time of the day? You may be struck by the sun!"

"That is my own concern."

"You wish me to attend to the matter at once?"

"Certainly!"

"I had better wait until Valentino returns—some customer may come to the inn."

> "The village sleeps, dolt! You will please me by attending to it at once."

Pedro Jorge groaned as he got his sombrero and waddled slowly to the door and out toward the corral. Never in all his life had he witnessed such a *siesta* hour.

Once he had been in a revolution, and the soldiers would not even fight in the heat of the day. This terrible Don José—!

Valentino returned with the intelligence that the man would have his cart at the door within a short time, though he believed that Valentino must have misunderstood the *hidalgo's* instructions, for no real gentleman traveled at such an hour, according to the cart man. Valentino hoped that the remark would soak in, but it appeared to bounce off Don José's back.

Presently Pedro Jorge appeared with the horse, and spoke not a word as he got bridle and saddle and put them on, but his groans and grunts were eloquent.

"You are excellent men, though much too fat to work properly," Don José said. "Place the trunk in the cart when the man arrives."

The cart did not appear for half an hour, and then the driver looked at Don José as a man looks at a curiosity. Pedro Jorge and Valentino put the trunk in it, and Don José gave his instructions. The cart was driven away.

Some minutes later Don José, having smoked another cigarette, got on his horse and followed.

CHAPTER XV

DON JOSÉ TELLS A STORY

LATE that afternoon Don José rode slowly up the driveway at the Roberts *hacienda*, humming his eternal song of youth and love, and the heavy cart lumbered along after him, the driver almost asleep on his narrow seat.

Don José stopped before the veranda steps, dismounted, handed the reins to a *peon* who stood near, and hurried to the door, which opened at that moment to allow Roberts to step out.

"Ha, *señor!* I have accepted your very kind invitation, you see!" Don José said. "It will give me the greatest of pleasure to remain at your hospitable house for a few days, and I trust that I shall be a welcome guest."

"You can bet you're welcome!" Roberts exclaimed. "You are welcome because of yourself, and also because you caught that rascal of a Juan Lopez. It makes me shiver to think of it! The scoundrel might have slain me or the members of my family and ransacked the place. One moment, Don José!"

He called for servants and ordered that the trunk be carried to a certain room, after which Don José paid the driver of the cart and dismissed him. And then Roberts served Don José with cakes and wine and took him for a fresh tour around the *hacienda*.

Roberts had a wholesome pride in the place, and his chest swelled as he indicated the improvements he had made, and showed Don José what a money-maker the *hacienda* was getting to be. He showed him the men working in the orchard—and Don José unconsciously made an unfortunate remark which he was destined to remember afterwards.

"There's a strapping fellow!" he exclaimed, indicating a man at work in an irrigation ditch. "Larger than the usual run; eh, *señor?* Taller he is and with a greater breadth of shoulder. What an excellent soldier the man would make!"

The *peon* heard him and snarled, showing his yellow and uneven teeth, and he muttered curses as Don José walked on with Señor Roberts. Other men working near had heard the words, too, and they glanced at one another with sudden suspicion and fear.

After that Don José sat on the veranda talking to Dorothy and Mrs. Roberts, pleasing them with his quaint courtesy. He discounted the idea that he had flirted with death for a day, and declared that the experience had been stimulating.

"A man must have his bit of excitement now and then—is it not so?" he asked. "A bit of a fight here and there but keeps the blood from getting sluggish. In the good old days, when my father was young—"

Don José ceased speaking, and smiled as if at a happy memory. The women waited patiently.

"Ah, those were the days!" he continued presently. "It would not do to mention names, of course, but I have heard, it seems to me, of an adventure in this very vicinity, perhaps in the neighborhood of this very building."

"A romance?" Dorothy asked.

"Decidedly," said Don José. "There lived a young blood of noble family who thought an hour wasted in which he did not drink a gallon of wine, make love to a *señorita* he never had seen before, or create a new enemy. He was the delight of the countryside, it has been said.

"Ha! How his eyes did flash; how he could ride and wield a blade—for that was in the days when a gentleman used only the blade and scorned to use his pistol, with its smoke and noise, except against the natives and such inferior folk.

"There came to the vicinity—so runs the tale—a similar youth, also of good family and great energy. His people founded a *hacienda* and started to mingle socially with the others. And there was a certain *señorita*— In all such cases, it appears, there is a certain *señorita;* is it not so?

"This one was of the loveliest; she had grace and charm, and her hair was like the wings of a raven, and her eyes sparkled and flashed their messages even as the wireless flashes them now.

"Nothing more natural, of course, than that both youths should become enamored of this pretty *señorita*. How could they help it? Ha! And so they wooed her, and her parents sat back and awaited the outcome since either young man was eligible, and there was little choice between them when it came to blood or fortune."

"An interesting situation," Mrs. Roberts purred.

"The rivalry grew intense, the two youths spat at each other like two strange wildcats, but they never came to a clash. And because the clash was delayed all thought it would be a great one when it did come.

"Finally there arrived a day when these two youths appeared at the *hacienda* of the *señorita's* father at the same moment. They always had avoided that before, you see."

"Wise young men," said Mrs. Roberts.

"Indeed, yes, *señora*," replied Don José. "The father of the *señorita* appeared and strove to ward away trouble, fearing the name of his fair daughter might be bandied about. But one of the young men did not seek trouble. He had a clever idea. He would demonstrate to the *señorita* and her father what manner of man his rival was.

"Now there could be no question of birth, and breeding, his family and his fortune, of course, but— Have you ever noticed—you especially, *señora*—how a man who appears to be perfect at a first glance, has some damaging flaws in his character that are revealed afterward?"

"Indeed, yes," said Mrs. Roberts.

"He may be a man among men, and yet not exactly the sort of man to make a woman happy. Has he cowardice in his make-up, either physical or mental? Is his temper too quick under fire? Has he a lack of faith in humanity? Is he loyal to his friends under all circumstances? Ha! Is there avarice in him? Is he the prey of jealousy? Does he believe in square dealing? Those are the little things that count, you see?

"A man may be a man, but if he has some of those flaws in his character, sooner or later his wife will lose respect for him, and thereby lose love for him also. And one of the young men who wooed the *señorita* had some of those flaws. The other set out to demonstrate the fact."

"Did he succeed?" Dorothy asked.

"Ha! Did he!" cried Don José. "He forced the other man to show a trace of cowardice in a critical moment. He taunted him, courteously, of course, and betrayed his quick temper. He made him jealous to such an extent that he even questioned the *señorita's* goodness. He showed that his rival was avaricious, and would swindle a man if he got the chance. And when the *señorita* realized all these things she sent the man away.

"But before he went the other youngster told what he had done, and offered to fight it out if the other insisted. But the other did not insist. He had been shown that he was not a worthy man, and so had lost confidence in himself—and a man who has not confidence in himself cannot fight for anything whatever, or for any cause!"

"And the others—were married?" Dorothy asked.

"It seems to me that I have heard they were," replied Don José, "and lived happily ever afterward. It goes to show that a maid should look closely at the man who would make her his wife."

There was silence for a moment, and then Mrs. Roberts sighed; and then to their ears came the sound of drumming hoofs, and Hugh Hankins galloped up the driveway, for he had come to eat the evening meal at the Roberts house. He showed his surprise at seeing Don José sitting on the veranda.

Hankins scarcely greeted them, and hurried on into the house, declaring that he had business with Roberts.

"I see that this Don José is here again," he said to the owner of the *hacienda*. "Is he pestering you?"

"On the contrary," Roberts replied, laughing as he bent back from his desk. "I asked Don José to come and visit us for a few days. He came this afternoon with his trunk."

"His trunk!" Hankins gasped.

"Oh, he had to have his trunk—a man like Don José must change apparel at least thrice daily."

"I'd be careful, if I were you, Roberts!"

"But consider, Hugh! Don José captured Juan Lopez. Think of me having a scoundrel like that managing the *hacienda!* He might have slain us all and robbed the place afterward. I'm indebted to Don José for catching the man."

"He doesn't act right!" Hankins declared. "He still keeps his name to himself, and he hasn't stated his business. I don't like the looks of it!"

"Rot! He has come to have a sentimental look at the home of his ancestors."

"You believe that stuff?" Hankins asked. "He had his look the first day he was here. Has he said that it is the home of his ancestors—said so in as many words?"

"Perhaps not—and I have not asked him. I merely took it for granted, and I am sure that I am right. It is a delicate subject—I can't question the man as if he were a *peon*."

"Why not?" Hankins asked.

"A man like this Don José—a man of high blood and great family connections?"

"You're being fooled, Roberts!" Hankins declared. "I tell you I know the tribe. Haven't I worked in Central and South America for years; haven't I had to handle them? He's running a big bluff, and for no good purpose. He's a greaser, pure and simple, and some day he'll bust!"

"You said that before, Hugh. And you thought he had 'busted' when the merchant was murdered, but we have found out differently. A man couldn't be a *peon* and act as this man acts. And it isn't only his actions—it is his general manner, the way he speaks, the way he dresses and looks. He's a gentleman, Hugh, and you should be able to see it. You're sore because he fooled you out at the barn and got away—and because Dorothy had helped him."

"Nothing of the sort!" Hankins declared. "I can read men, and I have read this Don José!"

"He is the essence of politeness and courtesy. I suppose he is a little unusual in some things—hot-blooded, eager for adventure and excitement, ready to fight at the drop of a hat—"

"Or to make love!" added Hankins.

"Ah! So that is what is the matter!"

"It's enough!" Hankins said. "I tell you that Dorothy is getting infatuated with the fellow. What chance have I against him, even if she has given me her word? He stands for romance, and Dorothy is a romantic girl. I haven't got a chance, and that's what I'm asking for—a white man's chance! He twirls that confounded silk handkerchief, and rolls his eyes, and plucks at a guitar-string. And I'm a prosaic business man! It isn't fair! All I'm asking is a white man's chance—"

He stopped, because Roberts was roaring with laughter.

"You'd better not let Dorothy know that you are jealous," Roberts said. "The girl is sensitive—she'd say you didn't have faith in her, and it would be all off. Wake up, Hugh. You won her too easily, you didn't have any competition. Now you have it. Be romantic yourself. See every trick of this Don José's and go him one better. You want a white man's chance, eh? Take it!"

"What's that?"

"Take a chance! Instead of moping around here, get into the lists and fight. Great Cæsar's ghost! You've got a chance to make the girl love you more than ever! You won her once when there wasn't anybody else around. Win her again in a stiff competition and you'll have a love that— Oh, Heaven! I wish I was a youngster again! I'd show you whether I'd have a white man's chance or not!"

"I suppose you haven't heard from Boston again," Hankins said, by way of changing the subject.

"No; I haven't."

"When is this Mr. Blenhorn due to arrive?"

"I haven't the slightest idea, but they promised to let me know in plenty of time so I could meet him in Quebrada."

"Let us hope so. If he has to eat a meal or spend a night at Pedro Jorge's inn he'll have a proper grouch and turn in a bad report on me for spite. Funny business! Have to let a perfect stranger judge whether you'd make a girl a good husband!"

"It is necessary," Roberts said. "It isn't only the money—it is carrying out the wishes of Dorothy's father. And she loved her Dad and will see that his wishes are obeyed. Come along now, Hugh; we'll join the others and eat."

They went out on the veranda. Don José was in close conversation with Mrs. Roberts. Dorothy was standing at the end of the veranda looking out across the orchard, and thinking. She was digesting Don José's remark that a maid should look closely at the man who wanted to make her his wife.

CHAPTER XVI

A BARGAIN IS MADE

JUAN LOPEZ and Agustin Gonzales spent the day in the *carcel*, entertained by the glares of the jailer, who furnished them with what food the law allowed, which was not much.

They were entertained by the populace, too, which was of the opinion that it was entertaining itself, but was wrong. Children stood a short distance from the *adobe* building and glanced at the barred window behind which were the two men who had steeped their hands in the blood of a human being and were liable to face a firing-squad or be hanged because of it.

Old women walked close to the window and saw the faces of Juan Lopez and Agustin Gonzales peering out, and the old women hurled imprecations and reminders of an imminent ignoble death, and some other things, among which were bits of rock and handfuls of dirt.

Certain *peons* who had worked at the *hacienda* of Señor Roberts in days gone by and had felt the sting of Juan Lopez's tongue took this occasion to relate to the erstwhile *superintendente* that the day of retribution was at hand and that they would be there to see his untimely end.

Juan Lopez and Agustin Gonzales received these kind attentions in an amiable mood. They began to realize that they had acquired a reputation. They were murderers, and men and women feared them. They suddenly were famous, persons of some consequence instead of common members of the mob. The tirades of the townsfolk were appreciated by them.

But their predicament was not. During the latter part of the afternoon they held a conversation in low tones, so that the prisoners in the adjoining room could not hear. Incarceration would lead to a trial, they knew, and a trial would lead to a sentence and undoubtedly execution. Juan Lopez and Agustin Gonzales had no wish to die either by facing the rifles of a firing-squad or by dropping through a trap.

It was a time that called for wit and strategy, and Juan Lopez, being the man of brains, was supposed to formulate some plan for their escape.

They already had inspected every inch of their prison room. The walls were of thick *adobe,* hardened until it was steel. The roof was of the same, with Spanish tile over it. The floor was hard, too, being of a mixture of cement and soil. There was but the one door, which opened into the corridor. It was a strong door, made of steel, and the hinges were upon the outside. Moreover, it was doubled-barred and locked.

Granted that they could get through that door without being detected they would not be at liberty. They

could only walk down a long, dark corridor and come
to a similar door that guarded the entrance to the
jailer's office and reception-room.

Even were they through that they would have to
overcome the jailer or his assistant, who was on guard
at night, and solve yet another door. Escape that way
did not present many possibilities.

The guard did not enter the prison room, and so
there was no chance of overpowering him and taking
away his keys. He thrust water and food through an
aperture in the door, and did not even give the prisoners a chance to grasp him by the hand.

There was but one window in the prison room. At
first, Juan Lopez had entertained hopes of that window,
but his hopes were dashed to earth now.

The steel frame of the window was set in cement
and *adobe*, and a man would have difficulty digging
around it even if he possessed tools—and Lopez and
his accomplice did not have as much as a pocket-knife
between them. Their tools consisted of a rusty nail,
with which Agustin Gonzales had fastened a tuck
in the rear of his trousers, to make them tighter
about the waist so they would maintain their correct position.

The window was large enough to admit the presence
of a man's body, but there were half a dozen steel
bars in the way. Juan Lopez had examined those bars,
and had given an exclamation of disgust because the
contractor who constructed the *carcel* had used such
excellent material instead of submitting to graft and
making a generous profit out of the job.

And so Juan Lopez sat down on one of the bunks

and considered the matter. Unless his fertile brain achieved a miracle, death stared him in the face. The trial might be held any day and judgment would be swift, with the townsfolk eager to witness an execution.

Finally Juan Lopez achieved a plan. He whispered it to Agustin Gonzales, and Agustin said that he would pray the saints to make the plan successful. Who had a right to pray, he asked, if not a man with blood on his hands?

So when the jailer served the evening meal, which consisted of a beaker of water and some cold *frijoles,* Juan Lopez stepped nearer the door and spoke.

"We would see the *magistrado,*" he said.

"On what business?" the jailer demanded. "The *magistrado* cannot answer to your call at every hour of the day."

"Guilt is heavy on our souls," Juan Lopez explained. "We are bothered with horrible visions and cannot sleep unless we tell everything to the *magistrado.*"

"Ha! You wish to make a confession?" the jailer asked. "You wish to save the country the expense and bother of a trial?"

"What sense is there to a trial in court when a man is guilty?" Juan Lopez asked, his face mournful. "We wish to confess, and then, perhaps, the saints will allow us to sleep. You will send at once for the *magistrado?*"

"*Si!*"

"And bid him come to us with all haste, even if he be drinking wine at Pedro Jorge's place, for it is in our minds now to say these things, and if we have time for reflection we may change our minds. Men have done as much before."

The jailer hurried away, and Juan Lopez smiled at Agustin Gonzales knowingly. The jailer, he knew, was glad of the chance to send for the *magistrado*. He thought that it would hasten the day of execution when he, the jailer, would be a sort of master of ceremonies. And perhaps his grandeur and the necessity of the state for his services would be impressed upon a *señorita* who, at the present time, was inclined to make soft glances at the station-agent instead of the keeper of the *carcel*.

The jailer put the guard on duty and went himself to find the *magistrado*. He went first—and last—to the inn of Pedro Jorge, and there he found the official drinking wine and speaking of his own importance, as the jailer had expected.

He whispered in the *magistrado's* ear.

"Ha!" the *magistrado* exclaimed. "So the guilt is heavy on their souls, eh? If I allow them to confess, the execution can be held in a few days. But I had anticipated presiding at a clever trial. I had expected some measure of glory in this matter. However, one must think of the law and justice. I shall go at once to the *carcel* and hear their confessions."

It was quite dark when they reached the *carcel*, and lights were burning in the office and corridors. The jailer led the way to the prison-room.

"I suppose that I must enter," the *magistrado* said. "But do you stand just outside the door, ready to fire should these scoundrels attempt violence."

The *magistrado* went inside and glanced sharply at Juan Lopez and Agustin Gonzales. The men sat side by side on one of the bunks, with sorrowful faces; they appeared like men who could not sleep.

"What have you to say to me?" the *magistrado* asked.

Juan Lopez bent forward a little and spoke in whispers that the jailer could not hear, though he strained his ears to do so. Agustin Gonzales made not the slightest move; he appeared to be lost in thought.

"*Señor,*" Lopez said, "we have asked you here to listen to us admit that we are guilty of this crime."

"Ha! That settles it, then!"

"One moment, *señor*. Do you not desire to hear some of the particulars?"

"It is not at all necessary—your admission is enough, and I am busy this evening. I shall call in the jailer to be a witness to your words."

"Wait, *señor*—we robbed as well as killed."

"That is true."

"We were overheard talking at the *hacienda,* and so it became known that three thousand *pesos* of our loot was buried beneath the floor of Agustin Gonzale's hut."

"The money was recovered by Señor Roberts and turned over to me," said the *magistrado*.

"And of course many men know of that, and so you must account for the money."

"Naturally. It will be held for the heirs of the dead merchant, and should no heirs be found it will go into the federal treasury."

"Ha! And for your zeal you get nothing!" Juan Lopez said.

"That is a sample of the injustice of the times," the *magistrado* replied, "but I fail to see in what manner it can concern you."

"Listen, *señor!* Agustin Gonzales and myself got six thousand *pesos* when we robbed the merchant's desk. The old fool kept all his wealth by him."

"What is this?"

"The truth, *señor!*"

"And where is the other three thousand *pesos?*"

"Ha!" exclaimed Juan Lopez. "Do you not wish that you knew?"

"You have hidden it?"

"Undoubtedly."

"And now that you have confessed, you will tell me where to search for it?"

"That does not follow at all, *señor*," Juan Lopez said. "Perhaps in revenge for being put to death we shall keep our lips sealed, and the money never will be found. Think of that, *señor!* Three thousand *pesos* in excellent currency left to rot in the ground! Would not that be a shame? Think, for instance, what a man like yourself could do with three thousand *pesos*. Let it be supposed for instance, that, you have been dipping into the public funds, and that this mysterious Don José is in reality an official about to make a careful investigation—"

"This talk is nonsense!"

"I said only let it be supposed that such is the case, *magistrado*. If you were in that predicament, three thousand *pesos* would be like a fortune from heaven, would it not? The missing funds might be replaced and possibly there would be a little left over in the way of clear profit. A man may do any half-dozen of a hundred things with three thousand *pesos*. Does it not seem a shame to let good money rot in the ground when it might do so much good?"

"You are determined to let it rot?" the *magistrado* asked.

The truth of the matter was that Juan Lopez had guessed correctly, and that the official was low in his funds. Scarcely ever an inspector came to Quebrada, and the *magistrado* had allowed himself to grow careless. And now, if this Don José actually happened to be a federal official—

"Would you appreciate it, *señor,* if I saw that you received the three thousand pesos?" Juan Lopez asked.

"Naturally. I could add the amount to the merchant's estate and make an accounting of it."

"Ha! That would be scarcely necessary, *señor.* Nobody would know that you possessed the money. It would be said always that the amount had been either hidden or destroyed. Or, the public in general might not even know that the stolen money amounted to six thousand instead of only three."

"What is your meaning?" the *magistrado* asked.

"Speak lower so that the pig of a jailer may not hear," Juan Lopez warned him.

The *magistrado* bent nearer and by that movement Juan Lopez knew that the official was prepared to talk business.

"You have said that you will appreciate it if I hand over to you these three thousand *pesos*," Juan Lopez said. "But how much will you appreciate it, *señor*? Enough to aid two men to escape?"

"A *magistrado* cannot be expected to aid murderers to escape the consequences of their crimes!"

"Ha! You are speaking to two very wise men now, *señor*, and not to a crowd of *peons* in Pedro Jorge's inn for political effect. Please remember that."

"Even were I the least willing to listen to such an abominable proposition, the thing could not be done," said the *magistrado*. "It would be impossible."

"Explain," said Juan Lopez.

"There would be too many difficulties in the way. Not because I dream for the slightest instant of doing such a thing, but just to show you how impossible it would be, I shall relate a few facts."

"We are all ears, *señor*."

"In such an event, I would have to save my own face; is not that true? How could I aid you to escape? Could I order the jailer to unlock the doors and let you go free? Could I render him unconscious and unlock them myself? I should be detected in the treason."

"And I had thought that you were a man of nimble wit," Juan Lopez said. "All that would be necessary would be a crowbar placed against that wall, so it could be reached from the window and brought into the room."

"And what could be done with a crowbar?" the *magistrado* wanted to know.

"The steel bars in the window could be pried apart to admit the passage of a man's body. About midnight the moon will not shine on this side of the *carcel*. I watched it last night after you had put us here, and I know. We could get through the bars and slip through the shadows to the rear of the store. If it happened that the two *rurales* had been given a few *pesos* by a grateful *magistrado* because the desperate criminals had been captured, it also would happen that they would be at Pedro Jorge's place, and undoubtedly very drunk."

"What else?" the *magistrado* asked, wetting his thick lips with his tongue.

"Were the escaped prisoners to find the horses of the two *rurales,* with their saddles and bridles on, waiting just outside the gate of the merchant's corral, they might find it possible to be in the hills before dawn."

"I suppose they might."

"And that would be all there was to it."

"Ha!" exclaimed the *magistrado*. "You are forgetting the other part. There is an evident fault in your brain work. If I were scoundrel enough to submit to such a plan as you have mentioned, how should I receive my reward?"

"Nothing would be simpler than that," Juan Lopez replied. "We will say that the bargain is agreed on and that five hundred *pesos* are passed over immediately to bind it; and—"

"Ha!" said the *magistrado*, starting to get up.

"Not quite so fast, *señor!* Do not think that you can

search me and find the five hundred *pesos*. I can hand them to you almost instantly, but you might search from now until the end of all time and find not the slightest trace of them. I am not boasting. Try it— and I talk of the plan no further!"

The *magistrado* sat down again quickly.

"We will assume that the five hundred is paid, and that the crowbar is left where I said as soon as possible," Juan Lopez went on. "The *rurales*, we will assume, are drinking at the inn, their horses are ready at the corral. We will even assume that the escape is made successfully."

"And then?" the *magistrado* questioned.

"Ha! And then those who have escaped hurry to the residence of the *magistrado*, who will see to it that there are no servants near the *patio*. They will meet the official there, and they will hand him the remainder of the promised money—twenty-five hundred *pesos*—a fortune, *señor!*"

"Is it in your mind that I am a fool?" the *magistrado* asked. "I suppose, after you have escaped, you would hurry over to my house and give me the twenty-five hundred."

"We shall not break faith with you, *señor*. Besides, we have to go to your house to get the money."

"How is this?"

"Sit down again, *señor*. You might dig up every foot of ground in your *patio* and tear your house to bits, and yet not find where we have hidden it."

"I'll have nothing to do with any such proposition."

"Think but a minute, *señor!* We will surely hand you the twenty-five hundred *pesos*, in addition to the five hundred you will receive before you leave the *carcel*. That is an excellent price for a crowbar and a few other little attentions. If you do not agree, you do not even get the five hundred."

"I can search you and this room—"

"And divide with the jailer if you find the money?" asked Juan Lopez. "Think of the good you could do with three thousand *pesos, señor!*"

"I am afraid to trust you!"

"You need not be, *señor.* I swear by all the saints that you shall receive the five hundred now and the twenty-five hundred additional at your house soon after we have escaped. And I swear, also, that if you do not have the horses waiting as I have said, we will return some day and slay you, even if we are captured and executed for it afterward."

"If I make a bargain, I stick to it!" the *magistrado* declared. "But I hate to take your word!"

"Is it agreed?"

"It is agreed," replied the official, "as soon as I get the first five hundred *pesos.*"

"Then bend forward, *señor*, and shield me from the door. That jailer is watching us closely."

The *magistrado* bent forward and Juan Lopez took a package of bills from beneath his belt.

"Do not grieve that I have fooled you," he said. "Could I take them from the hiding-place with the jailer watching? See that you keep to our bargain, *señor*, and we'll keep it also!"

"I am to put the crowbar against the wall beneath the window as quickly as possible. I am to see that the *rurales* drink at Pedro Jorge's, and I am to have their horses ready so you can escape on them. That is all?"

"*Sí, señor!* If any persons are watching our window, to torment us if we show our faces, you can send them away, saying that we have confessed and that a *padre* is with us. And as soon as we are free, about the hour of midnight, say, we will come directly to your house and give you the twenty-five hundred *pesos*. You are to have the coast clear there, and wait for us at the end of your *patio*."

"It is agreed!" the *magistrado* said.

He had slipped the bundle of currency into one of his pockets, and now he got upon his feet.

"Think it over until to-morrow morning," he said loudly, so that the jailer could hear. "If you come to your senses I'll visit you again in the morning."

And then he stalked to the door, and the two prisoners remained sitting on the bunk, holding their heads in their hands. The jailer let the *magistrado* out of the prison-room.

"Did the wretches confess?" he asked. "I thought possibly you would call me in as a witness."

"They are willing to confess the murder and robbery, but they are not ready to say where they have hidden the remainder of the merchant's money," the *magistrado* said. "I have refused to accept their confession until they are prepared to tell me that. "And I have refused to let them have a *padre* to soothe their

troubled breasts until they come to my way of thinking. You will make sure that no *padre* visits them
without my permission."

"You are a stern and just man, *magistrado!*" the
jailer said.

CHAPTER XVII

HOW TWO ROGUES KEPT FAITH

THE moon started to swing toward the horizon, and the side of the *carcel* in which was the window of the room wherein Juan Lopez and Agustin Gonzales were incarcerated became dark.

Juan Lopez had been pacing the floor like a man entertaining a troubled conscience, in order that the jailer might see him and appreciate it, if he took the trouble to peer through the aperture in the door; but now and then his pacing took him near the window and always he glanced out.

About two hours before midnight, on one of these trips, he saw a dark shadow slipping toward the building. He stood beneath the window and almost held his breath until he heard something being placed against the wall. Then he put his hand through the bars, reached down and grasped the end of a crowbar.

"He has not broken faith with us," he hissed to Agustin. "And by the same token we shall not break faith with him!"

And then he laughed lightly, and had there been a light in the prison-room a watcher could have seen Agustin Gonzales grin in a knowing manner.

Agustin walked close to the door, to stand there listening, and Juan Lopez, the stronger of the two, began to pry the bars apart. It was no easy task, for they had been well set, and the *carcel* was practically new. But he exerted all his strength, stopping frequently to listen and to look through the window, and in time one of the bars gave a trifle.

That encouraged Juan Lopez and he worked feverishly, knowing well that this was their last chance. If they could not engineer an escape to-night they were doomed to be condemned to death.

The perspiration poured from his face and neck and arms, and he fought to keep from gasping when he breathed and worked on. Now he had bent two of the steel bars far apart, but was unable to dislodge them at either end, and so he tried to bend them more, to make a space through which a man's body could pass. He thanked the saints that neither he nor Agustin Gonzales had thick hips.

He could tell from the shadows that it was close to the hour of midnight. Not a sound came to his ears from the village. He could glance across the plaza and see the inn, and that there were lights burning there, and he supposed that the *rurales* were still spending the money the *magistrado* had given them, and would be in no condition to take up a pursuit for some time to come.

Finally he had the bars as far apart as he could get them, and Agustin Gonzales crept away from the door and across to him and looked up at the hole.

"It will be a tight fit," Juan Lopez said. "But a

man who faces death can make himself small in the shoulders. I shall go first. Warn me if anybody comes near the door."

They put a bench beneath the window, and then Juan Lopez got upon it and thrust his head between the bars. He urged himself forward, tugged manfully and finally got his shoulders through. Then he let himself down the side of the wall and Agustin left the door to take hold of his feet and aid him.

Since Juan Lopez had made the passage safely, it stood to reason that Agustin Gonzales could, since he was much the smaller man. He got his head and shoulders through the bars quickly, and Juan Lopez grasped him by the arms and pulled him on through. They stood side by side in the darkness against the wall of the *carcel*, free at last of their prison.

There was no sound to indicate that they had been observed. It appeared that there was nobody moving about the plaza. And yet they were cautious as they hurried away from the *carcel*, keeping in the shadows as much as possible, and wishing that there had been no moon at all.

They left the plaza and circled it carefully, and so approached the residence of the *magistrado* from the rear. They slipped to the corner of the dark *patio* and waited against the wall.

"*Señores?*" a voice near them whispered.

"Is that you, *magistrado?*" Juan Lopez asked.

"*Sí!* Make no noise!"

They crept through the darkness until they had reached his side, darkness so dense there in the *patio* that they could not even see his face.

"You have brought the money?" he whispered.

"You shall have it, *magistrado*, as we promised. You did your part, and we shall do ours. Did we not say that we would hand you twenty-five hundred *pesos* when we came here?"

"You did. Where is the money?"

"Tell us first—are the horses ready?"

"Saddles and bridles are on them, and they are tethered outside the gate of the corral, waiting for you."

"And the two *rurales, señor?*"

"They are as drunk as pigs at the inn of Pedro Jorge. I gave them money enough to keep them there until morning."

"Then you have, indeed, done your part," Juan Lopez declared.

"The money! We cannot remain here talking all through the night," the *magistrado* complained. "In order to make good your escape, you must ride hard before the dawn!"

"Take us into your office," Juan Lopez said. "I cannot give you the money here."

"What nonsense is this?"

"Take us into your office—quickly! It will not take more than a few minutes. And we are anxious to be on our way to the hills!"

"I shall do no such thing!"

"There's a good reason, or I'd not ask it. And if you do not take us into your office, we shall go away and you shall get nothing. You understand?"

"I shall give an alarm—"

"We could choke you to death in an instant!"

Juan Lopez informed him. "Take us into your office and you shall have the money!"

"Follow me closely, then," the *magistrado* said.

He did not pretend to understand this business, and he was beginning to grow afraid. This was what came of making deals with murderers and thieves, he told himself. He had been a fool to listen to them! But the money—ah, there was the bait!

He opened a door softly, and led them through a dark hallway and to the office. There were heavy shades and curtains at the windows, and so the *magistrado* struck a match and lit a tiny candle.

"That will be light enough to serve, and it is all that I dare risk," he said. "Now give me the money you promised. Where is it? Concealed beneath your clothing? You have dug it up since leaving the *carcel?*"

"We promised to hand you twenty-five hundred *pesos*, did we not?" Juan Lopez asked.

"But certainly! Make haste!"

"Open your safe!" Lopez suddenly commanded, pointing to the strong-box in one corner of the room.

"I shall not! What madness is this?"

"Señor Magistrado," Juan Lopez said, "you have been collecting taxes recently. Also, two days ago Señor Hankins paid you several thousand *pesos* due the government for his mining concessions. You see, I know all about it. And you have not had a chance to send this money on to the proper authorities, and so it must be in your safe at the present moment."

"You—you would rob me?" the *magistrado* gasped. "You are breaking faith—"

"We are not! We promised to hand you twenty-

five hundred *pesos,* to hand it to you tonight, and we
shall do so. But now we wish you to open your safe."

"I shall not!"

Juan Lopez stepped close beside the cringing official, reached down, and clutched him by the throat.
At the same instant, Agustin Gonzales picked a knife
up from the *magistrado's* desk and started forward.

"Open the safe instantly, or we slit your throat,"
Juan Lopez threatened. "And make but the slightest
sound, and you are a dead man. You understand,
señor?"

The trembling *magistrado* understood.

"I ask but one thing," he said.

"What is that?"

"That you bind and gag me after looting the safe."

"We will agree to do that, *señor,* since we planned
to do it anyway."

The *magistrado* bent over the safe and began working at the combination. It would not be so bad after
all, he told himself. If they robbed the safe, and then
bound and gagged him, he was saved. For with the
safe looted, how would the higher authorities ever know
how much had been in it? How would they ever be
able to say that the *magistrado* had been short in his
accounts? There would be no profit in it, but at least
he would be safe.

Presently he swung the door open and stepped back.
Juan Lopez ransacked the safe completely, and the
haul was a rich one. He had been right—the *magistrado* had not had time to send Señor Hankins's money
on to headquarters. His eyes glittered, as did those
of Agustin Gonzales. Here was a haul worth while!

They could ride to the States and live like kings in
Arizona. They could dress like gentlemen and travel.
There seemed no limit to the possibilities.

"You made an oath by the saints—" the enraged
magistrado was saying.

"That we would hand you twenty-five hundred *pesos*,
eh, *señor?*" Juan Lopez said. "And we intend to do
so, and keep our oath. In just a moment—"

He counted the bills out rapidly made a little pile of
twenty-five hundred *pesos*, and handed the money to
the *magistrado*.

"There you are, *señor*," he said. "There is the
amount I promised to hand you. I did not say that
I would not take it from your own safe first, did I?
I dislike to give up that much money, but I am a
man of my word, and the haul will be an excellent one
as it is. Moreover, it is a good thing to keep an oath.
Put the bills away, or those who find you will find the
money also, and wonder how we happened to overlook it. Quickly!"

The official put the money beneath the edge of a
rug. Afterward, if the money was seen, he could tell
a tale about sneaking that bundle of bills from the
thugs while their backs were turned, and so be a
hero.

"Tie and gag me well, but be merciful about it!"
he said to the thieves. "You may tear some strips off
that rug by the window. Slash it with a knife."

They worked swiftly, and Juan Lopez bound the
official's hands behind him, and then lashed his legs
together, and finally tied him to the legs of the heavy
desk. Then he prepared a gag.

"It has been a pleasure to deal with you, *magistrado*," he said. "And because of the friendly feeling we have toward you, let me whisper in your ear a word of advice."

"Well, *señor?*"

"This Don José—you know little concerning him, eh?"

"Almost nothing."

"I thought as much. He has been out to the Roberts *hacienda*, as you know. Beware that man, *magistrado!*"

"What is the meaning of that statement?"

"I heard him holding speech with Señor Roberts. This Don José is playing a crafty game. In the first place, he is a high government official, and he has evidence that you have made false and incomplete returns of taxes the past three years or so."

"What is this?"

"He told Señor Roberts as much," Juan Lopez lied. "He is here to get you, *magistrado!* He has been asking a multitude of questions. Some fine day he will come into your office, ask you a few that you cannot answer satisfactorily, and then have you thrown into the *carcel!*"

"Ha!"

"He will do this despite any bribe you may offer him, because there is a larger bribe coming to him. When you have been taken care of, he will appoint a new *magistrado*, one who will allow these Americaños to rob the government and have their own way in matters financial. You understand? And the Americaños will pay him much money for that. But first he must get you out of the way."

"The dishonest dog!" the *magistrado* exclaimed.

"We have hatred for the man, because of what he has done to us, and would gladly slay him, but it will be impossible for us to remain in this locality now, of course. But if you are a wise man, *magistrado*, you will seek out some *peon* over whom you hold the whip-hand, and you will offer him a generous reward for slaying this pretty Don José. Only after that has been done will you be safe. It is a nice plot, is it not?"

"The dog shall die!" the *magistrado* promised. "Gag me now and go!"

Juan Lopez fixed the gag. Then he put out the candle, and went with Agustin Gonzales through the house to the *patio*, and on toward the merchant's corral. They found the horses—the *magistrado* had kept faith.

"We did as we promised—handed the rogue twenty-five hundred *pesos!*" Juan Lopez said.

"And he will have this Don José slain," Agustin added. "It is a pretty night's work."

They turned westward and rode toward the distant hills.

CHAPTER XVIII

BLASTS OF HATRED

JUAN LOPEZ and Agustin Gonzales rode like the wind into the distant hills, but did not turn toward the border in the north, knowing that, if there was a pursuit, the trails toward the north would be the first to be followed. Besides, they had work to do before they quitted the vicinity of Quebrada; and in the hills they could find shelter, water, and food, and descend out of them now and then to go ahead with their business.

For, according to their manner of reasoning, they had a right to place their entire stock of troubles on the shoulders of Don José. Had he not beaten them in the plaza? If he had not done that, would they have attempted to waylay him in the little ravine of the shadows? If he had not conquered them there, would they have thought of slaying and robbing the merchant to get money and to have the crime fastened on Don José? And if they had not slain and robbed the merchant would they now be fugitives?

Ha! There was everything simple in that method of reasoning. And it all led to this—that Don José should pay for the situation with his life, with a little torture beforehand, if such a thing proved to be possible.

Far up in the hills they stopped at the hut of a herder of sheep, a man they knew well, and who had been in Quebrada the day before. They kicked in the flimsy door and routed the man out of bed and forced him to light a candle. The man was terrified, because here were two murderers, according to all report, and he did not know what fate had in store for him.

"Get us food, *señor!*" Juan Lopez commanded. "And do not tremble so, for we have no wish to harm you. We consider that you are a dear friend."

"*Si, señor!* You escaped?"

"But certainly! The *carcel* has not been constructed that will hold the pair of us. And after we escaped we robbed the safe in the office of the *magistrado,* and tied and gagged him, and left him so in his office. It has been a profitable night."

"And you wish food, you say?"

"We do. Some to eat at this moment, and some to carry with us. We shall even give you payment, to show you that we consider you our friend. And we shall give you certain information, too, that you may pass along to the men you know."

"Concerning what?" questioned the herder of sheep, feeling relieved and starting to get food.

"Concerning this pretty Don José, who is now in the vicinity of Quebrada," Juan Lopez said.

"Ha! What of him?"

"He has little to say concerning his name and business, has he not? Perhaps there is a reason. He is at

the *hacienda* of Señor Roberts now; and before we
were taken to the *carcel*, I overheard him talking to the
señor. And what do you suppose his business is, eh?"

"I know not."

"It would be well if you and the rest of the countryside knew. You are comfortable here, are you not?
You do not have much labor, and you are paid fairly
well. And you rest when it so pleases you, and have
excellent food, go and come when you like, and are
in no danger. Is it not so?"

"It is, *señor*."

"Ha! But suppose, my friend, that your freedom
was taken away, and you ate only the few scraps that
were thrown to you, and got very little money, and
came and went only when another man said that
you might. And suppose you were put in constant
danger of violence and of losing your life. What then,
señor?"

"But how could such things be?"

"In the army," said Juan Lopez.

The herder of sheep dropped the pan he was holding, and his face turned white.

"The army?" he gasped.

"I have overheard this Don José talking, *señor*. He
is an officer of the army, no less. He is in the vicinity
of Quebrada to look over men as he would cattle, and
he will pick out those who are able-bodied and strong.
And then, on a certain day, soldiers will get off
the train and those men he had selected will be
forced to leave their homes and go into the army, for
revolutionists to shoot at. How shall you like that,
señor?"

"By the saints—"

"This Don José knew that I was aware of his true identity, and so he plotted to have me arrested for the murder, and Agustin Gonzales also. Do you understand now? He expected to have us executed so we could not spread the alarm. And now that the saints have been good to us and we have escaped, we cannot remain to warn all the people, of course. But you can warn them, *señor*."

"The beast!" said the herder of sheep.

"Don José does not care. He is an officer, and will wear a fine uniform and sip wine while you poor devils face bullets. Ha! If the men of the countryside but knew!"

"They shall know!" said the herder of sheep.

"Ha! That is the manner in which to speak. See to it that you spread the news well, *señor*. Here is a bill that you may use for expense-money. It would be well if the men of the countryside banded together and descended upon this fine Don José and did him to death. That would be the best manner of it, for with such a mob no single man afterward could be held to account."

Juan Lopez and Agustin Gonzales then ate the food that the herder of sheep had prepared for them, and accepted the two packages of it that the man had ready. And then they rode deeper into the hills, for the dawn was near.

The herder of sheep started down from the hills shortly after the hour of dawn. He stopped at a hut here and there, and he told his intelligence in whispers, and he left white-faced men behind him. They

had heard of federal recruiting officers before, knew
that they did not stop to consider whether a man was
single or had wife and children to feed, and that a
soldier's life was that of a dog.

Each man that the herder of sheep told made it his
business to relate the tale to others, and so it spread
throughout the countryside like a prairie-fire raging
before a high wind. It traveled to every *hacienda*, even
to the *hacienda* of Señor Roberts, and there a big man
remembered the words he had heard Don José speak—
that he would make an excellent soldier. He called the
attention of others to it, and so the rumor became a
certainty.

Juan Lopez and Agustin Gonzales circled the small
valley, always keeping to the hills, and made their way
down the opposite side, spreading the report. It took
them only two days to have more than a hundred men
more than willing to slit the throat of Don José, else
fire a bullet into his body from ambush.

About this time, too, a certain powerful *peon* began
murmuring that this Don José should be slain, as he
was a menace to the country. Those who heard him
did not know that he had some of the *magistrado's*
money in his pocket, nor did they care, since his ideas
were similar to their own.

Juan Lopez and his accomplice were changing their
tale to suit conditions, too. Now they were working
in a district where some of the men owned small farms,
and from there they told that Don José had come from
the capital to look around and see where a few more
dollars could be squeezed from the people in the way

of taxes. If this Don José lived to make his report, the tax officials would be around soon, they said, and those men who had a few dollars in the way of profits would have to turn them over.

Don José himself remained ignorant of all this, for none of the men spoke to the Americaños of such things, and so there was none to inform him. And he was not taking the time and trouble to find it out for himself.

He was the life of the Roberts *hacienda*. His quaint courtesy won the Señora Roberts, and Roberts himself liked him, and the Señorita Dorothy Charlton found him very agreeable indeed. He rode abroad with her a great deal and Señor Hankins scowled when he heard of it.

It was on the third evening of Don José's visit that Señor Hankins spoke to Roberts in his office.

"I'd watch that Don José, Roberts," he said. "I don't like the fellow at all. And he is in Dorothy's company entirely too much to suit me."

"Nonsense! It is nothing but ordinary courtesy."

"How long does he intend to remain?"

"He hasn't said. And I cannot very well ask him to leave, after having invited him here."

"Well, I hope that nothing ill comes of it," Hankins said. "He's a greaser, all right!"

"And sooner or later he'll bust, eh?"

"You've said it!"

Shortly after that he found Don José alone on the veranda, and it appeared that Don José wished to talk business.

"You are a business man, Señor Hankins," he said. "You know business conditions well, I doubt not."

"I believe that I do."

"That mine of yours—is there any stock for sale?"

"You are thinking of investing?"

"Possibly. I have some funds that will be idle within a month or so. And funds should not be allowed to remain idle, eh, *señor?*"

"You are right there!"

"I imagine that your mine must be an excellent one, and due to be profitable, else you'd not trouble yourself with it. If it is possible to invest money there—"

"About how much?" Hankins asked.

"Oh, says fifty thousand *pesos* at least."

Hankins's eyes narrowed a trifle for a moment, and his face took on a slow flush, but Don José evidently did not notice this. Hankins cleared his throat and looked across into the orchard.

"You want my advice, Don José?" he asked.

"If you'll be kind enough to give it to me."

"I am afraid that you cannot invest in the mine you have mentioned at this time. The company has ample funds, and the development work has reached the stage where profits are beginning to pour in. But I happen to know of another property that would make an excellent investment."

"And where is that, *señor?*"

"Some of my associates have a claim not far from the principal mine, known as the Golden Harvest. It is rich, we think—possibly richer than the present mine. Scarcely any development work has been done on it, for we have been too busy with the other. But soon the work will start."

"I understand, *señor*."

"Get in now, Don José, before the price of the stock increases. Invest all that you can command. You'll probably double your money within two years."

"Can that be possible, *señor?*"

"It is possible. Of course, it is not a certainty; but if I were you I'd go into it. The Golden Harvest probably will live up to its name."

"You could attend to the matter for me?"

"Of course, Don José."

"I believe that I'll do it," Don José replied. "I'll have to send for the money, of course, and it may be, say, ten days before I have it in my hands."

"I'll see that the stock is held for you, Don José. Fifty thousand *pesos?*"

"Perhaps," said Don José, "you had better make it a hundred thousand, if the mine is to be that good."

Don José changed the subject then. There was a pleasant glow passing through Hugh Hankins's veins. A hundred thousand *pesos* from this Don José would not be so bad. He could tell exactly what would happen to it.

"If I have your gracious permission, I shall ride over to-morrow and take a look at your mine," Don José said.

"Come over by all means!" Hankins replied. "I'll be glad to show you around. We have some great improvements over there. You'll be enthusiastic."

That was what Hankins desired, of course—to get

Don José enthusiastic. A man with enthusiasm and money would be a boon to any mining company. So Don José rode away from the Roberts *hacienda* the following morning, but not alone, for Dorothy insisted on going along. They galloped slowly down the highway toward Quebrada, intending to stop at the inn for luncheon and then continue to the mine.

Don José talked and sang as they rode, and appeared to be filled with the love of life. Dorothy said little, but she smiled continually and seemed to be happy. It seemed that she always was happy when in the company of Don José, and that was beginning to bother her.

She wondered whether she had made a mistake giving her word to Hugh Hankins. There could be no thought of marriage with Don José, of course, she told herself, if he was of another race; and yet the fact that she felt as she did in his presence seemed to tell her that her heart was not wholly Hankins's, as she felt it should be if she wedded him.

They came in sight of the village, and here and there they passed the *adobe* hut of some native, set close to the edge of the road. Don José noticed that children gave him one glance and then ran away, and that the women stared at him peculiarly and clutched their babies to their breasts. And he noticed, too, that here and there a *peon* gave him a black look, a look of hatred, in fact.

"It appears that I am not a popular personage and I had thought the contrary to be the case," Don José said, laughing a bit and wondering a great deal. "There must be some excellent reason for all this apparent hostility on the part of the good folk of Quebrada. I do not relish these black looks."

"Pay no attention to them, Don José; the people are peculiar at times," Dorothy said.

But she was worried herself, for generally the people of the village adored her, and she had caught several glances of hostility that she could not understand. She did not dream that it was because she was riding with Don José.

They dismounted at the door of the inn, and Don José tethered the horses to the hitching-rack there. There were several men loitering about the plaza, and Don José noticed that they glanced away when he looked at them.

He threw open the door of the inn, and they entered and started toward the table in the corner. Pedro Jorge was sitting at one end of the bar, intent upon doing nothing at all. Valentino was on duty serving wine to some half-dozen men of the village.

"Ha! Valentino!" Don José called.

"Ha, *caballero!* And a good day to you, *señorita!*" Valentino called in answer. "It does my old heart good to see your smiling face again, and that of Don José, too."

"Give us some luncheon, good Valentino, and wine. And serve the men here with wine, too, and place it to my account."

He had placed a chair for Dorothy, and she had seated herself, and now Don José turned to survey the men before the bar, to see whether there was any there to whom he had spoken before, that he might give him a more personal greeting.

He was startled to notice that there was a black scowl on a face here and there, and that half of the men had turned away from the bar already, and the others were gulping down their drinks, so that they could hasten away instead of waiting to drink the wine that Don José had ordered for them.

"Have wine with me, *señores*," Don José said again, thinking that they had not understood his invitation. "I like to have good men about me when I drink— strong, hearty men, broad of shoulder and lean of hips, good soldierly-looking men—"

A snarl of rage interrupted him. It came from a big *peon* who was halfway to the the door. The others expressed hatred in their faces and started to leave the place. Don José stepped across the room and stood directly before the door, his chin thrust forward, his hands clenched at his sides, his eyes blazing.

"What is the meaning of this?" he demanded. "I have asked you to have wine at my expense. Why these black looks? Are you attempting to cast insult upon me?"

Old Valentino was hurrying from the end of the bar, and Pedro Jorge had left his chair, somewhat alarmed. Valentino was attempting to attract Don José's attention, but the latter did not see it.

"Back, *señores!* Back and drink your wine!" he commanded.

The half-dozen men confronted him—mean, surly, dangerous. Their eyes had narrowed until they were mere flakes of fire. Their nostrils were distended as they breathed heavily and quickly.

"We—we want no wine," one said finally.

"What joke is this? A man of Quebrada refuse good wine? What is the meaning of this attitude? Answer!"

"And who are you to command an answer?" one of them asked, with a sneer. "What is your name—and business?"

"You dare to speak in that tone to me?" Don José cried. "Have you taken leave of your senses?"

"We would take leave of the inn," the spokesman replied. "If the *señor* will step to one side—"

"I shall not step aside until I understand the meaning of these black looks. Is that understood by your dense intellects? Tell me now! Why have the children run from me this morning? Why have the women flashed their eyes at me in hatred? Why do you men wear surly looks and refuse to drink the good wine I have offered to purchase for you? These things demand an explanation and I intend to have it!"

"We shall leave the inn at once!" the spokesman declared, glancing around at the others.

They all were crouched before him now. And Don José saw that one of them was fumbling at his belt, and saw that there was a knife there. Even as he glanced at the man, the fellow whipped the knife out, balanced the haft of it in the palm of his hand for an instant, and then let it fly.

Valentino screeched in sudden alarm, and Dorothy, getting out of her chair, cried a warning also. But

Don José dropped his head quickly, and the knife flew over his shoulder, and the point of it was driven into the door, where it remained quivering. Then the six men rushed.

"Now is the time!" the spokesman shouted.

But they did not stop to consider the fact that Don José was an active man when danger threatened. He did not brace himself against the door to meet their rush—he went at them. Two steps forward he took, quick steps that gave him an impetus. Then he sprang straight up from the floor. Above him were rafters, and to one of them he clung. His feet shot forward as he swung, the whole weight of his body behind them.

He struck the first two men in the breast with his feet, and sent them sprawling back against the other four. He let go the rafter, and when he fell his legs went over another man's shoulders and hurled him half-senseless to the floor, gripping him by the head, holding him there.

Don José was upon his feet again in an instant, still between the others and the door. He rushed forward, and his fists shot out. Two men received blows against their chins, blows that they remembered for some time to come. Another knife was thrown, but Valentino shouted a warning, and Don José let the knife go past his head and clatter against the wall.

Valentino had worked his way toward the door.

"Back, scum!" he cried. "Come to your senses! You would attack a *hidalgo?* Ha! Be thankful if he does not slay you all."

Dorothy had run from the table and around the mass of fighting men. She came to the end of the bar, and saw Pedro Jorge's big revolver on a shelf beneath it. She knew that Don José carried no weapon, and resolved to give him this.

When Valentino shrieked at the men, they fell back for an instant, and Dorothy ran in front of them and reached Don José's side. She pressed the weapon into his hand.

"This is a terrible weapon, *señores*," Don José said. "I have heard it explode. It sends a bullet big enough to tear a man's chest to shreds. Back to the bar and drink your wine!"

They cowered before him, they went back to the bar. Valentino filled the glasses swiftly, though his hand was trembling, and the men picked them up. But their eyes continued to flash hatred at Don José when they looked at him.

"Drink!" he commanded, flourishing the revolver. "If ever I tell this tale, men will call me mad. Invite men of Quebrada to drink at my own expense and have them refuse? Ha! Is the world coming to an end? Drink!"

They drank, put their glasses down, and stepped away from the bar. They would not meet his eyes now, even to show their hate. And into this scene walked the *magistrado*.

"What is this?" the official cried. "You are threatening these good men of Quebrada, Don José, and in the presence of a *señorita?*"

"You probably will not believe it, *señor*, but I am

forced to threaten them to get them to drink free
wine," Don José replied. "It is almost beyond belief."

The *magistrado* took in the situation at a glance.
Here were surly men who would love to slit Don José's
throat, and they had been unable to refrain from showing their hate.

"Pay not the slightest attention to the fellows, Don
José," he said, in an oily voice. "We, who amount
to something, understand these little things. It is the
nature of the animals to sulk now and then and make
faces at their betters, is it not? Why waste good
wine on them?"

He whirled upon the *peons*.

"Go!" he exclaimed. "To your kennels, dogs!"

The men rushed for the door. The *magistrado* had
been crafty. He himself desired Don José's untimely
death, and he knew of the tale that was making the
rounds, that Don José was a recruiting officer for the
army. His words had been well chosen. Even now
the men were whispering among themselves in the
plaza.

"Did you notice it?" one asked. "The *magistrado*
as good as said that this Don José is a government
official. The *magistrado* would not speak with such
politeness to one who was not. This man must be
slain!"

Inside the inn, Don José had drawn Valentino to
one side and was speaking to him.

"Why this sudden hatred of me?" he asked.

"I do not know, Don José. I have not the faintest

idea. The dolts appear to have taken leave of their senses. But I can make an effort to find out."

"Do so, Valentino, and let me know the truth as soon as possible. And now hurry with the luncheon, for the *señorita* is famished,"

CHAPTER XIX

DON JOSÉ BUYS INFORMATION

THE luncheon at an end, Don José decided that he would not visit the mine of Señor Hankins that day, but would ride back to the *hacienda* with the *señorita*.

Dorothy thought nothing of this change in their plans, thinking it nothing unusual that Don José should neglect to show enthusiasm for a hole in the ground, and not knowing about the contemplated deal between Hankins and Don José. The latter made the change in plans cleverly, and himself scarcely knew the reason for it.

But he seemed to have a premonition that all was not well, and that to ride to the mine would be to subject himself to danger and Dorothy to a scene of violence.

After the heat of midday, they mounted their horses and rode back down the highway toward the north. They traveled leisurely, and Don José watched the trail ahead, and wished that he had worn his revolver, deciding that he always would do so after this. It was no country to travel about in without a weapon, especially if *peons* held enmity toward him.

They galloped along, breathing deeply of the bracing air, and Don José commenced humming the song

of youth and love again. Suddenly his horse gave a
snort of fear and darted to one side. Don José almost lost his seat. He clutched at saddle and reins
like an amateur horseman, and a bullet whistled past
his head.

He put spurs to his horse and dashed a short distance ahead to escape a second shot if one was intended. Dorothy's horse had been frightened too, and
had dashed on along the road. Far to the right, Don
José saw a puff of smoke showing against a clump of
brush.

"Ride on, *señorita!*" he shouted.

He turned his mount in the direction of the puff
of smoke, used his spurs vigorously again, and dashed
directly toward the clump of brush where his foe was
lurking. He bent over his mount's neck and watched
the spot.

A figure darted from the brush and sprang down into
a gully. Don José rode on, not sparing the animal
beneath him. Another bullet whistled past his head,
but he gave it scant attention. He had reached the
edge of the gully now, and found a cliff confronting
him, a sheer drop of some fifteen feet. Just below
him was the man, and he fired again, and again
he missed.

Don José left the horse's back in a flying leap, arms
and legs spread out. The man below had not been
expecting that, and he had no time to dart aside. Don
José struck him with full force, knocked the breath
from him, and rendered him half-unconscious. As he
struck, he glanced around quickly, but saw no other
foe.

"Get up!" he commanded.

He already had knocked the weapon from the other's hand, and it had fallen some distance away in the dust. He grasped the fellow by the neck and compelled him to stand. He was a ragged *peon*, who had the appearance of being very ignorant.

Don José glared at him, and the other would not meet his eyes. He appeared to be resigned to whatever Fate had in store for him. He had attempted an assassination and failed, and his would-be victim had him in his power. He made no pretense of fighting hand-to-hand with Don José.

Once more came the thudding of horse's hoofs, and Dorothy stopped on the brink of the gulch.

"You are all right, Don José?" she called.

"Yes, thank you, *señorita*. I have the fellow."

"And why did he fire at you?" she asked.

"I am about to ascertain that, *señorita*."

He forced the man to face him. "Here is where you tell me a few things," he continued. "Why did you try to kill me? Speak up! You are one of those men who did not wish to drink at the inn, aren't you? And you rode out here ahead of me, to fire from ambush."

"*Si, señor.*"

"You might have injured the *señorita*—"

"I was very careful."

"Why did you attempt to slay me?"

"For money," the man confessed.

"You mean that somebody offered you pay to kill me?"

"*Sí, señor.*"

"His name!"

The man glanced up at Don José, and then looked off across country, but made no reply. Don José waited for a moment, and then shook him roughly.

"Answer me!" he commanded. "What man was to pay you if you took my life."

"One who has good reason for wanting you put away, *señor.*"

"And you will not speak his name?"

"*Señor,* I dare not!"

"Why?"

"He would learn that I had betrayed him, and would punish me."

"Sit down!" Don José ordered.

He forced the man to sit on a rock, and he sat on another himself, and bent forward until his eyes were blazing into those of the other man.

"You like money?" Don José asked.

"Naturally, *señor,* and have little of it."

"How much were you to get for slaying me?"

"Fifty *pesos, señor.*"

"By the saints! Am I worth no more than that? You hear it, *señorita?* I am valued at but fifty *pesos.* Ha! And why did you not demand more, fellow? Is it an ordinary, half-day job for you to slay a man?"

"I did not demand more because I was not in a position to do so, *señor.* The man holds the whip-hand over me. He could have ordered me to do it without payment, and I should have been forced to obey. And he said that he would see I was protected from all consequences afterward."

Don José, watching the man before him closely, felt in a pocket. He drew out some currency.

"If you will tell me the whole truth, and make no further attempt to send me into the here-after, I shall make you a present of a hundred *pesos*," he said.

The man looked at the money, his eyes gleaming. "I—I dare not," he said.

"And why not?"

"The man would learn of it."

"Not from me."

"But he would punish me if I did not continue in my attempt to slay you."

"You have a family?"

"No, *señor*."

"If I made the amount two hundred *pesos*, you could go away from Quebrada, to some other part of the country where you'd be safe, and live like a king. You could purchase decent clothes, and perhaps start in some little business and not have to work hard with your hands any more, and half starve. Could you not?"

"*Sí, señor*."

"It is a bargain?"

The man hesitated a moment longer, and then held out a hand for the money. His face was beaming, his breath coming quickly, for hope had come to him again.

"One moment!" said Don José. "How shall I know that you are speaking the truth?"

"I swear that I will not tell a falsehood, *señor*."

"Here is the money. Now tell me the man's name."

"The man is the *magistrado* at Quebrada, *señor*."

"And why should the *magistrado* wish me dead?"

"He believes that you are a government official come here to punish him because he has robbed the government of certain tax money. If you are killed you cannot make a report saying that he is guilty and asking that he be arrested."

"This is foolishness. I am not concerned about the petty thefts of the *magistrado*. You have told me the truth?"

"I swear it, *señor!* Felipe Botello does not lie after he has sworn to tell the truth."

"So your name is Felipe Botello? Have you any further information to give me?"

"None, *señor*."

"Are you the only man appointed to slay me?"

"I believe so, *señor*. The *magistrado* knows that once I stole to keep from starving, and he threatened that if I did not do as he said he would put me in the *carcel* for that. That is why we made the bargain."

"Very well, Felipe Botello. I believe you. And, if you fear the *magistrado*, you'd better use that money getting out of this locality."

"I have a cousin up in Arizona, *señor*, and I shall make him a visit."

"That is a wise thought. Say nothing about having had this talk with me."

"I dare say nothing about it, *señor*. You are very kind not to slay me for having attempted to take your life. Had the revolver been a better one—"

"Let both of us thank the saints that it was not," Don José said. "Had it been, I should be dead now, and you'd not have two hundred *pesos.*"

"You are very good, *señor,* and I would give you a warning. Guard yourself well, for your life is in danger."

"I thought that you said you were the ony man—"

"The only one engaged by the *magistrado* to slay you. But there are others. Juan Lopez and Agustin Gonzales, the men you put in the *carcel,* told certain tales regarding you after they escaped. And so the men of the countryside will shoot you on sight, *señor.*"

"For what reason?" Don José asked.

"Do you not know the reason yourself, *señor?* I cannot say more without betraying friends, and I will not do that even for much money. I have warned you, *señor,* and that is all that I may do."

"At least, I thank you for that. You may go now, Felipe Botello."

"I shall leave Quebrada to-night and walk to the next station to the north and take the train there."

The man started to walk down the gully.

"You are forgetting your revolver," Don José said, tossing it at him.

"Are you not afraid that I shall use it again, at short range, *señor?* You have money on your person."

Don José met his eyes squarely. "I am not afraid," he said. "You are not under the orders of the rascally *magistrado* now, and I think that you are an honest man."

"Señor, you are indeed a *caballero!"* Felipe Botello said. "You may turn your back with perfect safety."

Don José did so, and without glancing around again made his way up the side of the gully to where Dorothy Charlton was waiting, and mounted his horse.

CHAPTER XX

DON JOSÉ REFUSES TO TALK

ONCE again the brilliant moon bathed Sonora in splendor. At the Roberts *hacienda* the men had built a big fire down by their huts and sat around it to laugh and sing. The laughter and song had a purpose, since it detracted attention from certain of the *peons* who were holding a council behind the big barn, at which all speech was in whispers.

Hugh Hankins had been at the *hacienda* for the evening meal again, and now it was over, and they were all sitting on the veranda enjoying the cool breeze that blew down from the distant hills.

Don José, it appeared, was delighted with all the world. He had said little about the trouble at the inn and on the road, and had belittled the adventure when Dorothy had spoken of it. It was not at all necessary, to Don José's way of thinking, to bother his host and hostess with his troubles. Later, he would attend to the matter in his own way.

But he did see fit to mention that he intended to make an investment in the vicinity of a hundred thousand *pesos*, and that he hoped the investment would turn out well and his profits from the enterprise be enormous. They asked him what it was, and he told

226

them without hesitation. Roberts glanced at Hankins from the corners of his eyes, and Hankins winked at the *hacienda* owner when Don José was not looking.

Immediately thereafter Hankins and Roberts retired to the latter's office, and Don José continued his conversation with the Señora Roberts and Dorothy; but before long Dorothy excused herself to go to her room, to read magazines just come from the States.

In the office, Roberts and Hankins faced each other across a table.

"What is this nonsense Don José is talking about making an investment?" Roberts asked.

"He intends putting a hundred thousand into the Golden Harvest."

"That will prove a golden harvest for you and the other promoters, but scarcely for Don José."

"He has looked over the property."

"Did you show him the assay sheets?"

"The very first thing."

"The genuine ones?" Roberts persisted.

"Well, I showed him some assay sheets," Hankins replied, grinning. "He seemed to be satisfied."

"The man knows nothing at all about mining," Roberts said. "He is taking your word that the investment will be a good one."

"That is his lookout, Roberts. The man is of age, and he should have common sense."

"But have you stopped to consider that Don José is my guest, and that you are swindling him while he is beneath my roof?"

"Oh, come now, Roberts! He is really forcing him-self upon you, isn't he? You know nothing about him. And, besides, the fellow is a greaser!"

"I think he is something more than that."

"We've argued that before. I tell you that I know the breed, Roberts. He's a greaser trying to play the gentleman. I have not the slightest doubt that his money is stolen, or else he has had a small estate left him and is playing *hidalgo*. I know these fellows bet-ter than you do."

"I grant you that."

"And the hundred thousand *pesos* would be better in a white man's hands. Do not feel the least anxiety about it. The process of separation will be a slow one. He'll be gone from here long before the blow hits him. Has he intimated how much longer her intends to re-main?"

"No."

"The fellow has his nerve with him. I'd be careful, Roberts, if I were you—as I have said before. He is a stranger. You don't even know his name. Why don't you ask him outright? Why don't you demand his business?"

"Oh, rats! He came here to visit the home of his ancestors, and he has plenty of money and seeks an investment in the neighborhood—that's all," Roberts said. "You'd have me think that Don José is a crim-inal."

"He may be, at that."

"If you are so eager to find out facts concerning him, ask a few questions yourself. You have an opening, since he wants to invest in your hole in the ground."

"Perhaps I shall ask him a few questions," Hankins said.

The door opened, and Dorothy came into the room. She closed the door behind her again, and walked up to the desk. She looked at her foster-father first, and then at Hankins, and neither of them relished her glance.

"I have been listening," she announced. "And I think that it is a shame! Hugh, you are going to rob Don José. That is what I call it—robbery—and that is what it is! You know that the Golden Harvest isn't worth the price of enough powder to loosen the rock. It is the joke of the country. And you are planning to sell Don José a hundred thousand *pesos'* worth of it!"

"He is not a child, Dorothy," Hankins said.

"He may be like a child when it comes to mines. He is trusting you, Hugh."

"What business has he trusting a stranger? If he loses his money, it will serve him right and teach him a lesson."

"Perhaps he trusts you because you are a friend of this house and he is a guest here."

"I never heard of such a thing!" Hankins said. "You talk as if I were taking bread out of an orphan's mouth. Don José is a man, and should be able to take care of himself and his affairs. And this is business!"

"Business!" Dorothy scorned.

"And you shouldn't bother your pretty head about

business, my dear. Let your future husband do that. How am I going to be able to buy you all the pretty things you deserve if I do not attend to business now and then?"

"I do not want pretty things that are paid for with stolen money," Dorothy said.

"Dorothy, I believe that you are taking this matter too seriously," Roberts put in.

"Worrying about a greaser's money!" Hankins added.

"He is not a greaser!" Dorothy threw up her head proudly and spoke with some anger. "He is a Spanish gentleman. I should think you could see the difference."

"Is there any?" Hankins asked. "It appears to me that you are pretty much interested in the fellow."

"He is our guest, and he has treated me with every courtesy," the girl declared. "And you shall not rob him! I'll tell him that the Golden Harvest is worthless."

"Dorothy!" Hankins exclaimed.

"I'll do it—unless you give me your promise now that you'll not sell him that stock!"

"Better leave business to men," Hankins said.

"Either I have your promise immediately, Hugh, or I tell him the truth. I'd rather be poor all my life than have you get money that way."

"This is nonsense, Dorothy!"

"Do you promise?" she asked.

"I suppose that I must," Hankins replied. "But, since I have promised, you are to say nothing to him—

you are not to intimate that I intended getting his money that way. I'm losing a good thing, Dorothy, and there would be nothing wrong in it. It is simply business. But—well, I promise."

"Thank you," Dorothy said; and then she left them.

Hankins bent over the desk. "You see, Roberts?" he asked. "She's showing entirely too much interest in the fellow. He's the sort that appears to a girl with a romantic turn of mind. No greaser, eh? She'll find out! He's due to bust one of these days. But what chance have I until he does, until he shows his real self? I want a white man's chance against his glamour!"

"Well, take it, as I said before," Roberts suggested.

"You'd better send the fellow away. There's something wrong with him. How about that attack at the inn? How about the man who shot at him on the road? When greasers set out to get another greaser like that, there is something wrong. I am going to find out his correct name and his business here. That story about visiting the home of his ancestors doesn't sound good to me."

"Suit yourself!" said Roberts. "But I think you're letting him worry you too much. The man's all right, Hugh."

Hankins left the office and went out on the veranda and maneuvered to get Don José alone, but did not succeed until Dorothy and Mrs. Roberts left them for the night. Roberts, sensing what was in the air, retired to the living-room, where he could hear without being seen.

"Regarding that proposed investment of yours, Don José," Hankins began, "I'll make the application for your stock immediately. By the way, what is your name in full? I'll have to put it in the application," you know."

"You may leave the papers in blank, *señor*," Don José replied.

"Would it not be better to put your name down at once?"

"That can be arranged afterward."

"The company will naturally be interested in such a big stockholder," Hankins said. "Some of the officers may wish to know who you are, you see. They always guard against certain interests gaining a foothold in the business. And what shall I tell them, Don José?"

"Only tell them that I am a man with a hundred thousand *pesos* to invest, *señor*."

Inside the living-room, Roberts chuckled softly, so softly that the two on the veranda could not hear.

"May I say where you are from, what connections you have in the business world, where you do your banking, and all that?"

"It is scarcely necessary, *señor*. Why should you go to all that trouble? Pardon me, but I do not feel like talking business to-night. Will it not be enough if I send for the money, and trade it to you for this stock? By the way, Señor Hankins, have you ever seen a prettier moon?"

"You will pardon me, Don José, if I speak plainly,"

Hankins said. "Being a—*hidalgo*—you will understand."

"What is it, *señor?*

"You are a guest here āt the house of Mr. Roberts, and on terms of more or less intimacy with his wife and foster-daughter. Do you not think that it would be proper for you to tell Señor Roberts something concerning yourself? Is it not a matter of pride that you give him proof of your standing in the world?"

"Why, I had not thought of that!"

"The information would go no further, if that is your wish. If there is some reason why you do not wish your identity known to the countryside, to the—er—officials—"

"You mean that I may be a fugitive from justice?" Don José asked, laughing lightly.

"Oh, I did not say that, *señor!*"

"Let us hope, also, that you did not mean it, *señor!*" Don José returned.

"I do not know whether I should conclude this business deal for you unless you are willing to talk more freely," Hankins said.

"Then do not trouble yourself further, *señor,*" Don José begged. "A man with money always can find investments if he is not too particular."

Inside the house, Roberts chuckled again. This Don José could be clever at times. Hankins did not seem to be acquiring much information.

Hankins left Don José sitting alone on the veranda and retired to the room that had been assigned to him. He felt that he was commencing to hate Don José. Why didn't Roberts force the fellow to leave the place? Why didn't Dorothy refuse to have anything to do with him, instead of talking with him, riding with him, and championing him at every turn?

And who was this Don José, and what was his business in the neighborhood of Quebrada?

CHAPTER XXI

A GHOST WALKS

Immediately after Hugh Hankins had entered the house and Don José knew that he was alone until such time as he decided to go to bed, he put his hand behind the bench upon which he was sitting and groped against the wall.

He brought forth a dry reed that he had found late that afternoon beside one of the irrigation ditches, a reed three feet long without a flaw in it, and with a hole through its center about a quarter of an inch in diameter.

Don José lighted a fresh cigarette from his dying one, inserted it in one end of the long reed, and placed the other end of the reed in his mouth, so that he had a cigarette-holder about a yard long. Then he leaned back against the bench, and smoked.

It was pitch dark at that end of the veranda now, and the only speck of light was the red, glowing end of the cigarette, and Don José kept it glowing by continual puffing, and now and then moved the end of the reed up or down an inch or so, as if he had been twisting the cigarette in his lips.

"We shall see what we shall see," Don José told himself.

The cigarette burned slowly until it was about half consumed. There was not the slightest noise except the faint rustling of the palm fronds in the soft breeze, and the low-voiced murmurings of the men down by the fire. This fire had been allowed to die down, and almost all the men had left it for their huts, and those who remained were sprawled on the ground, and probably would remain so until morning.

Suddenly there came a hiss not unlike that of a serpent, something flew through the air, the reed was slashed in twain, and the cigarette dropped to the floor of the veranda. At the same instant Don José gave a sharp groan, and slumped forward on the bench in such a manner that he came down heavily, as if he had struck the floor. And even as he did this, he was thanking the stars that the knife had struck against a pillow he had placed there, instead of clattering against the floor and warning the thrower that he had missed.

Don José made not the faintest sound now, but he was listening. For some time, no noise reached his ears, and then he sensed that a man was moving away from the end of the veranda.

"It worked!" Don José told himself. "I rather expected that. It is a good thing that the reed was long, and that the cushion was in the right place."

Now he got quickly to his feet, skipped to the railing at the end of the veranda, listened for a moment, and then dropped over and to the soft ground. His fine boots made no sound. He slipped around the corner of the house, keeping in the shadows and out of the moonlight, and was in time to see a dark form hurrying toward the nearest barn. Don José followed.

The trail led to the side of the barn and around it, and Don José was cautious now, not knowing what to expect. He came to the corner of the building and peered around it. Half a dozen men were squatting on the ground in a semicircle, and the man Don José had followed had just joined them.

"Well?" one of those in the semicircle asked.

"It is done!" the new arrival said.

"Then you succeeded?"

"*Sí!* The fool sat alone on the veranda after the others had gone in. Señor Hankins was the last to leave him. He sat there in a corner and smoked a cigarette. It seemed that he was determined to remain so all night, and so I could not wait, lest I grow nervous and my aim be bad."

"What did you do?"

"I prepared to hurl the knife. I waited until the cigarette was quite still—I could see the end of it burning—and then I threw the knife."

"Perhaps you missed him."

"Ha! I do not miss when I hurl a knife. He gave one grunt, like a fat big, and I heard him tumble to the floor. He gasped again, and then was silent. I waited for some little time, to see whether he would be able to move or call out, but he did neither. The knife was driven home in the correct place, *señores.* He is dead."

"We must be sure."

"Had I missed him, would I not have heard the knife strike against the wall of the house or on the floor of the veranda? I did not hear its clatter, *señores*. He is dead, and in the morning he will be found. And the knife is a new one, without a mark on its handle, and so it cannot be traced. It is done!"

He sat down in the semicircle.

"It is proper that we of the *hacienda* have done this thing," one of the others said. "The word has gone forth to slay the man, and since he is a guest here it is no less than correct that we should do the work ourselves, instead of letting some outsider get the glory. We have one bottle of wine remaining. We shall open it and drink in celebration, and then each man will go to his hut, and in the morning we shall be shocked when the tragedy is discovered."

The bottle of wine was opened in the simple manner of knocking off its neck with a stone, and the man who had just come from the house was given the first drink. He drank deeply.

"I am fortunate to have been the one selected by lot to do this deed," he said, as he passed the bottle on. "There are no slips when I am on a piece of work of this nature."

"Do you think you are the only one on the *hacienda* who can hurl a knife?" asked another, in surly tones.

"I can either hurl it or use it in the proper manner of fighting," came the reply. "If any man doubt it, he need only speak out, and there shall be a demonstration."

"Let there be no quarreling among ourselves," said the man who appeared to head this small band of assassins. "Drink your wine and cease your babble. It is growing late. We must get to our beds. Some-

body might go out on the veranda at any minute and
find the body, and then we may be suspected if we
are up."

"Not when to-morrow is a feast day, and we have
wine," said another.

"Then let us build up the fire and drink until the
morning. I shall go to my hut for more bottles, and
fuel."

He got up and strode away, and the others passed
the bottle again, emptying it.

Don José had heard the entire conversation from
the corner of the barn, and now an idea came to him.
Señor Roberts had taken him through that barn during their tour of the estate, and Don José had noticed
several things that he remembered now.

He hurried back from the corner of the building
and came to a window, which he swung back on its
hinges without making any noise. He crawled through
and made his way to a little room near the front door.
The door of this little room was not locked, for which
Don José was grateful. He went inside and closed
the door behind him. He was compelled to light a
match now, to find what he wanted, but he knew the
light could not be seen by those in the rear of the
building. He found a bit of candle and touched the
match to it, and then looked around.

There were the things he sought. There was a
bucket of whitewash, with a small brush in it. And
on a shelf were several bottles and jars filled with
chemicals.

Don José grasped the brush and dipped it in the

whitewash, and painted a broad band across his forehead, put white daubs on each cheek, and painted his throat white entirely. Then he took down one of the jars filled with phosphorus, which Roberts kept to make rat poison. He lifted out a stick, went to a cracked mirror in one end of the room, and drew circles around his eyes and mouth, put streaks across his forehead above and below the whitewash band, drew a line around his chin, and streaked the palms of his hands.

He dipped the backs of his hands in whitewash, then and went swiftly from the little room, through the barn, and out of the window, which he closed after him. He hurried to the corner of the barn.

The *peon* had returned with a few sticks of fuel and had thrown them upon the fire. He had brought bottles of wine, too, and they were circulating freely. Don José realized that the men were intoxicated. They had been drinking all evening, evidently, while they planned his death, all except the man who had been chosen by lot to accomplish it; and now this man was making an attempt to catch up by pouring wine down his throat.

"Simple matter," he was saying. "When I start to do a thing, it is as good as done."

"Boaster!" another cried.

"Well, I did it, didn't I?"

"Ha! And are you not afraid?" another asked. "How does your conscience rest with murder on it? Ha! Shall you be able to sleep?"

"Nothing can make me lose sleep," declared the knife-thrower. "Am I a weakling? I fear neither

man or devil! Is there anybody who dares say that
I do?"

He drank from the bottle again, and hurled it from
him empty. He wiped his mouth on the back of his
hand, and glanced across the fire to see whether another bottle was forthcoming.

His eyes bulged. He began to shake. He suddenly
was so weak that he could not move. He made a
peculiar noise deep down in his throat. The others
glanced at him in surprise, then looked where he was
looking.

It was a terrible thing they saw. Toward them
through the darkness walked the ghost of Don José.
Great rings of fire were around his eyes, streaks of
it were across his forehead and chin. And his face
and hands were ghostly white.

The portions of his face that he had not touched
with whitewash or phosphorus looked like splotches of
dried blood. He walked toward them very slowly, and
a short distance from the fire he stopped. One of his
hands came up. A forefinger pointed straight at the
boaster.

"Murderer!" Don José screeched. "Foul assassin!"

The words broke the spell. The man who had
thrown the knife gave a shriek of fear, plunged to his
feet, raised his hands far above his head, and dashed
into the darkness toward the orchard.

"Murderers! Murderers!" Don José screeched,
flinging out both of his hands as though he would clasp
the others to his breast.

Now there came a chorus of shrieks. The superstitious, intoxicated *peons* could not endure such a

thing. They turned and fled, tripping one another, fighting those who got in their way, babbling to the saints to have mercy and protect them.

They dashed along the line of *adobe* huts and continued toward the main irrigation ditch. Into that they tumbled, and scrambled up and went on, through the orchard, through the nearest field, toward the distant hills.

And Don José, leaning against the side of the big barn, was holding his hands to his sides and laughing so heartily that the tears were streaming down his cheeks, running through the patches of whitewash.

"This is all very well," he told himself, presently, when he was able to breathe normally again, "but it does not serve to solve the mystery. Why do these men seek to take my life? It is something that must be ascertained!"

CHAPTER XXII

ADVICE RECEIVED AND GIVEN

DON JOSÉ rose with the sun, as was his custom, bathed and dressed as quickly as possible, and hurried through the living-room to go to the veranda and drink in the invigorating morning air as the breeze swept down from the distant hills.

But as he opened the door he was confronted by Roberts and Hugh Hankins, and the former was storming up and down, beating the air with his fists and exclaiming against shiftless workmen and native labor and what it meant to a man of progress to have to contend with such.

"Gone! Gone! Every mother's son of them!" he was crying. "And those irrigation ditches not finished, and the rains liable to come on any day now, and some of the crops to be got under cover! Confound the ignorant, ungrateful beasts!"

"What is the trouble?" Don José asked, softly.

Roberts whirled and faced him. Hankins grinned as he looked at the man in the doorway.

"Not a *peon* on the place!" Roberts cried. "I cannot understand it. Their huts look as though they had been wrecked. The beds look as if the men who had slept in them had jumped up, seized their clothes,

and run away. Not one remains. And they have been
working well, too."

"Perhaps they saw a ghost," Don José suggested.

"The superstitious, ignorant— I beg your pardon,
Don José, but of course it is no insult to you. You
are not of their race. You have blood in your veins,
and they are part Indian, part Mexican, part negro,
part the Lord knows what! The ungrateful, superstitious beasts! I have given them good wages, good
huts, and easy work. To-day is one of their confounded feast days, and I even had provided wine
for them, and told them that they might make merry
all day and night if they did the morning's work and
cleaned up around the house. Why, they even left the
biggest part of the wine!"

"Ha! Then there must be something wrong," said
Don José.

"Not a man on the place! They left some time during the night. You can't trust 'em! I'll import some
good American farmers down here if I have to pay them
city wages!"

"Perhaps Don José has something to suggest," Hankins said. "He understands these people, no doubt."

"As Señor Roberts has said, I am not of their race,"
Don José replied. He had understood the implica-
tion. "All who speak the Spanish language are not
what you term greasers, *señor*."

"I didn't know there was a difference."

"*Señor!*" Don José cried.

Hankins had not slept well, and he was not in an
amiable mood.

"It is the customary thing among greasers for them

to be known only by their given name," he said. "And I have yet to hear your last name, *señor!*"

"You are attempting to insult me?" Don José asked, quietly.

"Bah!" said Hankins, and turned his back.

"Now you two are going at it!" Roberts complained. "Has everybody in the world turned imbecile?"

"I beg your pardon, *señor,*" Don José said quickly. "Perhaps I was too swift with my tongue."

"No, you were not! It was Hugh. The devil is in Hugh this morning because he had a nightmare."

"I don't feel well," Hankins said. "Beg your pardon, Don José."

"It is granted freely, *señor*. Let us say no more about it. Let us consider the unexpected departure of these—er—greasers. Can you think of no reason, Señor Roberts?"

"I cannot. I've treated them like white men. Beg your pardon again, Don José."

"You need not, *señor*. They are not my people. I consider that they did an unworthy thing to run away and leave you like this. But perhaps they merely have gone to some other *hacienda* for the feast day."

"Would they leave almost all their wine behind? I know them better than that. There's something in the air. Perhaps it is another of their confounded revolutions. What a country this could be under the rule of the States! Beg your pardon again, Don José!"

"And again you need not. I think, myself, that the United States government could make a great country of it. You found nothing to indicate why they had left?"

"I found some broken bottles around the ashes of a fire, and some streaks of whitewash on the end of the big barn. And somebody had been in the chemical room, because the phorphorus bottle was out of its regular place, though why the deuce any of them should want phosphorus is more than I can understand."

"It is a peculiar thing," Don José admitted. "Perhaps some inkling of the meaning may be obtained in Quebrada."

"Are you going to ride in to-day? Then I'll thank you to nose around and keep your ears open. Perhaps you can find out what the deuce it all means. I'll go inside and see about some breakfast. Thank heaven the women servants are here yet—they sleep in the house and didn't seem to catch the contagion from the others."

Roberts whirled around and hurried inside. Don José lighted a cigarette and glanced toward the hills.

"Don José, pardon me if I was too hasty a few minutes ago," Hankins said, having suddenly remembered the hundred thousand *pesos*. "I had a bad night—something I ate did not agree with me."

"You are pardoned freely. I understand what you mean. Sometimes I rise in the morning feeling as if I could slay my best friend."

"And business associates never should quarrel," Hankins continued. "We shall be business associates soon."

"That reminds me that I must send for the money when I go into the village to-day. You will have the stock ready?"

"It will be ready by the time your money arrives,

Don José. I'm going down to look around the barn now. Want to come along? We might find something that will indicate what has happened."

"Thanks, no. I'll smoke a cigarette and wait for breakfast."

Hankins ran down the steps and walked swiftly toward the big barn, and Don José grinned and sat down. He picked up the knife that had been hurled at him the night before, and which now had its point imbedded in a cushion, examined it, and then tossed it over the veranda railing. And then he sprang to his feet, bowing, for Dorothy had come out of the house.

Don José thought that she looked very beautiful this morning as the early sun touched her face with its splendor. And yet there was an expression in her face that seemed to indicate that she was troubled.

"Don José," she said, after they had exchanged morning greetings, "I am going to drop a word of advice, if I may."

"I shall be delighted to listen to anything that the *señorita* may tell me," he replied.

"And you will not mention afterward that I have told you?"

"I swear it, *señorita!*"

"Here is my advice—do not invest your money in the Golden Harvest claim."

"You believe that it is not a good investment?" Don José asked.

"I know that it is not, Don José. The claim is worthless. It is a joke in this part of the country. You will be swindled if you invest as much as a cent in it."

"But Señor Hankins—"

"Did he say it was a good investment?"

"But yes, *señorita!* He said that there was a chance for me to double my money. Just a few minutes ago he spoke of it again, and said that he would have the stock ready when my money came."

"I—heard him," she said. "Please say no more about it, Don José—but do not invest."

"Thank you, *señorita*. I shall take your advice and tell Señor Hankins that I have changed my mind. I shall wait a day or so before telling him."

Then she left him to go back into the house; and presently Hankins returned from the barn with the intelligence that he could find no clue, and they went in to breakfast. After the meal had been eaten, Hankins left for the mine; and Don José, having concluded his morning chat with Mrs. Roberts, mounted his horse and started for Quebrada.

Remembering what had happened the day before, he rode cautiously now, glancing ahead, behind, to either side, watching where the highway dipped into little ravines, searching with his eyes every jumble of rocks and clump of brush. And this morning he wore a revolver against his hip.

Finally, he topped the last hill before reaching the town, and saw the plaza in the distance, with more persons walking around it than could be found there usually. But that was no more than natural, since this was a *fiesta* day.

He galloped down the hill, past the *adobe* huts. Yesterday he had received black looks, but to-day he created a sensation. The children ran from him as before; but the women seemed to collapse in utter terror, and many crossed themselves as he passed.

Don José believed that he knew the reason for that. Already it had been spread through the countryside that he had been slain, and that his ghost was abroad seeking vengeance. He would prove himself to be a formidable ghost before the day was done, he promised himself.

He rode into the plaza and toward the inn of Pedro Jorge. The majority of the merrymakers were on the opposite side of the plaza, near the store, and only a few noticed his arrival, and these hurried away swiftly and said nothing to any one else.

It was evident that the merrymaking was at its height inside the inn, and that Pedro Jorge was reaping a harvest of profits. Raucous laughter came through the windows, loud jests, bursts of song, the tinkling of glasses.

Don José dismounted, fastened his horse to a peg at the corner of the building, and slipped along the wall to the nearest window. He glanced inside. Fully a score of men were there, drinking cheap wine. Don José looked for the *magistrado*, but did not see him. Both Pedro Jorge and Valentino were behind the bar, working like slaves, the perspiration streaming from their faces and necks and hands.

Don José peered around the corner of the building, waited a moment until some newcomers had entered, and then hurried to the open door. He walked inside, stepped swiftly to the left, and sat down in his usual chair before his usual table in the corner of the room.

The bright sunshine came through the window and touched his face; the remainder of his body was in the deep shadows.

His entrance had attracted no attention, for the men were crowding about the bar, and Don José saw that the man who believed he had slain him the night before was purchasing the wine. Neither Pedro Jorge nor Valentino saw him, for they were busy.

Don José waited until there was a lull in the din, and then struck the table with his fist.

"Service!" he cried. "Valentino!"

The noise was hushed instantly. As one man, those crowded in front of the bar whirled around. There was a moment of deep silence. And then came a chorus of shrieks and cries of terror. The answering hail of old Valentino was drowned. Glasses and bottles crashed to the floor. The crowd stampeded.

Don José sprang to his feet and put his hands before him on the table. That took the bright sunshine off his face, but the men in the room did not notice that. They had had one glimpse of him with the sun playing about his head like a halo, and that one glimpse had been enough.

They rushed for the door, for the windows. They fought one another to escape. Knives flashed, men shrieked from pain as well as from fear of the supernatural. Tables and chairs were overturned and wrecked. And then the crowd was gone.

"What in the name of the saints—" Pedro Jorge gasped.

"What is it, Don José?" Valentino asked. "What has got into the fools?"

"I should very much like to know," Don José replied. "You have found out nothing?"

"I have asked, but they will not talk to me; they know that I am your friend. Neither will they talk to Pedro Jorge, since you are really a guest at the inn."

"I am ruined—ruined!" Pedro Jorge wailed.

Don José passed him a bill.

"There is salve for your wounds," he said. "And since I seem to drive away custom, I shall leave you soon. Ascertain, if you can, why I am in the bad graces of the people of Quebrada. And, by the way, have you seen any of Señor Roberts' men? They all left his *hacienda* during the night."

"I have noticed two or three of them in the crowd," Pedro Jorge replied. "Why did they leave?"

"That is the question!" said Don José. "Some peculiar things are happening in the vicinity of Quebrada. Find me the solution, and I may be generous."

He hurried across to a window and looked out. The merrymaking had come to an end for the time being. Men and women were huddled together in the plaza, gazing with bulging eyes at the inn of Pedro Jorge.

"They must have taken me for a ghost," Don José said, smiling a bit. "I shall convince them that I am flesh and blood, and then they will patronize the inn again."

He stalked through the door and into the bright sunshine. He put his fists upon his hips, and bent back his head, and laughed long and loudly.

"Ha, men of Quebrada! Do you think that I am a specter?" he shouted. "Why did you run and leave

good wine? Can a ghost ride a flesh-and-blood horse?
Can a ghost fire off a revolver, as I do?"

He whipped out the weapon and fired a shot into
the air above their heads.

"Continue making merry!" he cried. "And those of
you who ran away from a ghost be ashamed of your
cowardice. How did you happen to think that I was
a ghost? What reason had you to believe that I was
a dead man? Buy more wine and drink it—you
need it to settle your nerves. And let it be known that
Don José has but played a little trick."

He walked toward his horse. Those in the plaza
were murmuring now. So they had been tricked!
They had been made to act as cowards. They had
thrown away good wine and had run! Don José well
understood the murmurings. He did not turn his
back to them as he went to his horse and mounted.
And after he was in the saddle he faced them and
laughed again.

"If those of you who left a certain *hacienda* during
the night return when the *fiesta* is at an end, I shall not
tell the owner that you ran away because you were
frightened at nothing," he said. "And if one of you
has lost a knife, he may find it at the end of the
veranda at the *hacienda* I have mentioned. Also, if
there be a man among you who wishes to furnish sport
and enliven this holiday by having a combat with me
with knives, let him step forward now! There is none?
Señores, á Dios!"

Don José rode slowly around the corner of the building. There were many in the crowd who had understood the words that he had spoken, and their

significance, and there were some who would have liked to take his life then and there.

But none such made a move, for it had been noticed that Don José's right hand had rested on the butt of the revolver he wore; and also a wholesome fear of him was in the hearts of the men.

CHAPTER XXIII

IN DEADLY PERIL

Don José returned to the *hacienda* of Señor Roberts. Now that the *peons* were aware that he was alive and was not rushing about the country in ghostly form, the chances were that they would double their endeavors to really put him in the world of ghosts.

Roberts was sitting on the veranda when Don José arrived.

"Find out anything about those rascals of mine?" he asked.

"I saw a few of them, *señor*, and I have an idea that they will return to their work when the *fiesta* is at an end."

"The good-for-nothing wretches! The imbeciles! Well, we can get along for a day, I guess, if they return tonight or in the morning. But I'll give them a talking to, all right! I'll make 'em think that old Satan himself is after them! Confound the fellows! They generally are worthless around a *fiesta* day."

Don José cared for his horse himself, and then spent the afternoon smoking cigarettes and walking around the place. He knew that there was some special reason for the enmity of the men of the countryside, and he wondered what it could be.

As a usual thing, a *peon* was servile in the presence

254

of a well-dressed man who had money, always looking
for a coin tossed out by way of a tip, always smirking
and smiling and holding hat in hand. But these men
were expressing downright hatred, were far too bold
for their regular natures.

Late in the afternoon, Hankins rode to the *hacienda*
again, and found Dorothy alone on the veranda.

"What did you do about Don José?" Dorothy
asked.

"Are you still bothering your pretty head about
business, my dear? Don't you worry—I'll attend to
the matter."

"You have told him that he cannot invest his
money?" she asked, looking straight at him.

"I have intimated that the company might not have
any stock to sell, have said something about a probable reorganization, and all that. Have to let him
down easy now, you see."

"I see," Dorothy said. She was glad that her foster-
mother came out on the veranda at that moment. And
Hankins felt uncomfortable, for he could not understand the look in the girl's face.

"I wish that Mr. Blenhorn would come," he said.
"Your father has heard nothing, Dorothy?"

"I believe not. Boston folk move slowly, I suppose,
when it is a question of coming to this part of the
world."

"He will think that this is an awful hole, I suppose," Hankins said. "He'll probably declare that it
is no fit place for a human being to live. He'll turn
up his nose at the dust and sand and rocks and greasers. He will be put out because he can't get his

Transcript at a corner newsstand. Let us hope that he'll not be put out so much that he'll turn in a bad report on me. I wish it was over with!"

"So do I," Dorothy said, but without smiling.

"Don José has said nothing about leaving the *hacienda?*"

"I believe not."

"The fellow has his nerve with him," Hankins declared. "I have told Roberts he should insist on knowing Don José's name and business. I don't believe this rot about visiting the home of his ancestors. And I do not believe that he is a man of noble blood. He is a greaser out for a fling at high life, playing the gentleman!"

"Why I don't see how you can say such a thing!" the girl exclaimed. "It is easily seen that he is a gentleman. He has not done or said a thing out of the way."

"Exactly! But some day he will. He's a greaser, trying to forget it for a time, but some day the greaser streak is going to show—and then he'll bust! I've seen 'em do it before. I've watched 'em play at being gentlemen—and all at once their true selves come out!"

"Any man's true self is liable to come out," the girl replied, looking out toward the orchard.

"You seem to be much interested in this Don José."

"Are you jealous?" Dorothy demanded, looking straight at him again.

"Not exactly jealous, my dear. But it would please me a great deal more if you would have less to do with him. Make the fellow keep his place."

Mrs. Roberts rushed to Don José's defense.

"Hugh, I am afraid that you have the wrong idea about this," she said. "He surely is a polished gentleman. And, as for keeping his family's name and business a secret, I suppose that he thinks it is romantic to have a mystery surrounding him. Naturally, he is of a romantic nature. And when the time comes, and he is leaving us, no doubt he will tell us the entire truth concerning himself. I shouldn't be surprised if we have been entertaining an angel unawares."

"Bosh! There are no greaser angels!" Hankins declared. "But I'll drop the subject, since it is evident that both of you are warm in the fellow's defense."

Evening came, and they gathered at the table for the meal. Hankins treated Don José with courtesy, remembering the hundred thousand *pesos*, and Don José himself proved the life of the gathering, as usual. When the meal had been finished, they went to the veranda, and Don José played the guitar and sang his usual song of youth and love and sighed at the moon. The scene was one of peace.

But all was not peace in Quebrada. Throughout the day the *peons* had been drinking, and most of the money for wine had been supplied by the *magistrado* through half a dozen men he held under his thumb. The *magistrado* was worried because Felipe Botello, the man he had ordered to slay Don José, was missing. Had Botello failed? Had Don José slain him instead, and hidden the body? Was this Don José to live forever, and finally descend upon the *magistrado* and order him to *carcel*?

So the *magistrado* took half a dozen other men into

his confidence, and gave them money to spend, and certain instructions to carry out. With wine coursing through their bodies, the *peons* became bold. They would gather and go to the *hacienda* of Señor Roberts, demand that this Don José be sent forth, and then they would slay him. He was a recruiting officer for the army, a man who took other men from the bosoms of their families, and as such was not entitled to live.

As the afternoon passed, they grew more emphatic in their speech. They grew careless, too, and cared not who heard and understood them.

Did this Don José have a friend to warn him? He did not! Was it not even being whispered that the *magistrado* would turn his face the other way when the killing occurred? It was!

They jammed Pedro Jorge's place, and old Valentino wondered where all the money was coming from, for usually the *peons* had little to spend. The *hacienda* owners generally furnished free wine on *fiesta* days to keep their men at home. But here they were in the village, and spending cash for their drink.

Valentino began listening intently whenever a group held conversation. He was kept so busy that he could not leave the bar and creep around among them.

Evening came, and a great fire was kindled in the center of the plaza, and there were music and dancing, and more wild talk. Valentino left the bar for a time, telling Pedro Jorge that he would return soon, and went out into the plaza, keeping in the shadows as much as possible, trying to get near some group who spoke seriously and in low tones.

Valentino knew that some trouble was brewing. It

might be a feud between men of two *haciendas*, or it might be another foolish revolution that had come out of the wine bottles, where so many of them came from, or it might have something to do with Don José.

And finally he crouched behind the bole of a palm and listened to the conversation of one group that appeared to be less intoxicated and more serious than the others. There was brains behind the project, for it was well planned, Valentino learned. Men were to leave the village by couples and threes, and as soon as they had gone some distance they were to make all haste to the Roberts *hacienda*. They were to hide along the road and wait.

Others were to ride there on horses, so as to be prepared if Don José made his escape. The house would be surrounded, and they would demand that Don José come forth. If he did not, they would enter the house and get him, and tear the place down to do it, if they were forced to do so.

In some manner, they were to get this Don José into their clutches and slay him. If any of the Americaños were injured—well, they were Americaños! And why? Because this Don José was a recruiting officer for the army, and a man who might raise their taxes, an official whose business it was to oppress honest men. Don José was everything bad.

For a moment Valentino trembled with horror and fright. Then he saw his duty clearly. He would have to warn Don José else the *hidalgo* surely would be slain. He knew that it would avail nothing to tell these men that Don José was not a government official. As a matter of fact, Valentino did not know

whether he was. There was but one thing to do—warn
Don José.

Valentino started to hurry away from the palm, and
in his eagerness he stumbled and fell. Instantly they
were upon him, had seized him, had their knives out.

"Ha! It is old Valentino!" one of them said. "He
considers this Don José a great man and his friend.
And he has heard our words."

"A knife across his throat or between his ribs—"
another began.

"We have nothing against old Valentino, and many
times he has slipped us wine when we had no money,"
the first man reminded them. "It is necessary only to
tie him up, keep him prisoner until we have done what
we contemplate. It is agreed?"

"Agreed!" they cried.

They tied Valentino's hands behind his back and
forced him to walk along, going away from the plaza
and keeping in the darkness as much as possible. They
took him to a hut on the outskirts of the village. The
hut was of *adobe,* and had strong doors and windows.
Valentino had his legs and feet lashed together, and
was placed in a corner of the hut.

"Two men shall stand guard," the spokesman said.
"You may draw lots for it, since all wish to go to the
hacienda and see the man Don José die. When one
returns with news of Don Josè's death, Valentino may
be released."

Valentino heard the door closed, and knew that they
were drawing lots outside. He heard the low curses
of the two men who were to be left behind for guard

duty, heard the spokesman giving them instructions, and then knew that the others had gone.

Valentino was almost frantic now. Was he to lie like a pig in a pen while Don José was slain? Was he to fail to save the *caballero?* He asked the saints for the strength of his youth, and tugged at the bonds. But his hands and legs had been lashed well, and the knots would not give.

For some time he remained silent, gasping for breath, almost sobbing because he could do nothing. And then he grew calm and glanced around. There was no lamp in the hut, but the moonlight streamed through a window. There was a table on one side of the room, dishes and utensils upon it.

Valentino caught sight of the handle of a knife. He rolled over on the floor until he was beside the table, and there he managed to get to his knees. He could look at the top of the table now, and he could see the knife. He got the handle between his teeth, lifted the knife off the table, and rolled toward his corner again. He dropped the knife beside him and examined it. He had hoped that it was sharp, but found that it was not. And he did not know how to make use of it.

But thoughts of the peril in which Don José stood unwarned came to him again, and he sought for a solution. There was a crack in the wall near the corner, and Valentino rolled over, grasped the knife in his hands, and with much difficulty succeeded in fastening the handle in the crack.

The crack was only a few inches from the hard dirt floor. Valentino turned and twisted until his lashed wrists were above the blade of the knife, and thus he began sawing at the rope that bound him.

It was difficult work. The knife gashed his wrists, and he was bending over in an uncomfortable position. The blade of the knife was dull, too, and slow to wear away the strands of the rope. But after a time Valentino felt the rope give and knew that he was succeeding.

He rested for a moment, went to work again. Finally the rope fell away from his wrists. He tore the cloth from his mouth. He sat up and rested his cramped arms for a moment. And then he removed the ropes from his ankles and legs as swiftly as possible.

He got up and paced the floor of the hut until the blood was coursing normally through his limbs and the tingling sensation was gone. He was free of his bonds, but not free of the hut. Outside, two men stood guard. And the others, he knew, already were on their way to the Roberts *hacienda*, and Don José, unwarned, was in deadly peril.

CHAPTER XXIV

WARNED TOO LATE

VALENTINO crossed the room to the window and glanced out cautiously, careful that the guards did not see him. He saw them sitting at the corner of the hut, their *serapes* wrapped around their shoulders—and they had a bottle of wine.

The moonlight was brilliant; there were no shadows on the side of the hut in which was the window. The door had been fastened on the outside—and Valentino had no weapon except the dull knife stuck in the crack in the corner.

It appeared to be a hopeless situation. It seemed that there was no possibility of getting away, of hastening to the Roberts *hacienda*, of evading those who would seek to prevent him giving a warning and getting word to Don José.

Old Valentino almost wept, for Don José was a man he admired, a *hidalgo* out of the past; he had brought to Valentino a renewed youth. And then he told himself that it would do no good to weep. Did he not possess more brains than the ignorant *peons* who guarded the adobe hut? And were not brains to be used by the man who possessed them?

He paced the floor for some time longer, scratching at his head and trying to think of some plan of escape.

If not interrupted he could dig beneath the rear wall of the hut, but that would take considerable time since he had nothing but the knife. Finally he decided to resort to a subterfuge. He stepped close to the door. And then Valentino began to groan, low at first, and then louder, to groan and moan like a man in agony. He almost wailed, and the guards at the corner of the hut heard him.

"The old man is ill," one said.

"Only uncomfortable—the bonds are tight."

"Listen to him groan," the other said. "I tell you there is something wrong. We'd better look in and see. We don't want the old man to die on our hands. It won't do any harm to take a look."

They got up and went to the door, and one of them let down the bar that held it closed. More groans came to their ears. They threw the door open and stumbled inside.

Then old Valentino, who had been beside the door, acted. One man stood some distance inside the hut; the other was just before the door. Valentino sprang, struck this man in the back, and hurled him against the other. In an instant he was outside the hut, had pulled the door shut, and had dropped the heavy bar in place. The guards were prisoners now.

But Valentino knew that he had no time to lose. Their shrieks might attract some *peon* who would unfasten the door—and one of the men was slim, and possibly could crawl through the window.

Valentino ran as swiftly as his old feet could carry his fat body. He kept to the shadows as much as possible, and made his way around the plaza toward the inn. He knew he had not a minute to lose. Perhaps already it was too late. There was a horse tethered near the end of the inn. Valentino did not know to whom the animal belonged, nor did he care. He untied the reins, sprawled into the saddle, and kicked at the beast's ribs with his heels. He dashed across the plaza and entered the highway and hurried toward the north.

It had been years since Valentino had risked himself in the saddle. Two decades before he had been a proper horseman, but he had long since lost all his skill. Now he could only cling and ride. He couldn't keep the stirrups—couldn't get an easy seat. But he could get speed out of the beast, and that was all that he desired.

He began watching the road ahead, for he expected to overtake some of the others before long. If he did not, it meant that he would arrive at the Roberts *hacienda* too late to be of any service to Don José. And if he did overtake them he didn't want to be stopped. He wished that he had a weapon—that he had stopped at the inn to get the big revolver that made so much noise and smoke.

He came to the top of a hill and saw horsemen far ahead of him. The men who had started out on foot would reach the neighborhood of the *hacienda* first, he knew, and would remain there in hiding until the others came, for that had been the plan. He was more than half way to the Roberts place now, and he was beginning to feel that he could not ride another mile, when he had five between him and his destination—and he was rapidly overtaking the horsemen in front.

One thing he guessed—that those horsemen would think he was one of their number who had been delayed in Quebrada and now was hurrying to be at the scene on time. That would help a little—and the horse he was riding was an excellent mount, strong and of good wind, able to do many miles at a fair rate of speed.

Again he was at the top of a hill, and the other horsemen, riding leisurely, were half way to the bottom. Valentino kicked his mount in the ribs again and dashed down at them. He swung the horse to one side, passed them, dashed on.

They realized in that instant that something was wrong. They shrieked after him and gave chase. Two other horsemen, a little in advance, stopped to ascertain the cause of the commotion. Even as they stopped, Valentino was upon them, had passed them— but he had been recognized.

"Ha! 'Tis old Valentino!" one of them cried. "Valentino has escaped from the hut and rides to warn the man!"

Now the chase was on in earnest. Valentino urged on his horse, kicked at him, tried to remember the tricks he had used in his youth to get speed out of a jaded animal. He held his distance for some time, and then the other began to gain slowly.

Valentino was in despair now. Was he to fail so near the goal? Was Don José to meet a terrible death because Valentino had failed? He sobbed as he kicked at his mount's ribs. He bent low over his animal's neck, for those behind were firing at him, and now and then a bullet whistled past his head. He was

afraid that the horse would be struck and the race
come to an end.

Now he swept around a bend in the road, and knew
that he was almost at his destination. He saw dark
figures running along the highway ahead of him, and
knew it was some of the *peons*. He heard the men
behind him shrieking to these *peons*, and knew that
an effort would be made to stop him.

On one side of the highway was a stone fence. Valentino, desperate now, turned the horse and put him
at the jump. It had been years since Valentino had
jumped a horse, but necessity compelled him to do it
now.

And then he was off the road and galloping across a
field straight toward the Roberts house. And some
of the horsemen were rushing up the curving driveway, and those on foot were closing in on the place.

"Don José! Don José!"

Valentino began shrieking the name, praying to the
saints that Don José, or some one in the house, would
hear. He was in the orchard now, the horse running
beneath the trees, Valentino bending forward to save
himself from being swept from the animal's back by a
low limb.

"Don José! Don José!" he cried.

The cry was shrill and seemed to cut through the
night. Valentino's agony was in it, the fear that his
endeavor had been for naught. He put the horse at
another fence and dashed toward the veranda, still
shrieking.

"Don José! Don José!"

He sprang from the horse's back and stumbled up the steps. He staggered across the veranda and began pounding at the front door. He was gasping for breath and tears were streaming down his fat cheeks.

Would they never hear him? Would they never come?

A light inside!

Valentino sobbed his gladness and shrieked again, and then the door was thrown open and Valentino stumbled inside, blinking at the light, looking up, trying to gasp out the warning. Roberts was before him, and just behind Roberts was Don José and Hugh Hankins. Valentino thrust Roberts aside and fell at Don José's feet.

"Fly, *caballero!*" he gasped. "Fly, *hidalgo!* They are coming—half a hundred or more! They will slay you!"

Roberts had closed the door.

"What does this mean? What does the man babble about?" he asked.

"Don José, for the love of the saints—"

"Explain!" Don José cried.

"I got away to warn you. All day they have been drinking and making ready. They are surrounding the place now—this place! Fly, *caballero!* They will slay you!"

"Who—and why?" Don José cried.

"The *peons!* Somebody has old them you are a recruiting officer for the army and they will kill—"

"Nonsense! You are unduly alarmed—"

"*Señor!* Don José! Fly, I pray you!"

"The man means it!" Hankins exclaimed.

"But I have nothing to do with the army—I'll tell them as much," Don José said.

"They will not believe you, Don José! You must go at once! Even now it may be too late! They are surrounding the place, I say! They have sworn to kill you! Juan Lopez started the rumor—"

"Ha! That murderer?" Don José cried.

"For the love of the saints, Don José!"

"Fly from a few *peons?*"

"Do you not understand? They have been thinking of this thing for some time—and they are mad with liquor!"

"So that is the reason?" Don José said. "That is why my life has been attempted several times recently?"

"There are half a hundred of them, or more, *señor!*" Valentino said. "I overheard all their plans. You haven't a moment to lose, Don José!"

Horsemen dashed up to the veranda. Loud voices were heard outside. A few shots were being fired.

"It is too late—too late, *señor!*" Valentino sobbed. "They are here!"

From outside came a hail.

"Inside the house! We see your lights! Send out this Don José, or we wreck the place!"

CHAPTER XXV

A DIVIDED PURSUIT

ALARMED by the sudden tumult, Mrs. Roberts and Dorothy Charlton rushed into the living-room. Behind them crowded half a dozen female servants, their eyes wide with terror. There was more promiscuous shooting outside, and again the spokesman made his demand:

"Stand back!" Roberts told the others. "I'll attend to this affair!"

He called to his wife and Dorothy that there was no danger, and for them not to be afraid, and then he walked across to the front door, unfastened it and threw it open. He closed it behind him again and walked to the railing of the veranda, where those in front of the house could see him.

"What's all this racket?" he demanded. "What do you drunken fools want?"

That was the usual method of dealing with *peons,* and generally it resulted in cowing them effectually. But they had been brooding over this business for several days, and also they were inflamed with wine. Roberts found that they would not be cowed now.

"We want this Don José!" one of the horsemen called to him.

"Why?"

"Give him to us—and we'll attend to him!"

"Why should you annoy my guest?"

"He shall die!" another shrieked. "He seeks men for the army! He shall die before dawn!"

"Are you fools?" Roberts cried. "He has nothing to do with the army."

"You cannot fool us!" the spokesman replied. "We have come for this Don José—and we will take him!"

Roberts shook a fist at them.

"Get off my place—every man of you!" he cried. "I shall not let you annoy my guest! And if you attempt any violence I'll shoot a few of you to make you have common sense! Get out!"

"We have come for this Don José!" the spokesman told him again, and a chorus of cries approved his words. "And we stay here until we get him. If you do not send him out to us, then we will come in for him!"

"You dare speak to me that way?" Roberts cried. "I'll have you publicly whipped! Make a move toward this house and you'll taste hot lead!"

"We are more than half a hundred, *señor*, and we are determined men. We intend to have Don José. If we have to wreck your place to get him, burn your house and barns and hurt some of you, then we shall do it. After all, you are Americaños!"

The last word was half a sneer.

"You drunken fools will be made to suffer for this!" Roberts promised them.

"We have nothing against you, *señor*. Give us this man and we will take him away."

"I'll do nothing of the sort! I protect my guests!"

"Then we take him, *señor!*"

"You try it at your peril!"

Roberts could see dark figures drawing nearer, running from bush to bush. He saw perhaps half a score of horsemen before the veranda, and more men were on the driveway and in the orchard behind the stone fence. If the rear of the place was protected as well as the front, undoubtedly there were half a hundred men on the place, as the spokesman had said.

"I am warning you for the last time—depart from my property!" Roberts said.

And then he whirled around and entered the house again and closed and bolted the door.

"Get your guns!" he told Hankins and Don José. "We'll give these fools a hot reception if they don't go away!"

"This is a serious business, Roberts," Hankins said. "Those men are angry and determined."

"Well what of it? Can't we defend ourselves?"

"And the women—"

"They must go to some safe, inner room, of course, where they will be out of harm's way."

"For Heaven's sake, Roberts, you're not going to fight them?" Hankins exclaimed. "They may burn down the place and kill all of us."

"What else is there to do?" Roberts asked.

Hugh Hankins whirled toward Don José.

"You are the cause of this mess!" he cried. "Recruiting officer, eh? And forcing yourself on this house —bringing trouble to it! Wouldn't even tell your name, eh? This is all your fault—you greaser!"

Don José faced him squarely.

"I am no more a greaser than you, *señor,*" he said "I do regret, of course, that I have been the cause of trouble."

"Regret! What good will regret do when the buildings are burned and our corpses are in the ashes?"

"Enough of that, Hankins!" Roberts exclaimed. "This is no time for petty animosities!"

"Petty animosities!" Hankins cried. "Are you going to try to fight them, Roberts? They'll kill us all!"

"Wouldn't you defend a guest?" Roberts demanded.

"If he was a friend—and a white man! But not a nameless guest whose business is unknown, not a man of an inferior race—"

"*Señor!*" Don José cried. "I cannot resent your words, since there are ladies present."

"You are dead willing to let other people fight your battles—risk their lives. Roberts, do the sensible thing! Send this man out of the house!"

"And let him be slain?" Roberts cried.

"That's his outlook! Let him settle his own quarrels!"

"Hugh!" Dorothy Charlton cried. She stood before him, her breasts heaving, her eyes blazing, fists clenched at her sides. "Is this the sort of man you are—the man I expected to marry? You would give another man up to death at the hands of those intoxicated wretches?"

"I'd make this greaser—"

"Hugh! Don José is a gentleman—"

"I notice you've been particularly fond of his company," Hankins sneered.

"You forget yourself, Hugh!"

"I'm not going to risk my life defending a man about whom we know nothing! I'm not crazy, if Roberts is! They'll burn the house—they'll kill us all if they once get started!"

"They may burn the house—and they may kill us all—but I'll never surrender a guest to such men as those!" Roberts declared. "If I did, I'd despise myself to my dying day!"

"And the women—" Hankins asked.

"Fight!" Mrs. Roberts exclaimed, grasping her husband by the arm. "Are we not human beings? Get your guns, you men!"

"Dorothy!" Roberts asked.

"There is but one thing to consider," she asked, looking Hankins straight in the eyes. "Fight!"

"Are you insane?" Hankins cried. "I'm going— and I'll take you with me! I'll tell those fellows that I have nothing to do with this Don José—as he calls himself."

"Hugh! You'd run away?"

"I'd be sensible—that's all. Why don't you rebuke this man here—this nameless fellow who has caused it all?"

"Pardon me, but I am not!" Don José said now, in a quiet voice.

They turned toward him. There did not seem to be the least nervousness in his manner; he was lighting a cigarette.

"I have no intention of letting those fellows batter the place to pieces and annoy all of you. If you'll keep them out, hold them off for a few minutes, I'll—"

"What would you do?" Roberts asked.

"Why, I am going to leave the house, *señor*. They'll follow me, and so you'll be left in peace."

"But they'll kill you, Don José!" Dorothy cried. "You cannot make the attempt to escape. They have surrounded the house."

"Ah, *señorita*, perhaps good fortune will be with me," he said. "And I do not care to bring disaster to the house of my friends."

"Don José—" she begged.

"Oh, let the fellow go!" Hankins exclaimed. "And for Heaven's sake let him go quickly! Those beasts will be at us in a minute—they're getting ready for it now!"

"One moment, until I get my revolver—" Don José said. He whirled around and ran from the room.

"Father, do not let him do it!" Dorothy cried. "It may mean his death!"

"Well, he brought it upon himself!" Hankins said.

"He is a gentleman, and he shows it!" Roberts declared. "You said that he was a common greaser, Hugh. A common greaser would have remained here and made us fight for him!"

"He is a greaser! He's still playing his game! But he'll bust yet!"

"I'm not going to let him do it!" Roberts said. "I'll tell him so! We can fight off those devils out there! You've been whining about wanting a white man's chance, Hugh. Here it is—the white man's chance! A chance to show the superiority of your race—a

chance to show that you're white and won't let a
bunch of real greasers dictate what you shall do. Get
a gun, Hugh! Get one—and we'll fight side by side!
We'll show that bunch of drunken *peons* that they're
dealing with white men!"

Roberts started toward the door to call Don José.
But there came a fusillade of shots from outside, and
two of the windows crashed in. The women cowered
in a corner. Hankins hurried over to the fireplace,
which afforded some protection from doors and windows.

"Last chance!" cried one outside. "Send out this
Don José, or we tear down the place!"

"Hankins, you can cringe in a corner if you wish—
I'm going to put up a fight!" Roberts said. "And I'll
not let Don José go out to those fellows!"

There were more shots, and more windows were
shattered. The men outside were shrieking now. Already they had fired a pile of hay, and the night was
red with flames.

Roberts ran to his own room for his revolver. In
the hall he met Don José.

"I can't let you do it, man—it's the same as sending you to death!" Roberts said.

"Don't worry, *señor;* I'll escape!"

"But how?"

"Delay them a moment—that is all I ask."

Don José had buckled on his belt, and the revolver
swung at his hip. He ran quickly through the hall and
started to mount a short flight of stairs. Then Dorothy
rushed in from the front room.

"Here, Dorothy, you ask him not to attempt it!"

Roberts cried. "It'll mean his death! I'm going in front and fight!"

"Please, Don José," the girl begged, as her father rushed away.

"I must, *señorita;* it is the only way. And something tells me that I shall escape!"

"Don José—"

"I can play a trick on them from the roof—get a horse and get away!'

"But they will shoot—they will follow—"

"I will not have my own good horse, that is true, but I think I can outwit them. Good-by, *señorita!*"

"José—"

"Every second is precious. They are beginning to batter at the front door. I must not delay."

An instant their eyes met, and then he rushed on up the stairs.

On the front of the house there was a second story consisting of two small rooms in which women servants slept. Roberts had added them after purchasing the place. Don José ran into one of these rooms. He hurried to the window and glanced out. Before him was the roof of the veranda covered with red Spanish tile.

He could see men on the driveway and in the orchard. The horsemen had dismounted, with the exception of the man who led them, and were helping besiege the place. The moon and the reflection from the burning haystack made the night almost as light as day.

Don José opened the window carefully and put out his head. He saw at a glance that probably none of the men would notice him if he kept close to the tiling. He crawled out, stretched flat, and worked his way to the edge of the roof.

He peered over. Directly beneath him was the leader of the *peons* on his horse. He was shouting directions to the others. More shots were being fired at the house, and Roberts was firing in reply.

Don José crouched on the edge of the roof—and sprang! He struck the rump of the horse, his arms went out and hurled the leader of the *peons* to the ground, he whirled the beast's head and kicked at his flanks. He shrieked in the animal's ear.

Cries of rage came from the *peons* as they started running for their horses to take up the pursuit. And then, from the rear of the house, came another sound of galloping hoofs, and they saw another rider dashing away from the house. An instant they stood puzzled, scarcely knowing what to do, while their leader shrieked at them.

And so, when the pursuit began, it was divided, for they had reason to believe that Don José was astride one of those fleeing horses, but they were not sure which.

CHAPTER XXVI

UNEXPECTED AID

THOUGH they shot at him from behind the fences, the trees, from the driveway in front of the house and from the orchard, Don José rode unscathed. He wished for his own horse, but he judged that the animal he rode was as good as any the pursuers had. And he did not think that more than a dozen or fifteen of the *peons* had horses. He had not noticed the second rider dashing away from the house, did not know the pursuit was divided.

The principal question was which way to turn. He would have to evade these men until their rage had died down and the effects of the wine they had poured into their stomachs had worn away. He could not do that by going to Quebrada, for if the recruiting officer story had been spread broadcast there would be men in the village ready to fire at him on sight. And every *hacienda* had its *peons*, and every mining establishment. They would be along the roads, in the fields and orchards, in the valleys and on the hills.

The hills seemed best. He would find fewer foes there, and there were better chances for evading them. There were places where a fight could be staged well, too, in case it came to that. Don José galloped toward the north until he came to the top of the first hill. He looked back and saw the foremost of his pursuers. He felt that he could out-distance them, but he would have to ride hard.

He dashed on, down the slope, urging the horse beneath him to its utmost. Finally, he reached a little trail that ran toward the hills, and turned into it. His pursuers would be puzzled for a time, and perhaps it would give him a chance to gain.

He passed a hut, and dogs howled an alarm. That would put his foes on the right track, he knew. There would be no chance of shaking them off until the hills were reached.

The trail began twisting between jumbles of rock, and always it ran upward and was rough. But now and then he struck a smooth, level space and forced his horse to do its best. He passed a *peon* making his way toward his hut home after the celebration in town. That was ill luck, he knew, for the man would put his pursuers on the right trail. He was climbing high into the hills now. Below him was stretched the valley. He was directly above the Roberts *hacienda,* and could see the burning haystack.

Half a dozen times he came to where the trail forked, and finally found himself in a network of paths. It was an excellent place in which to lose a pursuit, especially since jumbles of rocks gave good cover. He had not seen any of the men behind for some time, and when he stopped his horse for a moment to listen, he could not hear them.

Dawn was not far away now. It would be dangerous after daylight, he knew, if the men continued the chase, and he had little hope that they would not. He left the trail along which he was riding, and urged his horse over the rough ground, following a tiny ravine toward the crest. And finally he reached it, and found a little pocket among the rocks.

He had come to the end of the chase, he told himself. Here he could hide and rest, and rest his horse, too. It would be luck for his pursuers if they stumbled upon him. He dismounted and led his horse aside, where there was a spring. The spring bothered him at first—it might mean that this was a place men visited. But he saw nothing to indicate that it was visited regularly. He drank, and allowed the horse to drink, and then crawled to the top of the rocks and waited for the dawn.

It was not long in coming. The first red streak appeared in the east, the sky grew brighter, and then the sun seemed to shoot into the heavens. Crouching among the rocks at the crest, Don José looked over the country below him. Patiently he watched, but saw only a lone horseman making his way toward the valley and he began to hope that his pursuers had become scattered, and had given up the chase.

The mist rolled away from the hillsides, the air cleared, and he could see the entire valley spread out before him. He looked toward the Roberts *hacienda*. He strained his eyes and looked again, peering intently.

Something seemed to be wrong at the Roberts place. Clouds of dust-colored smoke were rising from half a dozen haystacks. And Don José could see little white puffs that he knew were caused by firearms. He guessed what it meant—the infuriated *peons* who had not had horses, and so could not join in the pursuit, had remained to besiege the place. They were enraged, intoxicated, filled with false courage and anger against the Americaños who had shielded him.

Don José's eyes narrowed, and his lips set in an expression of determination. There was but one thing for him to do in such a case—ride back and help fight the men off. Roberts had no place to look for help. There were only two *rurales* stationed in Quebrada, and it was doubtful if they would respond to a call for aid. They had little love for Americaños, and the *magistrado* would rather leave the *hacienda* to its fate than take sides against the *peons*. It would be an easy matter for him to say afterwards that the evil had been done before he knew anything of the trouble.

Don José turned his eyes from the distant *hacienda* and began looking at the trails and hillsides again, trying to locate his foes if any still lurked between the crest and the valley. His horse would be well rested presently, and he could start back.

He had not glanced behind him for some time, the scene in front demanding all his attention. He did not see a man's head show above a bowlder some paces away, did not note the expression of surprise in the man's face. Up there on the roof of Sonora, Don José anticipated the presence of no human being save himself.

The man's head disappeared, and a moment later it came into view again, and another beside it, and two evil faces regarded Don José with malevolence. One of the men raised a revolver he carried, but the other put out a hand and stopped the shot, and whispered in the other's ear.

Don José was almost satisfied that those who had pursued him had returned to the valley, else had followed a false scent to the north and by now were far away, questioning such men as they met and cursing because he had evaded them. He got up from the rock upon which he had been stretched, having decided to mount and ride to the *hacienda* by the most direct route.

"Hands up!" said a voice behind him.

It was a coarse, commanding voice. It seemed to threaten dire things. Don José could not dart to one side to cover, could not whirl around and whip out revolver and fire. He sensed that either move would result in disaster.

He extended his hands above his head, and then turned slowly. His eyes narrowed again, and his breath came quicker. He realized the grave menace that confronted him. Before him, covering him with their weapons, their faces wearing horrible grins of anticipation, stood Juan Lopez and Agustin Gonzales, the murderers.

"So, *señor!*" Juan Lopez said. "The saints are kind to us, we see. Unable to go down into the valley and search for you, to give you the punishment you deserve, you come to our little hiding-place and obligingly turn your back, that we may get the drop easily. What have you to remark about it, *señor?*"

Don José looked at them squarely, but made no reply. Nor did the expression of his face change.

"It is due to you that we are known as murderers," Juan Lopez went on. "Because of you, *señor*, we are driven from our comrades and the haunts of men. It appears that you have escaped the fellows who went to seize you because we spread the tale about you being a recruiting officer of the army. But in escaping them you have walked right into our hands. That is well. We would enjoy settling this little matter ourselves."

"Well, what are you going to do with me?" Don José asked.

"It would have been an easy matter, *señor*, to have shot you in the back a moment ago."

"And a deed I should expect a man like you to accomplish," Don José said. "It takes courage to look a man in the face. Murderers generally are cowards."

"You think so?" Juan Lopez snarled. "Call names, *señor!* Accuse as you please! Let your tongue bite and sting, if it can, for it will be the last time. Your cleverness ends here and now, *señor!* We could have slain you easily, but it suits us better to have you know we are going to do it, to anticipate it a little and perhaps shiver in that anticipation."

"Bah!" Don José cried. "You expect me to show fear? You expect to enjoy my cowardice, to laugh when I cringe? What is death? Ha! 'Tis but a new experience. Shoot—and within a flash of time I shall know more than a thousand—yes, ten million—men such as you! I shall be enjoying a new adventure— the greatest adventure of all. I shall be in the world of spirits. And then I shall see you cringe! Ha! That will be rare sport! I shall return to you, *señores*, shall haunt you—"

Agustin Gonzales's face grew white, and he crossed himself. Juan Lopez laughed scornfully, though with some nervousness.

"The merchant has not haunted us," Juan Lopez said.

"Ha! The merchant did not have a powerful personality, perhaps. But rest assured I shall haunt you! Your nights shall be sleepless. You will see visions of me, menacing visions! By day, thoughts of me will find your mind! You will hear shrieks and groans and the rattling of chains! Ill luck shall attend you! Whatever you touch shall be contaminated. Those associated with you shall know bad fortune and learn to shun you. And the visions will continue—until shrieking madness comes to your relief!"

"You cannot frighten me!" Juan Lopez cried.

"I shall frighten you then! You will scream and beg and pray to be rid of the fantom that pursues you. You shall—"

"Stop him! Stop him!" Agustin Gonzales screeched.

"Enough of your talk!" Juan Lopez commanded. "We do not care to listen to your ravings."

"And in the days to come you shall be forced to listen to them at all hours. I shall ride beside you when you travel the roads and trails. I shall sit on the foot of your bunk at night. My accusing eyes always will be upon your face. You never will be able to shut out the sight, no matter how dark the night, nor how tightly you close your own lids. 'Twill be a terrible punishment, yet one that you deserve! And I shall find the spirit of the murdered merchant, and bring him with me to aid in tormenting you. Ha!

He has heard my call already—there he comes now!"

Don José shrieked the last words and pointed to the rocks behind them. But the subterfuge was unavailing, for Juan Lopez had guessed it.

"Don't turn around! It is a trick!" he hissed to Gonzales. "You cannot fool us that way, *señor*. Say your prayers!"

Don José faced them without flinching. He could draw and fight, of course, but against such odds he probably would lose the battle—and it would be his last.

He almost exclaimed aloud. Another head had appeared over the rocks behind the two men. It was a fair head, a woman's head, the hair tumbled about it gloriously. It was the head of Dorothy Charlton.

"Hands up!" she cried, and covered them with a revolver.

They whirled around now, for they had not been expecting an attack from that direction. And, as they whirled, Don José acted.

His hand darted to his hip like the tongue of a snake. His revolver came out. He fired from the hip as fast as he could pull the trigger.

Juan Lopez was shot in the wrist, and his gun dropped to the ground. That put both his wrists out of commission, for the one Don José had shot that day at the entrance of the driveway was not yet healed.

His second shot struck Agustin Gonzales in the forearm just below the elbow. And then Don José was springing over the rocks at them, and greeting Dorothy with glad cries. He drove them back and stood over their weapons, forcing them against a bowlder.

"So, *señores!*" he said. "Thanks to the lovely *señorita,* you are outdone again. Shall I send your foul souls to the hereafter now, eh?"

"Mercy!" Agustin Gonzales shrieked.

"Did you have mercy on the old merchant? Would you have had mercy on me if the *señorita* had not put in an appearance so unexpectedly? You have aroused the *peons* against me, have you not? Why did you not ride into the north and go about your business after you escaped and robbed the *magistrado?* That pretty official will be glad to see you again, no doubt."

"And he will not, *señor!*" Juan Lopez said. "He will be afraid that we will betray him."

"Betray him?"

"He gave us the crowbar with which we worked our way to liberty," Juan Lopez declared. "We were to give him certain money for doing it. And we did—taking the money from his own safe first."

"That is the truth?" Don José demanded.

"I swear it, *señor.* And so you see the *magistrado* will not care to see us. Let us go, *señor.* Keep our guns and let us go. We will hasten to the north and not trouble you again. We will swear it!"

"I am afraid that I cannot accommodate you," said Don José. "Your words have sealed your fate. I have urgent need of you in my business, *señores!*"

CHAPTER XXVII

A WOMAN COMMANDS

HE warned them to remain standing with their backs against the bowlder, asking Dorothy to stand where she was and keep them covered; he searched them and took away their knives, and then he laughed and ran to his horse.

There was a lariat on the saddle, and Don José took it off and walked toward the two men again. There was haste in his manner, for he wanted to ascertain how Dorothy came to be there, and he was apprehensive of what was happening at the Roberts place. He lashed them well, so that they scarcely could move, and then turned to face the girl, extending his hands toward her and clasping hers.

"Thanks, *señorita;* you came at an opportune moment," he said.

"I am glad, Don José."

"But how do you happen to be here?"

"I rode away when you did."

"How is this?"

"When you started up the stairs, I thought that, if I were to leave the house at the same time, part of the men would follow each of us, and so you would have a better chance to escape. Father was in the front room, and so I got one of his revolvers and went to the back door. There was a horse standing only a few feet away."

"And you sprang upon it and rode?"

"Yes, Don José. Half of the men followed me, and I was compelled to keep ahead of them, so that they would not learn they were not following you. I finally escaped them in the hills, and I was making my way to the *hacienda* again, when I heard these men talking to you."

"And you saved me!" he said. "Ah, *señorita*, in all the world there is not another girl like you!"

He seemed to have forgotten the two prisoners. He sat down beside her on one of the bowlders.

"A certain gentleman we both know," he said, "is always wishing that he had a white man's chance. If I only had one, *señorita!* How I would strive to win you, how I could cherish you if I did! Is there no hope in all the world?"

"Don José, I—I wish I could say that there is hope!"

"But there is not?"

"How could there be, Don José? You know the story of my father's will, do you not?"

"And even did I possess your love I could not be judged a worthy man by those men in Boston?"

"They—they do not understand, Don José. They would see in you only an alien, and not the man I can see."

"Money is nothing—"

"It is not only that, Don José. I could exist with love and without the money, but it is my father's wish.

Can you not understand?   And—and we should not
be talking this way. Nothing can come of it."

"You love me!" he said softly, bending close to
her.

"*Señor*—"

"But I can understand," Don José said.

She turned her face away, and Don Josè sighed.
And then he sprang quickly to his feet.

"We are forgetting our prisoners—and we have work
to do," he said. "Juan Lopez, where are your horses?"

Juan Lopez scorned to reply.

"Have it your own way," Don José said. "If I had
one of your horses I could lash you to it and let you
travel that way. Since I have not, I shall pull you
along at the tail of mine—and the trails are rough and
dusty, and I intend to travel with some speed."

"Behind the rock!" Lopez snarled.

Don José found the horses, turned one loose and
led the other out. He forced the two men to mount,.
removing some of their bonds until they did so, and
then he bound their feet beneath the horse's belly,
lashed their hands behind them again, fastened them
securely in half a dozen different ways. He fastened
the end of the lariat to his own saddle, and once more
he addressed them.

"*Senores*, we are going to ride down into the valley,
and the journey will be a swift one. I cannot help it
if you are not comfortable, and would not help it if I
could. I might mention that we are liable to pass a
peon or two, and if you call out, or an attempt is made
to rescue you, I shall shoot both of you first and then
give attention to the others. "And when I shoot again

it will not be at the wrist or arms. I have made myself perfectly clear, *señores?* Thank you. There is nothing like having an understanding."

He aided Dorothy to mount, and so they started out. For the first half mile the going was slow, the descent over treacherous slopes and jumbles of stones. And then they came to the first real trail, and gathered speed.

Grunts and groans came from the men behind, but they made no effort to shriek for rescue. Don José did not even turn to look at them. He was watching Dorothy half the time, and the other half was watching the valley below whenever a turn in the trail gave him a chance.

Down and down they went until they were half way to the floor of the valley. Don José could see the clouds of smoke now, and saw men running around the house, and Dorothy saw them, too. They could also see little puffs of white smoke issuing from the windows of the big barn and guessed that some of the defenders had gone there and were besieged.

Now they were on a better and wider trail and forced their horses into a gallop. They passed a *peon's* hut now and then, and at times a child or woman would hear the drumming of the horses' hoofs and run to the doorway to look after them. Now Don José was riding with a revolver held ready in one hand, his every sense alert.

They came to the last slope and descended to a meadow in which cattle were grazing. Down the slope they dashed. They heard Juan Lopez and Agustin Gonzales grunting their discomfort behind them. They came toward a fence, and put their horses at it.

"For the love of the saints, *señor*—" Juan Lopez gasped, realizing what they intended to do.

But Don José did not stop. He motioned for Dorothy to take the jump, which she did, and then Don José eased his mount a little to give slack to the lariat, and then took the jump himself. The horse that followed jumped also, but heavily, yet he cleared the fence. Juan Lopez and Agustin Gonzales groaned because of the shock they received.

Don José and Dorothy galloped rapidly across the meadow, darted through a gate, and rode beneath the trees of the orchard. The scene was spread before them now. Somebody was firing from the house, and the *peons* were still surrounding it, firing now and then, but doing little damage. There was shooting from the barn, too.

Don José judged that the best thing would be to get into the barn, and Dorothy thought so, too, but Don José was almost afraid to attempt it, especially since they had prisoners who might be recognized, and an attempt made to rescue them. Inside the barn they could protect the prisoners and defend themselves; and there was Don José's horse, too, and other fresh and speedy animals that could be used if a run for the open had to be made later.

They could not hope to reach the barn without being seen. Nor did they. Several of the beseigers were at the point of rushing the door in an attempt to get inside. They heard the drumming of hoofs, recognized Don José and the *señorita*, quickly identified the two prisoners on the led horse, and greeted the arrival with raucous shouts that spread the intelligence to the others around the place.

Don José and Dorothy rode straight to the rear door. Don Josè began firing, making no deliberate attempt to slay or wound, but putting bullets so close to the men before him that they scattered for good hiding-places.

They came to the door, and Don José and Dorothy sprang from their horses, keeping the horses and their prisoners between them and the man who fired. The door was fastened on the inside; Don José pounded upon it.

"Open!" he cried. "It is Don José and *Señorita* Dorothy!"

The door opened a crack, the muzzle of a revolver showed, and then the face of old Valentino. The door was hurled back, and Don José thrust Dorothy ahead of him, and then led the horses inside. Valentino, uttering cries of delight and relief, barred the door again.

"Ha, Valentino!" Don José cried. "Here we are again without a scratch on us. And with the aid of the *señorita* I have caught the two murderers and fetched them back. "What has happened here? How do you come to be in the barn?"

"A lot has happened!" came the voice of Hugh Hankins. They saw him standing near a window, peering out.

"Has anything happened to Señor Roberts—or the *señora?*" Don José asked.

"You might well ask that—you, the cause of it all!"

Hankins snarled turning away from the window and walking toward them. "Only a part of the devils followed you; the others were angry and set fire to more haystacks. And they continued to keep the house surrounded, firing at it. Roberts and Valentino fired back at them. Just before dawn we decided it might be better to get into the barn, if we could. We could defend it easily, and the horses are here. If it came to the worst we could make an attempt to ride through them."

"And then—" Dorothy asked.

"Valentino rushed for the barn first, and got here without being seen," Hankins said. "Then I tried it, but the *peons* saw me, and I scarcely made the door. Roberts and his wife were afraid to follow, after that, and so were the women servants, for the men outside were watching."

"Anybody hurt?" Don José asked.

"Two of the *peons*, but none of us. Roberts has been firing from the house, and Valentino and I have been shooting from the barn."

"We have held them back, Don José, but they were preparing to rush us just as you came," Valentino put in. "Thank the saints that you are not wounded, Don José—and that the *señorita* is safe! But why did you come back, Don José, to face danger?"

"I thought that my services might be needed," Don José said.

"If I had my way about it you'd be handed over to those brutes and then they'd quit the *hacienda!*" Hankins said.

"I believe that you expressed those sentiments be-

fore, *señor*," Don José returned. "But it appears that
you do not have your own way about it."

"If I picked you up and threw you out to them—"

"Suppose you try it, *señor!*" said Don José evenly.
"We can send the lady into another room first. It
appears that you forget she is present."

"I cannot forget that you have caused all this!
Things have come to a pretty pass when a greaser—"

"*Señor!*" Don José cried.

"I have said it! A man afraid to even tell his name
and business! What have we here to do with your
quarrels? Why don't you fight your own battles?"

"Hugh!" Dorothy cried. "You forget that Don
José risked his life leaving the house to save us
trouble!"

"And forced you to ride out the back way, to divide
the gang, and thus made you risk your life!"

"What do you mean, Hugh? I went of my own free
will. Don José did not know of it until we met up
in the hills."

"Are you infatuated with the man?" Hankins cried.
"Be sensible, Dorothy! Look beneath the surface.
Forget his foreign birth, his romantic ways, and give
me a chance—a white man's chance!"

"You are unjust to Don José. When he saw you
were in danger here, he decided to return immediately
to help."

"Did he? Or was it because he thought that his
precious skin would be safer here? This is a pretty
mess. Suppose that Boston man walks in on us in
the middle of it?"

Dorothy turned away from him, half disgusted, and

crouched behind a grain bin, for the men outside were firing at the barn and house again now. And after a time the firing ceased, and a voice called out:

"Within the barn! Send us out Don José, and we will go away from the *hacienda!*"

"You see?" Hankins said, whirling toward him. "It is your presence that puts all of us in danger. Have you any manhood, any courage, any respect for women? Will you be the cause of all of us being murdered by those wretches?"

Don José faced him squarely for a moment, his eyes narrowed to two tiny slits. Then he wheeled toward Valentino.

"Valentino, my horse is in the third stall from the end!" he cried. "Saddle and bridle are just outside the stall. Get the animal ready!"

"Don José—"

"Get him ready!" Don José cried.

"*Sí, caballero!*" Valentino answered mournfully; and he started toward the stall.

"You shall not do it, Don José!" Dorothy exclaimed. "You risked your life once for us, and you shall not do it again!"

"Ah, but you risked yours, too, *señorita,*" he replied. "And this Señor Hankins questions my manhood and courage."

"It is madness—and you shall not do it! I command you to remain here, Don José!"

"If the *señorita* commands—" Don José began.

"Dorothy, you must let him go!" Hankins cried. "If he does not, all of us will be killed. Think of your foster-parents! Think of yourself!"

"Is it the part of justice and fairness for one to think only of oneself?"

"Dorothy, I must command you!" Hankins exclaimed. "You shall not throw away your own life and those of others for this greaser!"

"Let that be the last time you speak that word in connection with me, *señor*," Don José warned. "You take advantage of a lady's presence. I may meet you some time when there is no lady near."

"I command you, Dorothy!" Hankins said again. "As my future wife, I must ask you—"

Valentino, the tears running down his fat cheeks, led out Don José's horse.

"Attend to that brace of murderers, Valentino," Don José told him. "We'll see them handed over to justice later. And stand you by the door and be ready to throw it open when I command. I'll try to dash through them and so get away."

"You shall not!" Dorothy cried, running beside him and clutching him by the arm.

"Dorothy!" Hankins commanded.

"I must, *señorita*," Don José said. "Your future husband has the right to ask—"

"He is not my husband yet. He has not been passed on!" the girl said. "Even if he were, I'd not let you risk your life a second time, Don José!"

"What is this man to you?" Hankins cried. "Do you think more of his safety than you do of your own, mine, of that of Roberts and his wife? Dorothy, are you mad?"

Don José had mounted the horse. Dorothy clutched at the reins.

"Don José, you must not!" she said, ignoring Hankins. "Stay here with us, and fight. They will not go away—those men outside—if you ride through them and escape. They will be more infuriated than before."

"There is something in that," replied Don José.

"I command you to remain, *señor*. Are the commands of a woman so light in weight that you disregard them?"

"Valentino, open the door and let this fellow ride out!" Hankins cried.

"Valentino, you'll do nothing of the sort!" Don José said. "The lady has commanded—and I remain!"

He got down from the horse.

CHAPTER XXVIII

LOVE CONFESSED

DON JOSÉ sprang to work. He forced the murderers to get down from their horse and lashed them in a corner in such manner that they could not get free and would be in no danger from stray bullets.

Then he looked to the weapons, retaining his own and one he had taken from Juan Lopez, and giving Valentino the one that had belonged to Agustin Gonzales, so that Valentino would have two. He paid not the slightest attention to Hugh Hankins.

He ran to the front of the barn and glanced through a window, keeping back in the shadows so he would not be seen by those outside. The *peons* were almost ignoring the house now, giving their attention to the barn.

It was Don José they wanted. But Don José noticed that their enthusiasm and rage were waning. The wine had died out of their bodies. But fresh arrivals added fuel to the flames of their wrath. For there were fresh arrivals—the story of the siege evidently had been carried around the countryside and to the town, and the *peons* were rushing to see the excitement and perhaps take a hand in the battle.

Don José emptied his revolver at them, scattering

his shots well. They were told by that better than
by words that Don José was not going to be sent out
to give himself up. Cries of rage answered his fusillade, and they sought better cover and began pouring
a hail of bullets at the doors and windows of the barn.

"I can watch the rear door and window, Don José,"
old Valentino said at his elbow. "If this Señor Hankins will but watch the two windows at the side—"

Don José whirled around and saw that Señor Hankins was talking to Dorothy. So he gave his attention
to the window again, having reloaded the revolver he
had emptied.

"Why did you do it, Dorothy?" Hankins was demanding. "Has this fellow hypnotized you?"

"Could I send him out to death?" she asked.

"He would have escaped. And suppose he had not?
Who is he that we should concern ourselves with him?
A nameless greaser! The cause of all this terrible
muss! Which is worth the more—his life or ours?"

"You seem to think a great deal of yourself," she
said.

"You've let the fellow infatuate you, because he has
grandiloquent ways and wears unusual clothes, and all
that! Can't you see beneath his veneer? Throw
aside the glamour of romance that is about him, Dorothy. Remember that we are betrothed."

"If you had taken the right attitude at first—had
helped him fight—"

"Ally myself with that fellow! In Heaven's name,
Dorothy, you treat me peculiarly for a woman who is
to be my wife! If that Boston man comes here—"

"It will make no difference," she said.

"You mean that you do not care for his verdict? You mean that you'll marry me anyway? But that would be throwing good money away, and if things go right we can gain his consent."

"The girl looked at him scornfully.

"Hugh, you are a good man as men go," she said earnestly. "You are an excellent mining engineer, and no doubt the woman who becomes your wife never will know want. Men like you. And you are substantial."

"But what—"

"Wait a moment, Hugh. I used to think that you were perfect, but my eyes have been opened. You were the only man of our class here, and it was not so difficult for me to imagine that I had fallen in love with you."

"Imagine?" he cried.

"Yes," she answered. "I felt proud when you asked me to be your wife. But I do not feel so proud now."

"Since this Don José showed up, eh?"

"Hugh! That in itself is a flaw in your character. And there are other flaws. I do not say that you are the wrong sort. But you are the wrong sort for me, Hugh!"

"Dorothy! What do you mean?"

"I mean that—here is your ring, Hugh. I hope that you'll always have good fortune, but I have no wish to share it."

"You are imagining things!" he cried. "What have I done? You are inventing excuses—"

"I can explain," she said. "I have found out several things in the past few days. I—I looked for

them, Hugh. I wanted to see if you really were the
man I wanted to have by my side throughout my life—
and I decided that you are not."

"Well, what flaws have you found?" he asked. "Is
it that I am not as handsome as this Don José, do
not ride and shoot like a fiend, and all that rot?"

"Hugh, do you not give me credit for having more
sense than that? In the first place, you deceived me
—lied to me—broke a promise regarding having Don
José invest in the Golden Harvest. You promised that
you'd not let him, and you deliberately went ahead
with your plans. I overheard you. It showed me that
you are deceitful, and that you do not insist upon
square dealing in all things."

"That's business—"

"Yet it is a flaw that I cannot overlook, Hugh—
you lied to me, and you would have swindled a man
to get money. And I have seen flashes of something
almost like cowardice the past day. I'll not say
that you are a physical coward, but you have shown
that you are a mental one. You have a quick temper
—cannot control yourself. You lack faith in humanity—"

"Perhaps I wouldn't believe that this fellow is a
high-born *hidalgo* and almost a king—"

"Not exactly that—it was just the way you spoke
and acted. And you have no loyalty. Don José was
my foster-father's guest, and you would have betrayed hospitality. You have shown jealousy, too and
I cannot endure that."

"Because I loved you—"

"If you really loved me you would trust me, and

with complete trust there can be no jealousy. Perhaps some women would overlook these things, perhaps I am too exacting, but I cannot help it. It is useless, Hugh. My eyes have been opened—"

"And who opened them?" he snarled. "This Don José! This greaser with his pretty ways! This nameless fellow who perhaps is the scum of the earth! You have fallen in love with the cur—"

"Hugh! Is this the way to speak to me?"

"It's true, isn't it? You've fallen in love with a greaser! That'll be nice news for your Boston friends!"

"Leave me, Hugh! I cannot—endure—"

"Ashamed of it already, are you? In love with a nameless greaser! In love with—"

"Hugh! Go away!"

"You don't like to listen to the truth; is that it? Well, I am forced to speak plainly—"

A hand gripped him on the shoulder.

"The lady has requested that you leave her," said Don José's voice in his ear.

Hankins whirled upon him. He found the muzzle of one of Don José's revolvers pressed against his stomach.

"This way, *señor*—over to the corner," Don José said. "I cannot have ladies insulted in my presence. And you should be guarding a window."

"I'm putting up no fight to help you save your skin!"

"We can have no possible traitors in camp, *señor*. You'll not help in the fighting? Very well, then!"

His hand swooped down and took away Hankins's weapon.

"Go into the corner, and remain there!" Don José commanded. "And do not make a treasonable move, *señor!*"

"I'll have a settlement with you for this—and other things!"

"All in good time, *señor*. There is fighting to be done now with those beasts outside."

"A greaser calling other greasers beasts, eh?"

"I shall remember that remark, *señor!*"

The voice of old Valentino reached him:

"Don José! They are rushing!"

Don José dashed away from Hankins's side, to the window, and began emptying one of the revolvers. The rush was stopped almost as quickly as it had begun, but there was danger that it would be attempted again at any moment. The *peons* had attained positions of advantage nearer the barn.

Roberts was firing from the house now and then forcing the men to take cover from that direction, also, and it helped a great deal. Valentino held back the charge in the rear. Don José saw that almost a hundred *peons* were about the place now, and all had joined in the fighting. He knew that some of them had come out from the town.

And he even caught a glimpse of the *magistrado* as he darted behind the bole of a tree. He guessed that the official was making a half-hearted effort to get the men to cease, while in reality he hoped they would succeed in getting Don José.

They rushed again, and again they were forced to take to cover, but closer to the barn than before. Soon they would be at the doors, and then the defense would have to be made from the inside. They could build a barricade in a corner, hold it as long as possible, possibly until their ammunition was exhausted, and then—

Don José threw a glance at Hankins, who remained in the corner, waiting. He half expected Hankins to make some sort of a move, but the man did not.

"When you are ready to fight, you may have your gun, *señor*," Don José called.

"When I'm ready to fight, I'll ask for it!" Hankins replied.

Again a rush—and once more Don José and Valentino stood it off. Don Josè began looking around for the best place to build a barricade, for it would be necessary soon now, unless a miracle happened, and Don José did not expect a miracle. He turned to the window again to observe the enemy. He felt a touch on his arm and found Dorothy beside him.

"There is danger, *señorita*—" he began.

"They will get inside?"

"I fear so."

"And then—"

"We'll get behind those packing cases in the corner, and make the best of it, *señorita*."

"And that may mean—" She could not speak the word.

"We cannot tell, *señorita*. I shall do everything possible. But say the word and I'll ride out and face them now. It would save you and the others—"

"But not you, *señor*."

"What of that? Death is but a beautiful adventure."

"*Señor*, you must not! José—"

"The name is beautiful on your lips, *señorita*."

"Ah, do not call me *señorita* always. Call me Dor-othy!"

"But Señor Hankins may object."

"He has nothing further to say about it, José. I am done with him; I have returned his ring. Oh, José, you opened my eyes! Do you remember the little story you told of the two *caballeros,* how one showed up the bad qualities of the other? You have done that with Mr. Hankins, José. You have opened my eyes."

"You may change your mind, *señorita*."

"No; I am awake now. And call me Dorothy!"

"It sounds much sweeter in Spanish," he said smil-ing down at her. "Dorotea!"

"It is—sweet," she said.

"And you are worthy the name. Dor-o-te-a!" he breathed.

"*Señor,*" she said, her lips trembling. "José! If we are about to die, there is something—that you should know. But I cannot force myself to say it. Can you not guess it—José?"

"Ah, if I might dare guess it, *señorita*. If I dared to say how I love you—how I have loved you from the first time I saw you in the plaza at Quebrada! If I dared try to make you love me in return!"

"Try, José? I do—now!"

"*Señorita!* You must not! There will come some man of your own race—"

"I cannot help what my heart speaks, José."

"But naught can come of it!"

"I realize that," she breathed. "It is as you once

said—they think every Spaniard is a—a greaser.
Those men in Boston—they would never consent."

"Think you I would waste a single moment dream-
ing of that money?"

"I am sure that you would not. Nor would I, José.
I could be happy with you in a hovel. I know it!
But there is another thing. It isn't only the money,
José—it is my father speaking to me through those
men in Boston. It is his last wish—and sacred. But
I love you, Don José, with my whole heart! I shall
go on loving you until I die, though it is hopeless.
Oh, why aren't things different? If you were—were
not what you are, José!"

"But I cannot change!"

"I love you, José! And Hugh Hankins with his
continual prating about a white man's chance! Oh,
Josè, if only you had—a white man's—chance!"

CHAPTER XXIX

DON JOSÉ "BUSTS"

Don José's glad cry startled the murderers, old Valentino, and Hankins. His face was alight. He whirled and clasped Dorothy in his arms, crushed her to his breast, rained kisses upon her flaming face.

"What's the meaning of this?" Hankins cried, running to them.

Don José whirled to face him.

"The time has come!" he cried. "Miss Charlton loves me! The world is fair!"

"You greaser!"

"No greaser, Hankins! I'm white! Get me? I'm as white as you, and maybe whiter! You haven't been contending against a romantic greaser, but a white man. You've had your white man's chance right along, and you've lost! The play is over!"

He threw his *sombrero* from him, tore off his jacket and threw it away, began rolling up his sleeves.

"I'm white—and I fight for the woman I love!" he cried. "I'm a greaser, am I? I'm due to bust one day, am I? The day has come! One side!"

He looked to his guns, called to Valentino to bring his horse to the front door.

"Nameless, am I?" he cried. "I'll give you a name presently that will explain!"

"Why not give it now?" Hankins sneered.

"Very well, I shall! You know me as Don José, eh? Don is an abbreviation for Donald, is it not? And does not José stand for Joseph in Spanish? My family name? It is Blenhorn! Donald—Joseph—Blenhorn! Do you get it?"

"The man from Boston!" Hankins gasped.

"Exactly! A trusted employe of the firm that handles Miss Charlton's affairs. It happens that I have traveled extensively and am supposed to be able to read men. And so they sent me down here to read you, Hankins! I read—and I disapproved! I've been a mining engineer, too. Oh, you didn't fool me with your Golden Harvest! I've spent years in Latin countries. And so I decided to play *hidalgo*, to watch you without you suspecting and being on your good behavior. You would be off guard, still waiting for the man to come from Boston. I tried you out, Hankins! I tried you out at the inn. I tried you elsewhere. I told Miss Charlton nothing, except that I related a tale that might have caused her to think a bit. And I showed you up, Hankins! You're what the world calls a good sort of man—but you're crooked in some ways. It all came out easily. I didn't know exactly how to do it at first, but when I heard them saying at the inn that I was the scion of a noble family come to visit the home of his ancestors, the rest was easy."

"And so you ran me down so you could win the girl and the money yourself," Hankins sneered.

"I was honest in it. I let all of you think I was a greaser. I never made the slightest effort to win Doro-

thy's regard until I had let her decide herself whether
you were the man she wanted. I am glad she made
the decision herself, for I should have been forced, in
justice to my employers, to send in a bad report on
you. No report is necessary now. Oh, it was easy!
I knew the language, the manners, the customs. I am
burned brown by the sun, because I returned recently
from a year in Central America. I had only to play
the part, and you—you, Hankins, damned yourself in
the lady's eyes. And now we have come to the end of
the play. She says that she loves me; do you hear?
And I have kept faith. I turned my back upon her
when my heart was full of love and I wanted to pour
the story of it into her ears. I'm a white man! Valentino, my horse! Stand ready to open the doors!"

"José, what would you do?" the girl cried.

"Call me Donald!" he begged. "Call me Don!
What would I do? End this farce of a siege. Those
fellows have made enough noise! Get back in a corner
where no bullet can strike you. Kiss me first! Hurry,
Dorotea—there is no time to lose. Ready, Valentino?"

"Don! You'll be hurt!" Dorothy cried.

"Not a bit of it! A bullet couldn't strike me now!
I have something for which to fight! I'm a white
man—and those fellows out there are greasers!"

"Don!"

"Away from the door, sweetheart! Valentino, stand
ready to let me in again. I'll be back almost
immediately!"

He ran to the window and looked out again, then
dashed forward and vaulted into the saddle. He
whipped out one of the revolvers and held it ready.

"Here's where I bust!" he cried. "Now, Valentino! Swing open the door!"

The door flew open!

And Donald Joseph Blenhorn, bent low over his horse's neck, flew out. He fired as he rode, fired at both sides, at men lurking behind rocks and trees and fences.

He jumped his horse over the nearest stone fence, and was in the orchard. The *peons* shrieked that he was escaping again. The few who had horses rushed toward them.

But Don José did not urge his horse through the orchard and to the broad highway. He galloped along a line of trees, bent from his saddle, threw an arm around a man crouching behind a rock, and jerked him on the horse before him.

It was the *magistrado*.

He turned his horse back toward the barn. He was riding like a fiend, and the magnificent animal responded to his commands. Over the fence again they flew, the *magistrado* hanging from the saddle and shrieking for mercy. For fear of hitting the official, the *peons* held their fire. Valentino threw the door open again—they were inside!

"My day to bust!" Mr. Blenhorn cried, springing from the horse. "You stand there, *magistrado!* Stand there against the wall, toad—grafter—crook! The hour of reckoning is at hand!"

"*Señor—*"

"Silence—and listen! I know how you ordered me killed. I got it from Felipe Botello. And I've got Juan Lopez and Agustin Gonzales back there in the

corner—see them? And they've told me how they
bribed you to help them to escape, and then paid you
with your own money. I'm wise to all your crooked-
ness, *magistrado!* You thought I was a government
official ready to send you to the *carcel* for theft, eh?
And you let those poor fools think I was a recruiting
officer, and hoped they would put me out of the way!
Now I've got you!"

"Mercy, *señor*—"

"Stand up, hound!"

He put the muzzle of a revolver against the *magistrado's* nose. The smell of powder was still in it, and
the odor made the *magistrado* suddenly ill.

"I'm going to blow off the roof of your head! Say
your prayers!"

"Mercy—"

"Beg—that's it! Well, I'll give you a chance. I'm
a white man—an Americano! I'm the man they were
expecting from Boston, and my masquerade has been
a jest. Understand that? Go outside—tell those men
the truth! If they don't leave this *hacienda* pronto,
I'll put a bullet through your head! You've got influence with them—you can do it! Tell them the
truth—make them go away. Go out and stand directly beneath the window and say it. If you try to
run away, I'll have your life! Do you understand?"

"*Sí, sí, señor!*"

"Quickly!"

He opened the door and thrust the *magistrado* out.
The firing ceased suddenly as the *magistrado* raised
his hands. The *peons* feared the official; he could put

them in *carcel* on charges that had no merit. To his friends he was kind in regard to taxes.

"*Señores! Amigos!*" he cried in his cracked voice that was doubly cracked now because of his terror. "Listen, *amigos*, for the love of the saints!"

Then he shrieked the story at them, using considerable eloquence to force home the point and make them believe, for he knew Don José's head was in the nearest window, and in fancy he could feel a hot bullet piercing his back.

They came from behind the rocks and fences and trees to listen. They did not believe at first, but gradually the *magistrado* won them over. They felt cheated of their prey, felt that the battle had been for naught.

Then Don José strode boldly to the door.

"Ha, *señores!*" he cried. "It has been a pretty fight, and you should be rewarded. Go your ways! And go to the inn of Pedro Jorge at your earliest convenience. I will arrange it that you all have free wine for three days. Old Valentino, the assistant, is here now, and I give him the order before you all. So go!"

They hesitated a moment, and then one of them cheered. And then they threw their battered hats into the air, and began laughing and joking, and the perspiring *magistrado* turned to Don José with great relief.

"It is over—they will trouble you no more," he said. "Have mercy on me now."

"As for the attempt you had made on my life, I shall forget it," Don José replied. "As for the other—there are your murderers, and you are an official. Do with them as you think best. I wash my hands of the entire affair.'

He turned back into the barn, and a happy girl ran out to meet him and be clasped in his arms. He kissed her again—this time slowly, gently, lingeringly.

"Sweetheart!" he breathed.

"I'm so happy—Don!"

"May you always be!" he said.

Then he saw that Hankins was walking toward him. He kept his arms around Dorothy and watched the man.

But Hankins had good streaks in him as well as bad. He put out his hand.

"It is all in a man's life," he said. "I guess you are the better man, Blenhorn. I congratulate you—and I wish you both joy."

"Thanks—it is appreciated!" Blenhorn said, and clasped the other man by the hand.

Hankins went out. A mystified Roberts stood with his wife on the veranda. The *magistrado* had gone to the corner to hold speech with the murderers. Blenhorn anticipated that the official would allow them to escape on the road to town.

He led Dorothy to the door, and they looked after the disappearing *peons,* and then up at the house, and Dorothy blushed again when she saw her foster-parents regarding her with amazement.

But she was bold in the knowledge of the love that had come to her. She put up her lips and was kissed again, and Mrs. Roberts gasped in horror.

"Now I suppose some man will have to pass on your eligibleness," Dorothy said, laughing a little.

"Say nothing about that, or I shall call you *señorita* again. Those men in Boston have known and trusted me from boyhood. I'll just make a report on myself!"

Dorothy crept closer within his arms.

"Kiss me again, and then we must do some explaining," she said. "Father and mother think I am giving myself to a greaser. Kiss me—my white man!"

Old Valentino wiped away a tear as he looked after them.

"If he isn't a *hidalgo,* he should be!" old Valentino said. "I might have guessed the truth that time when he interrupted a siesta hour!"

THE END